YOUNG JOAN

Other Books by Barbara Dana

YOUNG JOAN

A novel by

Barbara Dana

Based on the life of Saint Joan of Arc

HarperTrophy®
An Imprint of HarperCollinsPublishers

HarperCollins®, 📚®, Harper Trophy® are registered
trademarks of HarperCollins Publishers, Inc.

YOUNG JOAN
Copyright © 1991 by Barbara Dana

Library of Congress Cataloging-in-Publication Data
Dana, Barbara. Young Joan: a novel / by Barbara Dana;
based on the life of Saint Joan of Arc.
p.   cm.
"A Charlotte Zolotow book."
Summary: Joan, a girl growing up in the French country-
side during the Hundred Years' War, begins to hear voices
telling her she is destined to reunite her torn country in
opposition to the English invaders.
ISBN 0-06-021423-6 [lib. bdg.]
ISBN 0-06-440661-X (pbk.)
1. Joan, of Arc, Saint, 1412-1431—Juvenile fiction. [1.
Joan, of Arc, Saint, 1412-1434—Fiction. 2. France—
History—Charles VII, 1422-1461—Fiction.] I. Title.
PZ7.D188Yo   1991   90-39494
[Fic]—dc20   CIP
                                                  AC

Typography by Steve Scott

First Harper Trophy edition, 1997.

To the spirit of Joan

Contents

Prologue   xi

PART I

1   Home   3
2   The War   8
3   Island Castle   17
4   The Dream   25
5   The Wish-Fulfilling Tree   29
6   The Prophecy   34
7   The Voice in the Garden   45

PART II

8   The Call   55
9   Peddler Man   65
10   Philip Mouse   75
11   Fireflies   83
12   Return   91
13   Saint Michael   99

PART III

14   Catherine   109
15   Notre Dame de Bermont   119
16   The Mission   129

17   Joyful Counsel   137
18   Picnic   147
19   Another Place   154
20   Daughter of God   161
21   Hauviette's Plan   169
22   Pony Cart   179
23   Knowing   185

PART IV

24   The Walk   195
25   The Gray   203
26   Father's Dream   214
27   Uncle Durand   224
28   Simon's Fear   234
29   The Siege   242
30   God's Choice   250
31   Burey   260
32   Vaucouleurs   268
33   Friendship Stone   276
34   Ungiven Vow   286
35   Neufchâteau   295
36   Toul   304
37   Question   310
38   Wooly Lamb   320

     Epilogue   331

black belt. "Hurry," he said. "Jean, get your shirt."

moved to the door. "I will get the sheep," I said.

"Why make difficulties when all is one?"
—Joan of Arc

Prologue

When I was nineteen, or thereabouts, I spent quite some time in prison. They kept me in two different towers. I tried to escape from the first one. It was a high tower of sixty feet, but I jumped and hurt my ankle. After I hit the ground I was unconscious, so I could not run away.

When I first woke up the pain was very great. I was afraid because it hurt so much. My leg was swollen, and I thought it would burst. I lay on the cold stone floor in fear and pain until I remembered to give my pain to God. As soon as I did this all the pain went away, and so did the fear. I felt like I was floating in the arms of my Lord.

They said I jumped to kill myself, but this is not true. It is not my place. God decides when I am to leave this earth, and only God. Who am I to have a better idea? I jumped because I wanted to go and help all the poor people still fighting and giving their lives to save France.

My Saints told me not to jump. I did wrong to disobey them. They knew best, as they always do. I thought that they were merely trying to save me from injury. I have never minded injury for a just cause, so I decided to jump. I tried to use my mind to understand their message, but that is not the way. I can only use my heart. I beg their forgiveness.

After I gave my pain to God, as I lay there in the Lord's embrace, I thought I might be dead. I had no fear. I remembered back to when I was a little girl. I was thinking about the farm, and my dear parents, and my brothers, and my sister Catherine, and Wooly Lamb, and the red dress I wore when I left. I know not how long I thought about these things.

Part I

"The angels often come among us.
Others may not see them, but I do."

1

Home

Our house was made of stone with a slanted roof and small windows. Sometimes, during the day, a lot of light would come through the windows, and it was especially warm and cozy inside. Even in the winter, when it got so cold, still the sun made it seem warm.

We lived in a small village called Domrémy. In front of our house was the road, and then the fields, with the beautiful grass and trees. Far across were the mountains. Through the fields went the river Meuse. In many places there were trees and bushes at the very edge of the river. At the offshoots of the Meuse it got very reedy. Sometimes, when it had not rained for a long time, I could jump across the reedy offshoot section in front of Hauviette's barn. Somehow my brothers were never there to see me do it. In their minds I was always Short Legs, their teasing name for me, and I could not jump across anything big.

Our family was very close. My father was tall, as big as the roof of our barn, and very strong, but he was gentle underneath, and careful with the animals. He worked hard, but always had kind words for us and for my mother. He ran our farm, and also he was a leading citizen of our village. He helped the mayor in many ways and also helped all the people in the village when disputes or differences would happen. He also held the lease to the big castle where we took the animals when danger came.

My mother was kind and good. She was my friend. Because I was a girl, I spent much time with her. She taught me to sew and spin. When I first started spinning and sewing I was not very good, but those things are hard for small children. At that time I could only spin for a short while before my fingers would ache, and I would get tiny cramps around my thumb and have to stop. Mother taught me many things, but first of all she taught me love of God. It was from her that I learned everything. She taught me the Pater Noster, the Ave Maria, and the other prayers. I learned my faith from no one save my mother. My father loved God too, but his mind would go to other things sometimes because he had such great responsibility. He would forget that God will care for us always.

Between my mother and father there was much respect. Hauviette said that in her neighbor's house the husband would sometimes hit or even beat his wife if he did not like what she did. In many families I think they were doing this according to the laws.

In our town the law was that the wife was a part of the household, belonging to the husband, and had to be "kept in line." This is how they said it. The husband could beat his wife, but he could not kill her, a small difference at that point, if you ask me! In our house it was not like that. I never saw my father hit my mother, nor did my brothers or my sister,

Catherine, see it. There was a great love between my mother and father, and a great understanding. My father would often ask my mother, "Well, what do you think?" and she would tell him. Men should not beat women. The town laws were wrong. No person owns another. We each belong only to God.

I have three brothers and my sister Catherine. Jacquémin is older than the rest of us. By the time I was ten, he was living in Vouthon, where my mother was born. Soon after he left, Catherine got married. It was hard to let her go. We had always been as one, sharing the same room even. For a time I missed her greatly. She married a nice boy, who had a loving smile. His name was Colin. They moved to Greux, which was his town. Now, moving to Greux from Domrémy is almost like not moving because the towns are so close. Greux is only a step-walk away. I had to remind myself of this many times, and that Catherine was happy, and that her marriage was God's will. Then I felt better.

After that it was just myself and Pierre and Jean at home with Mother and Father. Older brothers can be blessings in many ways. They teach you things, but often they tease you. Pierre and Jean did both. I always liked their room. It was smaller than mine, but you could see the very back corner of the church from their window. I could see a piece of one of the Piney Bush Trees and sometimes the sky, but this was only in the winter when the big tree next to the far back Piney Bush Tree had no leaves. I thought it would be wonderful to see the church, but then I had the church in my heart. I did not need to see its corner from my window. My window was so small. Before I was seven, or thereabouts, I could fit through it by turning sideways, but after that I was too big.

Directly behind the house was Father's garden. If you stood looking away from the house, to the left, near the edge of the garden, ran the little brook that fed into the Meuse. Sometimes at night the brook sounded so loud outside my window. When I was very tired I did not hear it. There were many old, mossy rocks near the brook with sharp edges and carved-out places. The water must have made them like that after many years. I wonder how old they were.

To the right of Father's garden was the church. It was so comforting to be next to the church. You felt you could reach out and touch it. How I loved that garden! There were many trees. In spring there were flowers, and in summer came the vegetables, turnips for sure. My favorite trees were the three pine trees or Piney Bush Trees. I always called them that because they were so stout. I also loved the tall, gnarled Grandfather Tree with lots of vines, and the clumpy Troll Tree directly behind the house. These were my names for the trees. I never told anyone.

The Troll Tree could be climbed. Sometimes I would sit on the first ledge of the tree, the first heavy, twisted limb, and look at the church, waiting for the church bells. Also from this tree you could get a good view of the fields behind the house, and the barns, and the animals grazing. The tall, gnarled Grandfather Tree almost touched the roof on the tall side. One time Pierre and Jean climbed that tree and jumped over onto the roof. Father got angry when that happened. I was glad I had decided not to follow them. At the time it seemed exciting, but also dangerous in a meaningless way. I always felt that if you were going to do something dangerous, you should have a good reason for it.

2

The War

I was born during the great Hundred Years' War. From what I could see it was more than a war. It was constant attacks on the innocent people and animals by bands of brigands and thieves and soldiers turned into madmen. Father said the brigands and thieves were merely using a bad time to their selfish advantage, while some of the soldiers were half crazed. Others were following orders to break the backs of the French by weakening the people and destroying their means of survival.

The main trouble was that the English wanted to take our land. This was wrong. Our land was a gift from God. They had their gift from God in their beautiful English countryside, for though I have not seen it with my eyes I have heard tales of its beauty. All the French people who were born on French soil were surely put there by God. God must have intended for us to care for the land we found ourselves on. Not that we owned it. That is never true. All is God's. We own nothing, neither country nor town, nor house, for that matter. It only seems so. All is given by God, in trust, to care for while we walk the earth for a short time. And so God gave the French the French land, and the English the English land, because that was the way He wanted it to be.

From the first I heard of it I knew the English had no right to be in France, not if they were unfriendly. Some of the French people thought they did have a right, however. I know not why. These French were called Burgundians. They joined up with the English, making war on their own people, their brothers and sisters in France. Many of the French, called Armagnacs, who wanted to keep the land God gave them to care for, fought against the Burgundians.

All the people suffered greatly, and so, to the sadness of my heart, did the poor animals. Many times when I was little the Burgundians would come into the villages, attack the people, set fire to all the crops, and kill the animals. This upset me greatly. I heard many stories of these things. Although in our village it had not happened yet, always, beneath our thoughts, was the worry "When will it happen here?" It was no way to live.

The animals felt it too. There was an alarm bell that would sound in our village when danger was near, one ring from the north, two from the south. At the sound of the bell the sheep and cattle and other animals would run for cover. You could see the fear in their eyes. So often, in the deep of night, the bell would ring, and we would gather all the animals and a few things that we could carry, and escape to the Island Castle. When the danger was past my heart would be so full of gratitude to God for sparing the lives of my dear family, and of the animals who asked for nothing but to sleep and graze in peace.

Always I have loved animals. There was a common pasture in town where all the town animals grazed together. The different families would take their turns watching the flocks. Sometimes I would take my turn, and as it pleased God, it was my favorite task. When I was little I spent more time with the animals, but when I reached the age of understanding that changed. Mother needed me in the house. It was time for me to learn the woman things.

Of all the animals, the sheep were my special favorites, so sweet and comical, so simple in their ways. I loved their puffed-out bodies, their narrow legs, their flat ears pointing out to the sides. When they looked at me they always seemed to wonder what I was thinking.

Behind the house we kept the pens and sheds. That was where the barn was. Mostly the animals stayed outside, except on the coldest winter nights. Always, in the days, they would prefer the cold, sharp wind and the sunlight to the smallness of their barn quarters.

There was one night I especially remember. Although I did not know it then, on this one night began the many changes in God's plan for me. Oh, Catherine and Jacquémin left, and that was different, but nothing like the big changes that were to come. Before this night it was church, and Mother and Father, my brothers, and Catherine, my dear friends, the sheep and cattle, the birds, my stone house, Father's garden, the big iron soup pot, Mother's apron, her long brown hair put back, her loving smile, my cozy bed, the trees, my red dress, Father's hug, our valley, the spinning, and most of all, God. It was a rich, full life, with songs and love and changing seasons, and always the church bells, and the warmth of God's love, and the Saints protecting us. All beautiful, save the fighting. It was simple, and good, and all I thought that I would ever know. But God had other plans.

This night we were all in bed early, even Father, which was not usual. It was early spring. I was in my thirteenth year. It was a quiet night, and cold. I lay in my narrow bed, listening to the brook outside my window. I remember I was thinking, that night, about my dearest of true friends, Hauviette. She was younger than I was by some years. When Mother did not need me inside we were always together. Hauviette had a daring nature and always had ideas of good ways to enjoy life. She liked to dance, which was more to her way than mine.

That night I was thinking of her dancing in the large meadow behind her barn, and of how I was laughing because she did funny motions and tried to stand on her head. That was her mistake because she soon fell into the Meuse. Another dear friend, Mengette, was there was well, and Simon, the small boy who lived next door. He had been sick the year before. I did not miss a day to be at his side, to hold his hand, to bring him God's love and faith, because he was very much afraid.

After Hauviette fell into the Meuse we laughed so hard that we were too weak, almost, to pull her out. She was laughing too.

"The next time you do that, stay away from the river," I told her.

"I thought of that," she said.

After that we had to rush her inside because it was so cold.

I was almost asleep, thinking of poor, wet Hauviette, with her hair all in strings and dripping, when the alarm bell sounded. I always felt that sound in my stomach, and my heart would stop in fear. This must have happened to the animals as well.

The bell clanged. It took me a moment to return to breathing. I sprang up from bed as we were trained to do, grabbed my gray, patched dress, and pulled it over my nightdress. Then I grabbed my bed cover for extra warmth and ran into the kitchen. Pierre and Jean were standing there. Pierre had on his big shirt only. Jean had but his pants.

"Get dressed," I said. I was pulling my bed cover around my shoulders.

"We are dressed," said Jean. He was not really awake.

"You look not dressed to me," I said.

"Look once more," said Pierre.

"You have no pants."

"Get your pants," said Jean.

"And you, your shirt," said Pierre.

I grabbed my sack of provisions from the corner by the window. We always kept ready five sacks of important things to take with us to the island. Mine contained two metal pots for cooking and five bowls, one for each of us.

Father hurried into the kitchen, fastening up his thick, black belt. "Hurry," he said. "Jean, get your shirt."

I moved to the door. "I will get the sheep," I said.

"Hurry," said Father.

My heart was pounding as I headed for the pens. The alarm bell kept sounding. One ring, then quiet. They were coming from the north. That was good. The island hideout was south. Thank God. We had a chance.

I tugged at the latch to open the pens. It was so dark, the moon barely showing through the small breaks in the clouds. I could not see the latch. I pushed my fingers to remember how to open it without sight. The sheep clustered by the gate, pushing and bleating in fear. They had been through this many times before. They caught the terror in the hearts of the people and did not understand.

"Be still," I told them. "I will get you out."

Again the alarm. Pierre and Jean passed me with the cattle. Father hurried to my side. He carried his heavy sack, filled with food. We always brought enough for several days. "Let me," he said.

Just then the latch gave way. We moved the sheep out to join the cattle and Mother and my brothers on the road. The moon was brighter here. I could see the other villagers coming from their houses and yards with their provisions and their livestock, sheep, cattle, horses, hens. Simon carried his favorite goose. Simon's trousers were too large for him, his shirt too small. His trousers were fastened tightly at the waist with a piece of rope. He looked younger than his years, and he was only eight. His eyes were wide with fear for the safety of his beloved pet.

"My goose is afraid," said Simon.

"I know," I answered. "Place him in God's care."

"I place you in God's care," Simon shouted loudly at the unsuspecting goose.

The goose blinked, his thoughts inward.

"He does not understand," said Simon.

"Tell him with your heart."

"Hurry, Simon," said his mother. She moved up from behind, carrying a baby. She had a hold of another small child by the hand. This was Simon's sister, Aimée. She was tiny, stumbling in the dirt, crying, half awake.

We moved along the road. Around me there was much murmuring, not loud, but so much fear. My feet ached. One was cut already. The soles of my feet were strong and callused, but in the dark, in such a hurry, and with all the animals, it was hard to see the sharp rocks and stones and pointed sticks.

The alarm bell sounded for both towns, Domrémy and Greux. I thought of Catherine.

Let them hear the alarm! I prayed. Let them not be sleeping!

I thought of the stories I had heard of innocent people, their eyes put out, their feet cut off. I knew of no one to whom this had happened, but other things had happened, nearly as bad. My cousin's husband had been killed by a stone cannonball. I prayed silently for Catherine and Colin.

We moved on. You wanted to run, but that way there would be no control. The animals might panic and run off. You had to move them quietly, faithfully, constantly forward, a fast and steady walk.

Mother moved up by my side. She carried the sack with the blankets. "Joan," she said, "my baby." That was all.

We moved along silently together. My brothers and Father and I were moving the animals, surrounding them, each on different sides, always steady, always forward. My feet were hurting badly now, another cut, this time on the other foot. A cow had stepped on it, too, but you could not think of it, only of the poor animals, and of all your village friends in such great danger, and the enemy at our backs. How close? No stopping. No running. Only forward. Walk fast. Be silent. You must not draw attention. You were going into hiding. No one must know where.

The ewe before me stopped. At first I did not see this. I walked into her and nearly fell. The ewe turned, looked up at me, and bleated.

"Quiet!"

Another bleat, louder this time.

"Move! For God's sweet sake!"

Another bleat from my confused and frightened friend.

"Quiet now! Be still!"

"Hurry, Joan," said Mother.

"She will not move."

"She must."

People were passing me on both sides now, some knocking into me, not meaning to, not seeing. The ewe kept bleating. I wanted to pick her up, to carry her, but she was too heavy.

"Jacques!" shouted Mother.

Father turned back to see what was wrong.

"The ewe!" called Mother.

"Joan!" shouted Father. "Make her come!"

I bent down and grabbed the ewe by her thick, wooly neck, her coat, really, and pulled.

"We must go! We must!" I told her. "Please!"

She stared a long while, then bleated loudly in my face.

She must move, I thought. I cannot leave her. But if I stay Father will be angry. He will pick me up and carry me to save my life, but what of the ewe?

She stared at me, pleading.

People kept moving past, and also the animals.

"Joan!" said Mother. She had stayed at my side.

God help me, I thought.

I let all tension go from my body, let go my hold on the thick wooly coat, and gently patted the ewe on the top of her head.

All is well, I told her from my heart. We can stay here forever, or we can go. You decide.

I patted her once more. "As you will," I told her.

She turned then, and we followed the others.

3

Island Castle

At last we could see the castle. More than two hours of steady walking had brought it into view. It was a big castle, abandoned now, on an island in the Meuse. It had a half-circle tower to the south and two square towers to the north. These towers were used to look out for the approach of the enemy. Pierre and Jean were among those who shared the watch. Also Michel Lebuin, another boy from town.

The moon shone brightly as we moved the animals to the edge of the river. It was not deep at that place, and although it was cold, the water was welcome on my feet. They were cut quite badly now and almost numb. Also, my sack of pots and bowls was cutting into my shoulder from where the rope was carrying all the weight.

The animals were happy to cross through the water. They wanted to stop and drink, but you had to keep them going. They could drink on the far side of the castle, where they were less likely to be seen. We moved them through the river and to the other side. The water came up to my knees in some places. You could feel the relief in all the people and in the animals, too. They had been through this often. The Island Castle was always quiet, and although you never knew for sure, it felt safe.

We moved the flocks to the pasture, a space of sixty swaths, where we took turns watching them. That night I was in the first group. Pierre and Jean had gone up to the towers, so that left me, Michel Lebuin, and another boy from town named Henri. I moved off from them to pray, to offer my thanks to God for delivering us safely to the castle. But for God's grace, we never would have made it.

When I returned Hauviette was there. She had come with Simon and Mengette to look for me. We huddled together by the broken stone wall, on the cold grass, by the light of the bright, bright moon. I shared my bed-cover shawl with Hauviette because she did not have one.

"Where is the goose?" I asked Simon.

"In a place I made for him," he said. "I made it last time out of stones, around some grass, by the west wall. He can move freely there and rest, but he cannot get away."

"That is well," I said. "Did you give him some water?"

"I did," said Simon.

"I wonder how long we shall be here this time," said Mengette. She did not care for the outdoor life, so it was hard for her when we went to the island. I loved sleeping beneath God's stars, and all the beauty. I did not mind the cold or the roughness of the ground, but Mengette did.

"It could be forever," said Simon.

"I hope not," said Mengette.

"How could that be?" asked Hauviette, adjusting herself

under our shawl. "Forever is a long time."

"The longest," said Simon.

"So how could it be?"

"If the enemy comes right here to this castle and kills us, then that would be forever."

"Please," said Mengette. She pulled her long dress snugly around her knees. "Can we speak of something else?"

Hauviette ignored her question. "How is that forever?" she asked. "They would kill us fast. We would be dead. That would not take forever."

"Yes, it would," said Simon. "They would leave us on the ground to rot."

"Please," said Mengette.

"We would be here forever."

"Our spirits would go to heaven," said Hauviette.

"I meant a different thing," said Simon.

"What thing?" said Hauviette.

"You have it wrong."

"You see it as you look," said Michel, sounding very wise.

"I care not to see it," said Henri. "What about you, Joan?"

Henri was always trying to get me to join into everything when so often I wished to be quiet and think of God. Hauviette said he liked me and was going to ask me to marry him one day. I hoped not. I thought he was stupid. I tried to be kind, as he was, of course, a child of God, but he did not know that. He would often tease the animals, and this I could not watch.

"So, Joan," he persisted, "how is your mind on the matter?"

"What matter is that?"

"Do you want to think about death and dying and forever?"

"I do not mind."

"That is no answer."

"It is her answer," said Michel. "There is nothing wrong with it." Michel was slightly older than the rest of us, though not by much. To my mind he was very wise. His words were always sensible and filled with reason.

"Some people were tortured in Vouthon last week," said Simon. He was digging in the ground with a stick, poking at stones. "They were tortured over a slow fire."

"Please," said Mengette.

"How do you know?" said Hauviette.

"People said."

"Who said?" asked Hauviette.

"People," said Simon.

"What people?"

"Different people," said Simon. "Different people said it. They were tortured."

"Please," repeated Mengette.

"Over a slow, hot fire."

"All fires are hot," said Hauviette.

"No one listens to me," said Mengette.

"And some children were stolen. They would not tell where the cattle were hidden, so they stole them. They probably burned them, too."

"You know that not," said Hauviette.

"Nobody knows where they are."

"God is looking out for them," I told him. "Of that you can be sure."

"God again," said Henri. He always seemed offended when I spoke of God.

"She can speak of God if she wants to," said Hauviette. "You should try it. It might do you some good."

About then I left Hauviette with my shawl and moved off to look for Catherine. She and Colin were sleeping in a sheltered place on the far side of the castle. I let them sleep.

Later that night I was speaking with Father. We sat up on a small hill on blankets that Mother had set down for us. We had blankets around us, too, for warmth. Many of the people were asleep, at least those who were not keeping watch, or were not too frightened or too nervous to sleep. I remember asking Father to tell me about the war and the fighting, because there was so much I did not understand.

Father told me this. When I was born it was a bad time of civil war. The fighting was between the Burgundians and the Armagnacs. The Burgundians were the French people who wanted the English to take France. The Armagnacs were the French people who wanted to keep France for the French. These two groups wanted to rule the government of our king, Charles VI. The sad thing was that King Charles was very ill. The sickness was in his mind. He was tortured by problems only he could understand. It was said that he would roam the halls, howling like a wolf. He was once found cowering in a corner, believing himself to be made of glass.

When I was still quite small the English king, Henry V, took advantage of the confusion to once again stake his claim on the French throne. He had done that before and, in his mind, this was a good time to try again. He came into France and won a large battle, the Battle of Agincourt.

A little while later, when I was still small, the Burgundians captured Paris, so it was theirs and in the hands of the English. Right after that the Duke of Burgundy was killed. This frightened the Duke's son, who joined up with the English. Then it was more people on the English side.

The next year Charles VI, our king who had sickness of mind, was persuaded by his disloyal wife, Queen Isabella, to sign a treaty called the Treaty of Troyes. This treaty said that the king disinherited his son, the Dauphin, Prince Charles. It said that the heir to the French throne was Henry, the English king! This was a terrible thing because the king's true son, Charles, was given the job by God. His father had no just right to take that commission from him. Of course King Charles was sick of mind, so you could not blame him, but that did not make it right.

The very next year, as God would have it, both Henry V, the English king, and Charles VI, the French king, died. So who did that leave to rule France? The son of the French king, who was given the job by God? No. It was the English King Henry's infant son, a baby, who now ruled both England and France! God sets things right, and the people change it, and everything suffers. What we had then, as Father and I sat on the hill, was an infant ruling England and France and the true son of the French king, whose duty it was to take over for his father, now merely Dauphin, leader of the Armagnacs, who had become the national party of France. And more fighting, and more, 'til we could see no end.

"It is wrong," I said. "It is not the way God wants it."

"I know," said Father.

"And not because God is on the side of the French. God is not for the French. God is for justice."

"Some people see it differently," said Father.

"That does not change the truth."

Father looked at me and smiled. "You are right," he said.

I was glad that Father would discuss things with me.

Many fathers would not take the time to discuss things with their daughters, especially things that dealt with war or other serious subjects. Father was never like that. He always had respect for me. When I asked a question, he would always answer.

"The English have a terrible fighting plan," he said.

"What is that?"

Father breathed in deep, then let the air out through his mouth. He always did that when he did not like a situation. He looked out from our little hill to the valley in the moonlight. "We see it all around us," he said. "The soldiers are told, 'Set fire to everything, houses, churches, crops, orchards. Destroy the villages, kill the animals or take them for food. Burn everything. Break the spirit of the people so they will come to the enemy's side.'"

Just then Mother came with some bread for us and asked for Father's help with something. I do not remember what it was. They left me on the hill with my bread. It tasted good, so welcome after such difficult talk. I was looking off to the chapel at the east side of the castle as I ate. The chapel was made in the shape of a half circle and consecrated to Saint Peter. Soon I finished my bread. After that I went down to check on the sheep.

The sheep were fine. Michel was with them still, and Simon, too. Just as I joined them a strong rain came up. The sheep moved under the trees, and I ran off to the Saint Peter Chapel to get out of the rain and pray.

It was a small chapel. I always loved it there. You could feel the warmth of the prayers left by others. I prayed a long while. After that I lay down to rest. I did not expect to sleep, but I did. That was when I had the dream.

4

The Dream

I was in a big field. There was bright sun coming through the clouds in shafts of light. I was wearing a thin, pale-gray dress.

God is here, said a voice.

I know.

There was light all around, in the fields, in my head, coming from my body and my hands. It was very bright. In the middle of my forehead there was a jewel of light. It was blue-purple. I could see it as if my eyes were outside my body. Ahead of me the light was blinding. Again, the voice.

You must help the Dauphin.

Me?

It is your job.

How?

I could feel the light move into me and through me and out in all directions. I felt very big, as big as the sky. The light passed through me, but still there was light in my head and my hands. I woke suddenly, with a burning in my chest, and was very much afraid.

I thought a lot about the dream. The thing that worried me was that deep in my heart I knew it was not really a dream at all. I had had many dreams before that, some scary, some beautiful, some so real you could reach out and touch the things you dreamed of, awake, and be surprised to find it was not true. Other dreams would be so fanciful, like magic, a great make-believe story that no one could make up. Some would be funny with odd bits and pieces, glimpses of things that happened the day before mixed with things from years ago that you had completely forgotten. People you knew would be doing things you never saw them do, in ways you could never imagine, like Mother sitting in a tree saying, "I need my red hat," when I never saw her wear a hat of any color, or Pierre shrunken to the size of a turnip, sitting in a milking pail. There were familiar kinds of dreams, of me pounding on the church door when the bells are ringing, and no one lets me in. I had that dream once. I awoke so much afraid. My heart was pounding, but in minutes, or less, I knew it was just a dream. It was over. Somehow it needed to be, and now it was gone, released by God's grace. I could go to the church and find an open door. It was only a dream.

This was different. This dream, in the tiny Saint Peter Chapel on that cold spring night in the rain, was not a dream at all. This I knew with all my heart. It was real, a thing I must pass through, not over with the morning, but part of my life, a signal, a job to be done. I knew in my heart that God had given me a commission on that night. I know not how I knew, yet it was so. But what of the commission? Me? Help the Dauphin? It made no sense. How could I possibly help the Dauphin? I was a child, a girl, with no experience, no ways of the world. What could I do? I knew nothing that he did not know. I knew less. And he must have men to help him, with knowledge far greater than mine. I knew less than my father, my mother, my brothers, less than Catherine or Colin, less than Michel, less than almost anyone, except for Henri, of course, but that was not the point, and a very prideful thought as well. God, forgive me, but he was stupid! Enough of that. If strength was needed, why not ask my father or Pierre or Jean, some army captain or some soldier? What could I possibly do?

And then it came to me.

I could pray.

I was sitting under a large oak tree just outside the chapel. The grass was still damp from the rain, but the day was bright, with that clear, clean after-the-rain smell.

I could pray.

I leaned my back against the solid tree to think in comfort. I could hear the others talking on the far side of the chapel. The danger had passed, they said. The soldiers had not come as far south as Domrémy but had gone east at Pagny, then north to Toul.

I can pray, I thought. That is what God meant! That was His message, surely.

I knew the power of prayer. That I did know. Had I not prayed for Simon to be brought by God's grace through his fever, knowing all the while in my heart that this could be? Had I not prayed for birds with broken wings, for sheep with trouble at birth? And, as it pleased God, were these not comforted by His love? Then why not pray for the Dauphin?

Surely, that was it. That was my job in all of this. I could pray. When one knows the power of prayer one must use it. I must be mindful. I must pray for what I know in my heart is right, for the perfect outworking of God's plan for all the creatures, for Simon, for the birds, for the sheep, and no less for the Dauphin.

So there beneath the friendly oak I prayed my first prayer for the Dauphin. If it be God's will, I prayed, may great help come to the Dauphin. May he be strengthened, comforted, according to God's will. May he carry out God's perfect plan with ease and sureness.

On the way home I decided to pray for the Dauphin several times a day. No matter what else I was doing, no matter what my duties were, or how many others I had to pray for, I would never forget the Dauphin.

5

The Wish-Fulfilling Tree

Not far from our house, within view of Father's garden, on a hill to the south, in the beautiful oak woods known as the Bois Chenu, was my favorite tree. It was a huge and ancient beech tree by the edge of the forest. Many things were said about that tree. Some said it was the most ancient of trees, that it had stood proudly in its place since the memory of any man who walked the earth. Others said there had been fairies there. They said they no longer came in our time, but years ago had come there often. Others said it was a healing tree. A stream ran by near the tree, and it was said that many drank from the stream to be healed of illness. I saw some people do this, but I do not know if they were healed. Some called the tree the Fairies' Tree, some the Ladies' Tree, some the Big Old Beech. I called it the Wish-Fulfilling Tree. It had a remarkable beauty. One time when I was picnicking under the tree with some of my friends, I named it the Wish-Fulfilling Tree. I was sitting beneath it, and I was so filled with its protecting beauty. The thought came to me that any purely unselfish wish, made in true devotion and deep faith beneath God's tree of such beauty, was bound to come true. I felt this in my heart. Then

I named the tree. After that I remember thinking that any wish of that same kind made anywhere would come true, but since I had learned all this beneath the great beech tree, inspired as I was by its beauty, I gave the tree the name. Always when I came to the Wish-Fulfilling Tree, before doing anything else, I would circle it several times and make a wish, always sure that it be unselfish and always sure that God would grant it.

The same spring that I began to pray for the Dauphin, after the poor cattle were stolen, we had a picnic under the Wish-Fulfilling Tree that I especially remember.

It was a Sunday soon after Easter. I got up early to make bread for us to take. The plan was to go after Mass with Hauviette and Mengette. Simon wanted to join us, but he was needed at home. We would take bread, wine, nuts, eggs, and breadrolls. The agreement was that I would make the bread and bring the eggs, Hauviette would bring the nuts and a cloth to sit on, and Mengette would bring the wine and the breadrolls.

In the kitchen it was dark. The sun had not yet risen. I had a good view of things by the light of the fire, however. I loved our great big fireplace, the old familiar racks and hooks hanging over the fire to hold the cauldron and kettles. I remember Pierre especially loved the skewers and other utensils that hung on the sides. Sometimes he would play knights with them, using them as swords when Mother did not need them and did not mind. That morning he was asleep, though, as were all the others in the house. I kneaded the dough with full force and great joy, expecting the warmth of the day ahead.

After I made the bread I changed into my brown Sunday dress for Mass. Then I went out into Father's garden, where I sat up in the Troll Tree waiting for the church bells. I prayed for the Dauphin, and for a calf that was refusing to drink.

At Mass I was joyful knowing that I would make a garland at our picnic. I would offer it to Saint Margaret. Her statue in church was so beautiful, her blessing left hand, the drapes of gentle cloth in her robe, her soft and simple hair. I loved that statue.

After Mass we went back to our houses to get the food and the other picnic things. We then set off to "do the springs." That was how Mengette always said it. She said she had heard her mother say it that way, and she liked that way of putting it. "Let us do the springs," she would say, and that would mean picnic time for sure, beneath the Wish-Fulfilling Tree by the side of the stream.

It was already warm as the three of us carried our picnic things down the road toward the oak woods. Hauviette carried the nuts in a sack. She had tied the sitting cloth around her waist like a big skirt, which was her usual way. Mengette had the basket with her things. I carried the eggs in a cloth and the bread under my arm. We were quiet on our way, enjoying the freedom of God's beauty and our thoughts of the day to come. Soon we reached the woods on the hill, and there at the foot of the path stood the Wish-Fulfilling Tree. I was always surprised by its size and its beauty. I often thought of the tree in the cold months when we stayed at home. Always in my thoughts it was big and beautiful, but never did it match in my mind what it was in God's own truth, so proud, so green, so protecting, so timeless, so welcoming.

"Wait," said Hauviette. She worked at the knot in her sitting-cloth skirt. "Let me get this untied."

"We let you," said Mengette, switching her basket to the other arm. "By fact we want you to untie it. This basket is heavy."

I breathed in deep, joyful to be beneath the tree. I was joyful, too, about the breadrolls. Mengette's breadrolls were a special treat, to be remembered and desired long after eating. I was hungry, too. I went without breakfast on those picnic mornings to make a big appetite. The early hour at which I arose to make the bread put long hours to my empty stomach.

"Hold this," I told Mengette, handing her my sack of eggs. I still had the bread under my arm. "Why did you make it so tight?" I asked Hauviette. I reached out to help her with the knot.

"I wished it not to fall."

"You have your wish," I said, tugging at the knotted cloth.

"I wished it to stay clean."

"Dirty would have been better than this," I told her. "It will go on the ground at any rate."

"Hurry," said Mengette. "My arms are breaking."

"They are not," said Hauviette. "You always make so much of a thing."

"They are my arms," said Mengette. "I would surely know."

I opened the knot. "At last!" I said, and spread out our precious sitting cloth.

Hauviette popped a nut into her mouth and threw herself down onto the cloth, rolling around, exclaiming, "our cloth, our cloth!"

Mengette and I just stood there, waiting for her to calm herself and get up so we could set the food down. After that we all lay down in the grass, rolling over and over, just enjoying ourselves, and laughing and feeling dizzy. Then I got up to make my wish. I took a long look at the Wish-Fulfilling Tree, then began to make my wishing circles.

"Why do you always do that?" asked Mengette. She had stopped rolling. She lay flat and still, watching me as I circled.

"I am wishing," I told her.

"Can you not wish standing still?"

"I can wish any way."

"Then why make circles?"

"Why not?"

That started Hauviette laughing. "Why not?" she said.

"Why not?" repeated Mengette. "I suppose you are right."

"Joan is always right," said Hauviette.

"Not so," I said.

"You are very right," said Hauviette.

I am not right, I thought. God is right. I only get in the way. May it not be often.

6

The Prophecy

"I think the breadrolls should be first," I said, watching Mengette open up the basket.

"Breadrolls are more a dessert food," she said. She sounded overly serious, the way she often did, grown-up before her time. I think sometimes she tried to be as her mother. "I suggest the eggs," she continued.

I wanted the breadrolls. "How about this?" I asked. "One breadroll now, and then the eggs and the other things, and then all the rest of the breadrolls."

"I like that," said Hauviette. She was already dancing around the tree, caught up in a little made-up dance, humming quietly to herself.

"Fine," said Mengette, setting out the food.

We had a most wonderful lunch, stopping between mouthfuls to run to the stream and drink. The water was cold and clear, welcome beyond telling. Sometimes we would bend over, our knees on the soft, grassy earth, our hands at the edge of the stream, our faces in the water. Other times we would walk directly into the stream, water to our ankles, and stand, just feeling the wonderful coolness travel through our bodies. Soon we would bend, gather the water in our hands, then throw it on our faces. After that we would run back for the extra breadrolls, the tasty nuts, and sips of wine.

Toward the end of the meal Mengette mentioned the subject. "I became a woman yesterday," she announced, thoughtfully studying her breadroll.

Hauviette's eyes opened wide. "What do you mean?" she asked.

"You know," said Mengette.

"I do not," said Hauviette. "What do you mean?"

"We can discuss it another time."

"You cannot get away with that," said Hauviette. She gave Mengette a stubborn look. "What do you mean you became a woman?"

"I am no longer a child."

"You have taken a husband?"

Mengette looked in my direction. "You explain it," she said. I turned to Hauviette. As she was younger, I knew she would not easily understand. "When a young girl reaches our age, she usually begins her monthly sickness," I told her.

"What monthly sickness?"

"It is the same with the animals," I explained. "It is just as God would have it."

"Does it hurt?"

"Not in the way you would think," said Mengette.

"What way is that?" asked Hauviette.

"You explain it," said Mengette.

Hauviette looked troubled. The conversation worried her, you could tell.

"Do not be upset," I told her. "You have some time to get used to the idea. And remember, God sees all women through it."

"There is just a bit of blood," said Mengette. I think she wanted to prepare Hauviette so she would not be frightened when it came to her.

"Blood?" said Hauviette. She was turning pale.

"A bit," I told her.

"I do not care for that."

"It is not like a knife cut," said Mengette.

"Still I do not like it," said Hauviette.

"Did yours arrive?" Mengette asked me.

"Not yet," I told her.

"You must tell me when it does."

"If you like."

Hauviette was staring at the sitting cloth.

"Fear not," I told her. "Mengette has had her first monthly sickness, and she is fine. Your mother has had it, and your grandmother as well, many times over. When it is your turn God will see that you are ready. Leave it to Him."

Hauviette said nothing for some moments, thinking of what I had told her. Shortly, she nodded in agreement, took another breadroll, and ate. I could see that she was comforted, for the present at any rate.

We ate the nuts, and then it was time to gather the wildflowers and make the garlands for the tree and for the statue of Saint Margaret. We were singing all the while. Some were songs we made up. One went like this.

> We gather the flowers in spring,
> In spring. (This was Hauviette's added part)
> We gather the flowers and sing,
> And sing. (Hauviette's part again)
> The beautiful tree will be joyful today,
> As joyful as we are this Sunday in May.

Hauviette always liked to put in another "in May" after the "in May" at the end of the last verse, but that was not the way the song went. One "in May" was enough. Still, she would always add it, and the laughing would start. There was another verse, but I cannot think of it.

That day, as I sat back down beneath the Wish-Fulfilling Tree to make my garland, a tiny bird was watching from the branch. It wanted a bit of bread, I could feel, so I put some crumbs in my hand, then held it out before me. The others were very still and quiet as they watched the bird consider the bread.

"Come and eat," I told it from my heart. "I will not hurt you."

I waited as it thought about this. It did not move a feather. After much time, it looked left, then right, then flew down to the ground, just near the edge of the cloth. We all held very still. I was looking at it. I told it again from my heart, "No harm will come. This is yours for the taking."

The bird looked and looked, wanting the crumbs so deeply. More stillness. We waited. Then a look to the left, a look to the right, a few steps forward and a sudden, tiny jump onto the pale-blue cloth. I held my hand more still than still. "In your own good time," I told it. And then, just then, it flew into my hand, ate, and was gone.

After that I went off for a while by the stream to pray. Hauviette and Mengette were used to my doing this, and did not mind. Many times other friends from the village would tease me for this, like Henri, as I have said, but they did not know any better. This time I prayed for the Dauphin, and for the tiny bird, and for Hauviette to lose all fear of becoming a woman.

When I came back to the tree I had a surprise. There, under the tree with Hauviette and Mengette, was Simon with his little sister, Aimée, and Mengette's little sister, Marguerite. As usual, Simon carried his treasured goose.

"Hello!" I called out, running to meet them.

"Hello!" they answered.

Mengette was not pleased to see her sister, and was telling her just that as I came near the tree. "This is my time with my friends," she was saying. "Must I always care for you?"

"Not always," said Marguerite. She was carrying an old piece of cloth, with wool tied in it, and a face sewn on. The nose was missing. "Now we can play."

"Playing is the same as caring for you," said Mengette.

"Oh, no," said Marguerite. "Playing is fun. Taking care of me is dull."

"How do you know?" asked Mengette.

"You told me."

"You can play with Aimée," said Mengette.

"She knows," said Aimée. Then they ran off into the field.

Simon sat down, still holding his goose. I sat down too, to finish making my garland for Saint Margaret. Hauviette and Mengette had already placed their garlands on the Wish-Fulfilling Tree. They were making others.

"I named him," said Simon.

"Named who?" said Hauviette.

"His goose," I said, for the fact was clear. Simon had spent many days trying to name his beloved pet. He had thought of many names, but no name seemed just right.

"Guess," said Simon, stroking the goose's soft, white feathers.

"What?" said Hauviette.

"Guess," said Simon.

"Who could guess?" said Mengette. "It could be anything."

"I picked the perfect name."

"Potato," said Hauviette.

"Potato?" said Simon. He liked it not.

"You told me to guess," said Hauviette.

The goose blinked its round, steady eyes. It shifted itself to a more comfortable position in Simon's lap.

"What is your guess, Joan?" asked Simon.

"I have none."

"Guess."

"I cannot."

"Get ready," said Simon.

"We have been ready for days," said Mengette.

"It had better be a good one," said Hauviette.

"Just wait," said Simon.

"What is it?" said Hauviette.

Simon looked straight into my eyes. He paused. And then, "Nicholas," he said. He paused, waiting for my approval. He seemed almost to have stopped breathing.

"Nicholas," said Mengette. I think she was surprised.

"A fine name," I told him.

"Nicholas," repeated Mengette.

"I like it," said Hauviette.

"So do I," said Simon. "Do you like it, Joan?"

"A fine name," I repeated. "It suits him well." It had great meaning for Simon, and so I had to tell him twice.

Simon stroked the goose gently, then set him down on the grass by the edge of the cloth. The goose, or Nicholas, I should say, sat for a moment, then puffed out his feathers, got up, and went to the stream for a drink.

How beautiful it is here, I thought. The soft breeze, the warm sun, the smell of flowers. What a beautiful day. Nicholas's name day. I shall remember it always. I was working my fingers, weaving the flower stems for the garland. Over, under, twist. Over, under, twist. I looked up from my work at the rich green forest, so many kinds of trees, oak and beech, willow, aspen, alder, ash and birch, wild cherry and pine. I wove for some moments, not looking at my work. As with the spinning, my fingers knew the way. I was searching the deep woods with my eyes for the wild creatures. I never saw them this close to the edge of the forest, but I had been farther in with my brothers and had sometimes seen deer. I once saw a wild boar. It looked confused, as if it were late for something it could not remember. I had not seen the wolves, but I knew they were there, and heron, and many other birds.

I was thinking of the creatures when Simon mentioned the prophecy. He was stretched out on the picnic cloth, staring up at the leaves of the Wish-Fulfilling Tree. He had one leg bent up. The other was crossed over it. "Did you ever hear the prophecy?" he asked.

"Who are you asking?" said Hauviette. She was working on a garland, pink and lavender and blue.

"Anyone," said Simon. "Whoever may know."

"Not me," said Hauviette.

I thought back, but at that time could remember none myself.

"What prophecy is that?" said Mengette. She was making the smallest of garlands, tiny dark flowers laced so tightly. It would almost have made a necklace for Nicholas. Perhaps she had that in her mind. I never asked. She pushed a strand of hair from her face, then studied her work. "If you mean the one that speaks of the witch that comes from the north," she continued, "and all the lands will freeze and the crops will die and everyone in the valley will die from starving, I care not to hear it."

"Then why tell it?" said Hauviette.

She had a point.

"I never heard that," said Simon. He was alarmed. Mengette would have done well to keep that story to herself.

Simon sat up, searching all at once for Nicholas, who was foraging through some weeds by the edge of the stream. Marguerite and Aimée were playing nearby.

"Nicholas!" called Simon when his eyes had found the goose.

Nicholas turned to regard Simon, then back to the marshy reeds and bugs.

"Stay nearby!" called Simon.

Nicholas kept to his task, not returning a look. Simon watched for a moment, then, assured his goose would go no distance, he returned his gaze to Mengette. "Is it true?" he asked.

"You may never know with a prophecy," said Mengette. "Is that not so, Joan?"

"Not until it happens," I answered.

"That one had better not happen," said Hauviette.

"We shall hope not," said Mengette, sounding, once more, too old.

Simon bent both his knees up, holding them with his arms. "I meant a different one," he said. "Father told us at supper. It came from a long-ago prophecy. Part of it has already come true."

"The good part, I hope," said Hauviette.

"It was bad," said Simon. "But the part that will come is good."

"A blessing," said Mengette.

"Let him talk," said Hauviette.

"Do you want to hear it?" said Simon.

"We do," I said.

"Perhaps you know it already."

"Tell us!" said Hauviette. The suspense was causing her impatience.

"Here it is," said Simon. "Let me remember what my father said."

"You remember it not?" said Hauviette. She was almost shouting.

"I do," said Simon.

"Well, then?" said Hauviette.

"Give him time," I said.

Simon swallowed, pausing a moment. In his mind, I think, he was back to the time when his father had spoken. He proceeded in a careful voice. "Nine hundred years ago there was a man named Merlin who said this: 'France will be ruined by a woman and saved by a maiden from the oak forests of Lorraine.'"

I felt a shiver.

"I heard that," said Hauviette.

"Everyone has," said Mengette.

"Oh," said Simon. He liked that not.

I had heard it too, but had forgotten.

"Who was the woman?" asked Hauviette.

"What woman?" said Mengette.

"The woman who ruined France. Simon said the bad part has happened already, so who was the woman?"

"Queen Isabella," said Simon.

I remembered hearing Father speak of her at the Island Castle.

"She was bad and tricked the king," Simon continued. "She made him sign a paper."

"What kind of paper?" asked Hauviette.

"It said his son was not his son, and the king of England was the head of France."

"Why did he sign that?" asked Hauviette.

"He was mad," said Mengette. "Mad people do strange things."

"But who is the maiden?" said Simon. "Is it someone we know?"

"It could be anyone, at any time," said Mengette, in her grown-up way. "If, in fact, it be true."

Nicholas shook his feathers, held his bill high in the air, then moved sideways some steps along the edge of the stream. I watched him drink.

7

The Voice in the Garden

When I returned home, Pierre had a toothache. He and Mother were in the kitchen, near the fireplace, where she was tending to the pain. Mother was good with healing. Always, when Father would get headaches, she would cure them with her special mixture.

"You have a headache," Mother would say.

Father would always answer, "You know my head."

"I know more than your head," Mother would reply, "but that I know as well. Sit and I will cure it."

Then Father would sit on the small wooden chair with his head back, and his long legs stretched out until they took up half the room.

For Father's headaches Mother would apply a linen cloth, soaked in root of peony mixed with oil of roses, to where the pain was. This she showed me. I had to do it once for Jean when Mother was not well. It soothed the pain in little time.

This afternoon Pierre was the one in the kitchen with the pain. He was seated on the earthen floor, in the corner by the fireplace, his back against the stone wall, when I came in. Mother was on the stool. She greeted me with a hug as usual. "He has a toothache," she told me.

But I could tell. Pierre's mouth was swollen and still, holding Mother's toothache mixture—vinegar, oil, a certain spice, I forget the one, and the special healer, fireplace ash, rubbed on to start.

Pierre held up a hand. He mumbled a greeting through the mixture.

"Be quiet," Mother told him. "It needs more time."

Pierre hung his head down and stared at the floor. Mother sat back down on the stool. I sat down on the floor next to Pierre and touched his strong shoulder. I loved all my brothers, but truly, Pierre and I had a special love. He was nearer my age. Also, he did not tease me as much as Jean did. I never liked to be teased.

"I am sorry for your pain," I told him.

A mumble from Pierre.

"God will heal it."

Pierre nodded. He smiled a funny half smile so as not to swallow the tooth mixture. It tasted terrible! I knew from when I had swallowed some as a child.

I sat by Pierre, praying quietly for his pain to be eased. Then I sang him a tooth song, which I made up at the time. I do not remember how it went. Mother liked the song, and laughed. She joined in for a second time. Pierre could not sing, of course. He had only to listen.

After my song I told them of my day in the forest, of the beauty of the Wish-Fulfilling Tree, of the flowers, of our garlands, of Nicholas, and of the tiny bird that ate from my hand. Pierre's eyes told me that he liked my day, even through his pain. Mother said the day was truly beautiful.

After that Pierre sat some more in his tooth corner while I helped Mother prepare the evening meal, a thick and rich soup, with cheese and bread. Father and Jean were in the fields until after dark.

The next morning Pierre's tooth was healed. There was work to do with the sheep. They had to be washed. Now, any task with the sheep was my special joy, so Father always let me help. Mother, too, knew of my love for the sheep, and she would let me go. "The spinning will wait," she would say. "Go and help."

I was always so thankful.

We started early. First, we had to dam up the stream behind the house to make a washing pool. This took some time, as the stream always wanted to go its own way. Then Jean would get the gravel. There was a place nearby where gravel could be found. Jean would bring it in the heaviest of sacks to be dumped, while Father and Pierre and I would finish the damming up.

That morning, as usual, Jean made quite a thing of being the one to get the gravel. He said it was his muscles. "I am the strongest," he told Pierre. "You have not the muscles for it. I will get the gravel."

"I can carry gravel," Pierre answered. He never liked it when Jean called him little brother or said his muscles were small.

"Your muscles are small," continued Jean.

"My muscles are fine," said Pierre.

They had stopped their work, of course, to be free to argue. Father did not care for that. "Back to work," he told

[47]

them. "Joan and I must do it all. If you have such muscles, work!"

I kept quiet, collecting the branches and leaves and rocks and stones for shoring the dam. I always loved the work times with Father and my brothers. I loved their rough ways, so different from the measured peacefulness of Mother's kitchen. I loved that too, but being outside, working in heavy labor, with my brothers' loud voices and their strong ways, was a welcome time, an added spice to a nourishing, familiar soup.

Pierre agreed to let Jean go for the gravel, but not until he had made Jean swear that his muscles were not small and, in truth, were big enough to carry gravel at any time. I know not whether Jean believed that, but he said he did. He then went off to get the precious gravel. I never did imagine why he loved so much to carry it. I think it made him feel like a man. But that would come soon enough, with or without the gravel.

When the damming up was done Pierre and I went to get the sheep, while Father put up a rough fence in place in which to keep them. The sheep came easily. They knew well their washing time. Some liked it, I truly do believe, while others questioned the event.

The first thing was to clean all the foul and loose wool around the udder. You had to be careful. Father and Pierre and I worked at this.

Soon Jean approached with the gravel. It was still morning, without full sun, yet Jean was soaked from the wetness of a heavy sweat.

"How are your muscles?" Pierre called when first he saw him.

"Fine," said Jean. But he was out of breath and could not shout. "How are yours?"

"Ready for anything," said Pierre.

Jean dropped the gravel sack on the ground. Then he bent over, his hands on his knees, and stared at the ground, breathing heavily.

"Next time you had better let me do that," said Pierre.

"I am fine," said Jean, but clearly he wished to float in the washing pool and rest.

"You had better rest," said Pierre.

"I am fine."

"You rest," said Father, and that settled it.

Father and Pierre put the gravel in the pool. Then it was time for my favorite part. We each took a sheep, pulled it into the water, and standing in the washing pool, washed the sheep. Sheep swim well and appear not to mind the water. Sometimes they are stubborn at first, but once you get them in, they most often relax themselves and float. Even I could turn them in the water with no trouble. Clean wool was important, so we had to use washing lye and part the fleeces. This took some time.

I was working on a young one when a funny thing happened. Pierre was washing one of the older ewes behind the ears. The ewe liked not the washing, and reared up. Putting her two feet on his chest, she gave him a shove. Pierre went right over backward into the water. Of course, we all laughed. Father, too. He had a wonderful deep laugh that I would love to hear.

After each sheep was washed we released them one by one. They swam across the stream to the opposite side, rinsing themselves as they went, then climbed up the bank to drip off and dry. We always put hay there to console them. The lambs were noisy.

Later that day it was quiet. Father was meeting with some neighbor farmers, Mother was in the house, and Jean and Pierre had work to do in Greux. I do not remember what the work was. I was weeding in Father's garden. Always, in summer, there were so many weeds.

The sheep were in the small pasture behind the garden to the right of the barn, eating and resting after their busy morning. They were nearly dry. It was noon and very hot. I stood to look at them. I remember thinking they were too warmly dressed. Then I remembered that God had dressed them.

They cannot be too warmly dressed, I thought. It is God's way. It may appear that they are too warmly dressed, but I am outside their fleece and cannot know. A thing can look different than it is.

One of the sheep looked up at me. His ears stuck out in the funny way. His legs were so narrow, like tiny sticks from under his stuffy coat.

"Are you too hot?" I asked. I was hot myself and had a thirst.

He stared at me long, then went back to eating. The church bell rang its clanging sound, so full. I could always feel the bell in my chest where my heart was. I got down on my knees to pray. It had rained the night before, so the earth was soft. It felt good. A rock was at my knee, but I did not think about it. It was no bother as I was praying.

I looked through the trees, to the church bell tower, as the big bell tipped back and forth.

Joan.

I heard a voice. My heart did not beat.

Joan.

There was a great light between me and the bushes to the right by the church, a dazzling light. It filled everything and went out in all directions.

Daughter of God.

It was kindly, strong, a man's voice.

Jesus, I thought. Yes, but different.

Be good.

I try to be good, I thought. Am I not?

Be as you are. Go to church.

I go to church.

Be good. Go to church.

I became frightened. My heart pounded. It was beating so fast. I had never felt that. Not even when I rode the big gray horse behind Hauviette's barn the first time.

The light was fading. I was scared. It was such a big feeling. The feeling was in my chest, but it was too big. It was the church. It was God.

The light was gone. I tried to stand, but my legs were too weak.

Part II

"God must be served first."

8

The Call

My Joan life came in two pieces of time. There was the time before I heard the voice, that warm day in summer, and then there was the time after.

The dream in the Saint Peter Chapel was meant, I do believe, to prepare me for what was to come. It was an early message, a lesson, but I only partly grasped its meaning. I knew it was not really a dream, and this was true. I knew I should pray for the Dauphin, and this was true as well. But I wrongly thought that this was all I was to do. My Lord would show me otherwise.

Until that warm summer day when the sheep were drying and my hands were weeding, I was, in ways, asleep. I was as in a dream, a dream of love of God, of my beautiful family, of my church, a dream of God's creatures, of nature's treasures, of simple joy. I dreamed as well of war and struggle, of the hardships of all the poor people and the helpless animals. To me, this was the life that God had given, truly perfect with all the strife, somehow needed for wondrous, often unknown reasons. To me, this was all there was. But there was more to know. The voice was a call. It was my call to come awake, to open my mind to all the knowing in my heart.

The first time I heard the voice, the knowing did not come to my mind. I felt only a deep fear. I felt close to a thing of great meaning, but I could not understand. I wished only to be free of it because it pushed hard on my mind and somewhere said to me, "There is more to know. There are things to do. It will be frightening. It will be wondrous." I was very much afraid.

After the voice went away that day and the light ceased its brilliance, I tried once again to stand. Again I could not, so I sat down in the garden amongst the turnip greens and weeds and other vegetables. My head felt a lightness and I was somewhat dizzy. I put my head forward to the welcoming earth, then clasped my hands together behind my head, with my elbows to the earth, and waited. My fear was very great. Between my eyes there was a heavy pain. It was as if I had been struck. All things stopped, save the beating of my heart that was very loud. I could feel it beating strongly in my chest. Some weeds were scratching my nose as my head hung down. This made my nose itch. I lifted my head. I was looking at the side of the house. There was a wooden beam coming out of the stone wall. My head felt swollen.

If that beam had been swung against my brow I would feel this way, I thought. What happened?

I could not think. There was only the heavy pain in my head and the beating of my heart, a ringing in my ears, and the scratching weeds under my brown work dress.

What happened?

I looked over to the place where the sheep were. They were in one of their clumps, pushed close for no clear reason. If you pulled one away it seemed they would all fall over. Were they gathered tightly in fear? As always, it was hard to know what they were thinking. They looked concerned, but this was often their way.

What happened?

My hands had not the feeling of life in them. I lifted one, surprised that I could move it. My fingers were green and earth-brown from so much weeding.

What happened?

I sat still for some moments, still as a bird that has flown into a tower wall in a storm, not seeing, then finds itself on the ground, forgetting how to move.

Some crows flew over. They cawed their excitable caw-caws. I looked up to see their shiny blackness, to sense their sharp knowing.

Crows have big feet, I thought, remembering the crows I had seen in the meadow garden. But that was last year, or when? We were planting corn. The crows were noisy and excited. They knew what planting meant. Sentinels must have been watching, ready to spread the news of coming corn. Jean said crows are light in weight, surprising for their size. He carried a dying crow to a resting place in the wood one time. Where was I? He told me of it later, of how the crow had died, peaceful, and grateful for the shade.

What happened?

I forced my mind to work.

I was weeding, I told myself. I heard a voice. There, to

the right, by the church. And a dazzling light. What did the voice say? "Be good. Go to church."

The words ran through my mind.

Be good. Go to church. Be good. Go to church. I remembered the light, bright, blinding, like in the dream at the Island Castle. Was it the same light? Yes. The same voice?

I could not think. My headache had grown stronger.

I must lie down, I thought. But not here. I will injure the vegetables.

Slowly, I rose to my feet. My legs were still weak, as if I had run from Domrémy to Greux and back many times. I glanced at the sheep. They had parted from their group. Some lay down, legs folded under, chewing. Others stood. They bit at the grass, then sharply thrust their heads forward or back, snapping off the fresh grass with the force of their head movements. Some thrust their heads only forward, some only back. Forward or back. Forward or back.

I thought of my bed, of the dark coolness of my room, as I started toward the house. Then I remembered the weeding tools and the pulled weeds.

I must not leave them, I thought. Go back, bend over, pick them up.

Slowly I followed my mind's telling. Each thought was hard to form, each motion hard to make. I picked up the weed hook, then the crotch. I gathered the soft, lifeless weeds. Their work was done.

Move to the dung heap now and leave the weeds. Put the tools in the shed.

These things I did. Then I went slowly around the left side

of the house and in through Pierre and Jean's door. It was not a far walk, but it seemed to be. My knees were so unsure.

Mother was by the fireplace, snapping green beans. I stood in the doorway between Pierre and Jean's room and the main room, steadying myself at the edge of the wall. The room was moving before my eyes.

"Joan," Mother said, "what troubles you?"

"It will pass," I told her.

"Is it a headache?"

"Yes," I answered.

I asked her to remain at her work. I said that I would only rest a while, but of course that would never do. She got out the headache remedy and held the cloth to my head. After some moments she sent me to my room with the headache cloth to rest. I did not think to mention the voice.

I slept for many hours. I do not know how long it was. When I woke Mother was at my bed. The light was fading. It must have been late afternoon time. Mother sat on my narrow bed, not waking me, but there. When I woke I saw her face. She was surprised that I had slept for so long. It was never my way to sleep when the sun was out, only with a fever, and these I did not get but rarely.

"Are you well?" she asked.

"I am," I told her, for I felt much relieved. I had a weakness, but my head was clear and cool. I felt light and comforted. A weight had been lifted.

Mother reached out her hand and stroked my brow.

"Forgive me for sleeping," I said.

"You needed rest."

"There was work to be done."

"Your health is more important."

"I meant only to sleep for a short time."

Mother smiled. "It was a welcome sleep," she said.

"Yes," I answered.

After that, Mother returned to her inside work and I went to get water. I carried the bucket through the front yard and across the road toward the river. The afternoon sun was soft in its slanting way. There was a welcome breeze.

How beautiful it is, I thought.

I passed the rounded haystack by Hauviette's barn. The stack center came through the top. This was good for ventilation. We had it this way at our house too, but our first cut was not yet stacked. We would need to be busy.

I continued toward the river. Just ahead it made a gentle curve, and this was always my place for getting the water. To the right were the low bushes of alder and willow. To the left began the long row of poplar trees. A flock of wild birds left the trees and headed west. I turned to follow their path with my eyes. The sun blazed strong, a sudden flash of light. I remembered the voice.

The voice.

I had forgotten.

The voice.

I felt a shiver. I turned and continued toward the river.

The voice.

The fear was gone. I had only a floating, expecting feeling. Why had I been so fearful?

I could not recall. The voice meant no harm, that I could feel. It was somehow of God, as in my dream.

Was it the same voice?

I felt another shiver, but still, no fear.

It was. The same. But who?

I could not answer.

Jesus?

No answer still.

It felt like Jesus, I thought. But why would Jesus talk to me? He speaks in my heart, but surely He does to all who will listen. This was different. Why would He speak in tone to my ear? No one I know has ever spoken of this in their knowing. He speaks to the Saints, but not to the ordinary farm people. Why would Jesus do this?

I could not answer.

Was it Jesus? It was a man, strong and loving. Was it my Lord and Master? Could that be so? I love Him with all my heart. Surely, He knows this. With Jesus all things are possible. Where was He when He spoke?

Again, no answer.

His presence, His knowing, His love, these were well known to me. But His voice, as clear as Mother's or Father's, as clear as Simon's when he named his goose, such a thing could never happen.

As I approached the river, the grass, which had been stiff beneath my feet, was softening. The ground was darker now, moist. I knelt to collect the water in the wooden bucket. A peace settled over my mind. I vowed my pure soul and pure body to God's service for as long as He would have it so.

On my way back with the water I noticed a small group of townsfolk collecting by the side of the road. They were in front of Simon's house, which was next to the church on the other side. There was noise and much loud talking, but I could not hear the words.

Just then another small group was coming down the road from the north. It looked like mostly children. They were bent over, moving slowly. Were they injured? I could sense their concern.

The group by Simon's house moved up to meet the new group. I was closer now. I could make out Simon and his little sister as well, moving to meet the new ones. At that time Hauviette came running out of her house. She did not see me for I was behind.

"Simon!" she shouted. "What happened?"

Simon shouted back, but I could not make out the words.

I quickly brought the water in to Mother. She was spinning in her spot near the window, where I often sat with her. She worked so quickly, sure and steady, no need to watch her work. The light was fading now, but she could spin in the dark and often did.

I set down the bucket. "May I see to the trouble in the road?" I asked.

Mother kept on with her spinning. "What trouble is that?" she asked.

"Some people may be injured."

Mother stopped her work. "Is Father there, or Pierre, or Jean?"

"I did not see them. Hauviette is there and Simon and Aimée."

"Go then," said Mother. "Be careful."

"I will," I answered, and hurried out.

The group was gathered past the church, past Hauviette's house, on the river side of the road. As I neared them I could see that some were seated on the ground. Hauviette spotted me and ran in my direction. "Joan!" she cried.

I ran to meet her.

"Simon's cousin is hurt," she shouted, "and Michel's brother and Henri! They were fighting in Maxey!"

We joined the group by the road. There were several villagers, children and those grown, and an unfamiliar old man, bleeding, with clothes torn and a beard. Henri was off to one side with his mother. He sat on the ground. She sat by his side, holding his foot. Simon was kneeling by his cousin, Didon, who was not past my age. Aimée watched, crying, as Didon lay on the ground, bleeding from the head and the leg. Didon's eyes were open wide with terror. His pant leg was ripped to the waist. There was a long gash in his thigh, and just below the knee there was a deep wound. It was in a triangle shape, the size of a walnut, or only somewhat smaller. Inside one could see below the skin to the soft pockets, or sacks, the inside parts of the flesh as God had made it. There was much blood.

Mengette's father was there. He reached forward with a cloth to cover the wound. "Use this," he said.

Simon took the cloth and placed it on the wound.

"Tie it tightly," said Mengette's father.

I quickly knelt down to take Didon's hand. I knew him well. We once had played racing games by the river.

"Be still," I told him. "God is healing you even now."

"It hurts."

"Let go."

Mengette's father ripped his own shirt, then passed a piece of its cloth to me. "Use this, too," he told me. "For his head."

I held the cloth on Didon's head to cover the wound. It was above the eye. Next to me was Michel. He cradled his brother in his arms. The boy's eye was black and swollen closed.

Didon was quiet now. I held my hand tightly over the cloth on his head. I felt a love from my heart go out to cover his body. I closed my eyes to pray, still holding his hand. There was a blue-purple light. I prayed silently.

My Lord, if it be Your will, let this boy be healed now. May he be strengthened, comforted, made peaceful according to Your will.

I felt a tingling in my hands. Through the cloth, and from his hand to mine, there was a great heat.

9
Peddler Man

It was not long before the bleeding stopped. After that Didon's mother and father came, and then his mother cleaned the wounds with fresh, clear water from the Meuse. Simon had gotten some clean cloth from inside his house, and this was used to tie tightly over the wound under Didon's knee and also to place as a bandage over the gash on the thigh. The wound on the head was not severe. The bleeding had made it seem so. Didon was thankful for my prayers and caring, but I explained that it was only God.

Soon others from the village had gathered in the street, Mother as well. Everyone was helping the injured and asking questions. "What happened? More fighting? Were any killed?"

"Not this time," said Henri. He was still in pain and could not stand. Even though I thought he was stupid, I did not like to see him suffer. His mother was crying and this was sad. She held his foot gently as he spoke.

"We were in Maxey," Henri continued, "bringing milk, Didon and I and Little Gérard and the others from Greux. They started throwing stones."

"Who did?" asked Hauviette. She always liked to know the small facts of how a thing was.

"The villagers," said Henri.

"From Maxey," said Didon.

"Not again!" said Didon's mother.

It happened often. Villagers would come back bloody from Maxey, our neighbor village, where we should only have found love. So often it was the children who were injured.

"They were mean," said Michel's brother, Little Gérard. He was called Little Gérard not so much because of his small size, but more because his father's name was Gérard and the Little in front of the boy's name made it clear of whom one was speaking. Little Gérard was more frightened than injured. His eye was black, but he had the sight of it. "They were big and mean," he went on. "They called us Armagnacs."

"You are Armagnacs," said Hauviette.

"We are?" asked Little Gérard. He was only five.

"In truth, you are," said Michel. He held his brother gently in his arms.

"They made it sound bad," said Little Gérard.

"To them it is bad," said Michel in his reasonable way.

"Not to me," said Little Gérard.

"As one would expect," said Hauviette.

"What does it mean?" asked Little Gérard.

"It means you do not want the English to burn your house and torture and kill you and kill all your animals," Simon explained.

"That is not what it means," said Hauviette.

"Yes, it is," said Simon.

"Who wants that?" asked Little Gérard.

"The Burgundians," said Simon.

"The big and mean ones," said Aimée.

"That is not what it means," said Hauviette.

"Did they have knives?" asked Didon's mother. She was still cleaning the wounds on her boy's leg.

"They had knives," said Didon.

"And clubs," said Little Gérard.

"Dear God," said Mother. She hated the fighting. The year before a girl from Greux was killed in Maxey. The girl had gone there with her brother, who had been beaten badly. She was the daughter of Mother's good friend. Since that time Mother instructed us never to go to Maxey. She never liked it when Father went for business. He would go only rarely and, thanks to God, he was never injured there.

Soon the questions were answered and the villagers began returning with the injured to their homes. Michel told me good-bye, then carried his brother off in his arms. Mother hugged me before she left. "Thank God you are safe," she said.

"And you," I answered. Then I told her I would be in soon to help prepare the supper, for this we always did together.

After she left I noticed once more the unfamiliar old man with the beard and the torn clothes. Someone must have cleaned the blood off his face and hands, because there was none to be seen. Only a cloth tied on his hand and a cut below the eye could show he had been injured. He was sitting some small distance away, on a large rock, by the side of the road. He rested his elbows on his knees and stared at the ground. By his side, near the rock, were two large sacks.

Hauviette, Simon, Aimée, and I were all who remained. We watched the old man for a moment or two in silence. Then I moved toward him to speak. "Can I help you?" I asked, for I thought he might have some trouble, a stranger in the town with no one to help him.

He did not answer.

Perhaps he did not hear, I thought.

I tried again, louder this time. "Excuse me, sir," I said. "May I help you?"

The old man looked up from the rock. "Me?" he asked.

"Yes, sir," I said. "I see you were injured."

The old man nodded.

"Are you in much pain?"

"Enough," he answered. His voice was rough. He seemed to be tired from too many long nights in the cold.

"What happened?" asked Simon.

"To me?" asked the old man.

"Yes," said Simon. "Were you hit?"

The old man nodded.

"With what?" asked Hauviette.

"A club," said the old man. He held his head, returning his gaze to the ground.

"What happened to your hand?" asked Simon.

"Cut," said the old man. He waved his injured hand, but looked not our way.

"With a knife?" asked Simon.

The old man nodded.

"How did you come to be fighting?" I asked.

"I was passing through Maxey," said the old man. "I saw the boys in trouble."

I waited for him to say more, but he did not. He only shook his head. He still looked at the ground.

"Where do you live?" asked Hauviette.

"Me?" the old man asked. It seemed he never could believe we wished to hear his thoughts, or perhaps he was dazed in his mind from the blow to his head.

"We never have seen you," said Hauviette. She was still a small distance from the old man. I think she was afraid. "I wondered where you live," she added.

"Different places," said the old man.

"What kind of places?" asked Simon.

The old man shrugged as if to say it did not matter. He pulled at the cloth on his hand, looking at it as well, not looking to our faces to answer.

"Hello, old man," said Aimée. She was hiding somewhat behind Simon, small protection if you want my thought on the matter. "Are you sad?" she asked.

The old man looked at Aimée. He shook his head.

"You look sad."

"I do?"

"Yes."

The old man shrugged.

"You sound sad," said Aimée.

"I do?"

"Yes."

"Well . . ." His speech did not continue.

"What?" said Aimée.

The old man shrugged.

"You wait," said Aimée. Then she ran off.

"What are you doing?" Simon called after her. He may have suspected some mischief.

"You will see," called out Aimée. She ran into her house.

Simon sat down on the ground at the feet of the old man. "We are sure to be surprised," he said.

"Surprises are well to be had," said the old man, "if they are good."

Hauviette was watching the two large sacks by the rock. "What do you carry?" she asked.

"Things of use," said the old man.

"Are you a peddler?" I asked.

The old man nodded. I sat down at that time by his feet. They were in truth the oldest-looking feet I had ever seen, worn and rough from so much travel. I felt a sadness for him. Peddlers often came through the village trying to sell their wares, utensils for cooking, tools for the farm work and such. The townsfolk seldom had the money to buy, so the peddlers were often disappointed.

Hauviette moved up then and joined us sitting on the ground. "Have you seen much fighting?" she asked.

The old man nodded. "Too much," he said.

"Did you see anyone tortured?" asked Simon. The subject brought such fear to his mind that he often repeated it.

The old man was silent. He stared at his bandage. After a bit of time, he nodded.

"Were you ever tortured?"

The old man shook his head.

"If he was tortured, he would not be here," said Hauviette. "He would be dead."

Simon did not accept her reason. "Perhaps he was tortured and then for some cause they stopped the torture," he said. "Perhaps they tortured him to tell where cattle were hidden, or women or children, and when he told they stopped the torture, or perhaps they put him on a torture wheel like Saint Catherine and the wheel exploded."

"She was a saint," said Hauviette. "That is why the wheel exploded."

"Who knows," said Simon.

"I know," said Hauviette. She looked my way. "Am I not right?" she asked.

I told her I believed it was Saint Catherine's devotion to God that caused the wheel to break.

"Joan agrees," said Hauviette. "And to add to the matter, the Burgundians do not carry torture wheels when attacking a village, nor do the brigands."

"How can you be sure?" asked Simon.

"They would be too heavy."

"Would they be too heavy, Joan?" asked Simon.

"I do not know their weight," I answered, but told him as well that I had never heard tell of the torture wheel to be used in that way. It was more a thing for prisoners who had been kept in prison.

"What do you think, old man?" asked Simon.

The old man shrugged. "I have never seen a torture wheel," he said. "They torture more by fire."

I felt a shiver. Death did not trouble me, as I felt it would only bring me closer to God, but death by fire seemed to me most awful. I could not bear the thought.

"How did you escape?" asked Simon.

The old man lifted his head and stared off past the gooseberry bushes to fields beyond. "By God's grace," he answered.

"Surely," I agreed.

"When they burn people, do they burn them over a slow fire?" asked Simon.

"Death is death," said Hauviette. She was becoming impatient with Simon's many questions, uncomfortable too, I could feel, with the subjects they contained.

"Is it slow?" Simon repeated.

"I have seen it," said the old man.

"How long does it take them to die?"

"Leave the man be," said Hauviette.

"Is it quick?" continued Simon.

"Not quick enough," said the old man. Once more he shook his head. "A fortnight past at Bury-la-Côte the brigands attacked," he said. "They destroyed the town. Men, women, children, they all went."

"Were they tortured?" asked Simon.

"Let him talk," said Hauviette.

"They made a fort," said the old man. "They used the church. They surrounded the church with trenches, manned the bell tower with sentinels, piled stones to throw on the attackers."

"How many?" asked Simon.

"Stones?" asked the old man.

"Attackers," said Simon.

"The usual count," said the old man.

"What is that?" asked Hauviette.

"Thirty-five, forty, with a captain."

Simon moved closer to the old man. He gripped his hands around his folded knees. This was often Simon's sitting way. "What did they do?" he asked.

The old man glanced out over the Meuse.

"He may not wish to speak of it," said Hauviette.

Simon stared at the old man. He waited a bit, then spoke. "Do you wish to speak of it?" he asked. Simon was the most fearful of the three of us, and yet the one to want most facts of the tale. I think he wished to fill time's space with talk of danger. This done, in his mind, there would be no room for it to happen.

The old man drew a deep breath, then slowly let it out, the way Father did sometimes when he did not like a situation. He stared at the river.

"There is no need to tell us," I told the old man, for he seemed to be upset.

"I have seen too much," he said.

"Yes," I answered.

"Do you wish to speak of it?" asked Simon.

"Let him be," said Hauviette.

The old man looked at Simon, straight, with eyes that seemed to have no life. "The bell sounded," he said. "I hid in the bushes. The band came, thirty-five or forty, plus a captain, outlaws, exiles, all countries of rough men. They rode into the village. The villagers were in the church, or in their homes, or hiding in the fields. The men came, screaming. The sound was frightful. They went into the houses. They killed the women and children. They rounded up the cattle. They slaughtered the pigs, the chickens, the sheep. They smashed the wine vats. They stormed the church. They murdered those within. They burned the granaries. They burned the houses. They set fire to the fields. And then they left. They took only the cattle for food."

We all were silent. Even Simon had no more questions. I felt a heavy sadness. I felt then that I would rather die than go on living after such devastation of good people.

10

Philip Mouse

Aimée brought us back to right thinking. She came skipping from her house, holding something in her hands. "Here it is!" she called.

Simon knew at once. "Not the mouse!" he called.

"The very mouse," she shouted. "But truly!" She ran into the center of our circle and sat quickly on the ground.

"He has no mind for that," said Simon, glancing to the old man.

"He does," said Aimée. "You wait." She opened her hands and there in her palms one could see a trembling gray mouse. His nose was twitching, and not only that. Tied behind him was a tiny birchbark cart.

Aimée set the mouse on the ground. He moved carefully forward, his head low, his neck long, to sniff my hand. I remained still.

"Look at that," said the old man.

"I made the cart," said Simon.

"A good one," said the old man.

"From bark," said Simon.

"I see," said the old man.

"You pull it with a thread."

"I see."

"Woolen thread," said Aimée. "From our very sheep."

"Can he pull something?" asked Hauviette.

"Oh, yes," said Aimée. "Anything small."

"But not heavy," said Simon.

"But not heavy," said Aimée. "He pulled an acorn and also a thistle and many other things."

The mouse was sniffing my hand.

"Look at that," said the old man.

"Does he have a name?" asked Hauviette.

"Oh, yes," said Aimée. "His name is Philip."

"A fine name," said the old man.

"What does Nicholas think of this mouse?" I asked.

"He likes him well," said Aimée. "This morning Nicholas was under the tree and Philip brought him a beetle in his cart, and you know how Nicholas liked that."

I told her I did.

Philip moved forward now to climb upon the folds in my skirt.

"Where is he going?" asked Hauviette.

"He only knows," said Aimée.

Philip's scrambling mouse paws made my legs itch through the wool of my skirt. I had to laugh. This made Hauviette laugh as well. Simon put a small stone in the cart. This pleased Aimée greatly. "He brings you a precious treasure," she said.

"Look at that," said the old man. Then he smiled.

And so it was that one of the smallest of God's creatures, the tiny Philip Mouse, had brought us once again to peace and joy, to smiles and laughter, to the expression of God's true ways.

The sun was glowing red now. I remembered the supper. Mother would need my help. "Would you like to spend the night with us?" I asked the old man, as he had nowhere to stay.

"If it will be no bother," he said.

"It will not," I answered. "We have a warm bed for you and a nice supper as well. We often offer these to those in need."

"I thank you," said the old man.

I gathered Philip with his cart in my hands and gave him to Aimée. "Untie the cart now," I suggested. "Let him rest."

"I will," said Aimée. Lovingly she began to untie the thread.

With trouble, the old man stood.

His body is sore from the beating, I thought. He said good-bye to the others, then bent to pick up his sacks. I offered to help, but he refused. "I am used to these," he said. "I have them always."

"Shall we watch the fireflies tonight?" asked Hauviette.

I told her yes and we made our plans. We would meet after supper by the river. We would meet behind her barn, by the river's edge, to watch the fireflies. We loved the lights of these special ones. We would sit by the river, watching their glow, talking of things important and small. More often they were small. This was fun, for short times, in the presence of the wondrous lights. I never liked small talk in the daytime.

That night Mother and I prepared a large supper, a thick

soup of vegetables and beans, with some bread and wine and some delicious cheeses. Mother also made her special dessert pudding, which was welcome beyond telling. Each person would share a bowl with one other. When we had not company there was always an extra bowl left over. Pierre and Jean would most often share this, with Father dipping in for many spoonfuls.

"You have it," Father would say, but Pierre and Jean knew what he meant. "You hold the bowl between you and I will reach over" was more to the fact. Pierre and Jean would often joke of this to Father, but always in great fun. If Father had not taken his usual share of their extra pudding they would have been sad.

On the far side of the room was a place strewn with straw. Mother added herbs there for fragrance. She had heard that this was often done in Paris, and she liked the idea. I did as well. It helped to make the house cozy. This straw place was where the peddler man sat. While Mother and I did the cooking, he rested his bony back against the thick stone wall near the doorway to my room. Mother had given him a biscuit when first I brought him in, and some water. The old man ate the biscuit slowly, and with much thankfulness, as we cooked. The bone joints on his fingers were so large, his skin so rough. I noticed this as I watched him hold the freshly made white-flour biscuit. I wondered why he ate so slowly when one could tell he was so hungry. Perhaps he wanted the biscuit to last forever.

The old man was quiet until after Father and my

brothers returned from Greux. No one was surprised to find our guest, as I would bring ones like him home whenever possible. They were tired and hungry and we had food and beds, so this was only fair.

There was much to say as we ate. Father had heard the news of the fighting in Maxey, as had Pierre and Jean. Jean was troubled, as a close friend of his from Greux had been badly injured. He said he wished he had been in Maxey to give them what they deserved. Mother did not care for the idea and told him so. She said he could get killed for his trouble, and how would that serve his family, or his village, or even France? Jean did not agree. He felt that evil must be stopped by whatever means. Mother stopped eating then until Father told Jean that he would do nothing so foolish as to lose his life in a battle with neighbors gone mad.

"What about brigands?" asked Pierre.

"If they come to Domrémy, we will defend our village."

"Please God they do not." Mother spoke to herself. Then she had a bit more soup.

Father had some papers with him from Greux that he read by the light of the fire. He held the papers far from his face with an outstretched arm. This was his way to read. He said that since he was older he could not see the letters when he held the paper near. Mother could not read, but this outstretched arm was her way too with small work. One time she made a joke that older people need longer arms. It was good that her fingers knew the way with the thread and that she did not need her eyes for spinning.

As we had our pudding Father told the old man that the papers he read were signed by the people of Greux who were seeking further immunity from pillage. Father said that, to his mind, a lot of the trouble with the brigands came, in part, because the people had not gotten over the terrible sickness of earlier times. He said the Black Death had killed nearly half the people. It had broken the spirits of those remaining and caused much anguish and confusion. It was also a worry, as every so many years the sickness would return. The old man agreed that this was so.

I cleaned the supper things and after that I showed our guest where he would sleep. He would have my bed. I would sleep by the fire. This was always the way when travelers shared our house. I enjoyed the warmth of the hearth. I could also sense the comfort of these strangers in need as they rested. This brought great joy to my heart.

"You will sleep here," I told the old man. I could feel his tiredness as he regarded my narrow bed. To his thoughts the bed was as a piece of heaven.

"Who belongs here?" he asked.

"You do."

"I mean to say whose bed is this?"

"It is mine," I told him.

"Where will you stay?"

"By the fire."

The old man moved back some steps. "I will take the fire," he said.

"It is not just," I explained. "I have the bed each night.

You are on the ground. Tonight you have a bed."

He fought my way, but Mother came in then and helped us. She told him I was truly pleased that he should have my bed, for this was so. At last the old man agreed. Mother told him to lie down then and sleep, which he did. I went to join Hauviette behind the barn.

I walked a part of the way with my dear Pierre, who was heading to the bell tower for his night watch. Each night a different villager would take his lonely watch on the tiny square tower, ready in case of danger to ring the warning bell. The women of the village did not do this. It was only the men. This I never could quite reason out, but this was as it was. During the day the churchwarden would have the honored task, but for the night watch the job fell to those men of the town.

Pierre enjoyed his turn as night watchman. It had fallen to him but a few times as he was only recently of the age. Jean had taken his turn several times in the past years. When Pierre could share in this task with his brother he was truly pleased.

"Is it lonely up there in the stillness of the night?" I asked as we left our yard. We turned toward the church next door.

"No," he answered. "I only fear to fall asleep."

"God will not let you," I told him. "Ask for His help."

"I will," said Pierre. "If I should sleep the destruction of the village could lie by my hand."

"The destruction of two villages," I added.

"You need not remind me," he said. "I know too well."

"You will be alert," I assured him. "I have faith in you."

"Thank you," he said. "That will help."

We stopped at the church. "What do you think of all the night?" I asked.

"Different things," he said. "The danger, the stillness, the great sky, different lands, the farm work, my bed."

"Think not too much of that!" I told him.

He laughed. "A point well taken," he said.

A wave of love swept through me then for my dear, beloved brother, this brother who was my friend. Nearly still a child, he would spend this night alone on the tiny church tower, alone with his thoughts and the stars and the broad, black sky, guarding the safety of our village and the village beyond, our lives in his care. I looked at him there by the church, in the soft moon's light. His hair was rough, some parts not minding a neat way. This made him look so young.

"I love you," I said. "I love you so."

A redness came into his face. "I love you too," he said. "Take some sleep for me." He turned then and went into the church.

11

Fireflies

I moved down the road to meet Hauviette behind the barn. The village looked so peaceful in the soft, sweet light of the moon, the single street with the houses placed just on either side. I pictured the gardens behind each house, the fields beyond, divided into narrow strips for planting. In the distance I could see the beautiful hills. Many were crowned with vineyards.

I reached Hauviette's house, turned, and passed its side as I moved to the barn. There was not a sign of Hauviette.

She must already be waiting in our firefly spot, I thought.

I passed the barn. There behind it flowed our beautiful Meuse. Hauviette was waiting, just as I had thought, in our own special firefly spot. It was a private place, just behind the barn, and there, too, there was a break in the trees on the near side of the river. The trees on the far side were low, which gave us quite a view.

"Have you waited long?" I asked.

This frightened Hauviette, as she had not seen me coming. "You scared me," she said, as if to give me news.

I sat down at her side. "Forgive me," I said.

Hauviette reached down and pulled a long, reedy piece of grass from just by the edge of the river. She put the grass between her teeth. We sat some moments in silence. The river flowed swiftly here. I listened to its rushing way, to the sounds of the early night, the frogs, the crickets, and the other small creatures. A cloud passed before the moon, making so much dark, and then, the first firefly of the night, the first we saw at any rate.

"There!" said Hauviette.

"I see," I said.

"And there!" said Hauviette. "Were there two, or was the first one moving swiftly and we saw it twice?"

I could not tell.

"What do you say?" asked Hauviette.

We often played this game, trying to follow the path of the firefly in the glow of the afterlight, trying to sense its path. Most always we could not.

"I cannot say," I told her. "It seems to me as one, but this may not be so."

"A thing is often different than it looks," said Hauviette.

"Most often," I agreed.

"What makes the light?" she asked.

"I have heard they want to mate."

"Who told you that?"

"Jean."

"It must be true."

"Why?"

"Jean is wise."

"But not always right."

"Like you," said Hauviette.

"Like God," I said. "God is right, not I."

"He must be giving you the answers."

"The answers are for all," I said, "if only we would listen."

We were still then and quiet for a time, just watching the steady journey of the river.

"Do you like a boy?" Hauviette's question broke the stillness.

I was not sure I understood. I paused to form an answer.

"Do you like a boy?" she repeated.

"I like many boys," I answered. I still did not gather the meaning of her words.

"No," she said. "I mean truly."

I began to understand.

"I mean so when you see him you feel almost a fright, as when you crept up before."

"I did not creep."

"But do you understand?"

"I think so."

"You are older and I never heard you speak of these things, but Mengette did and already I feel them."

"I have felt them."

"You have?"

"At times."

"With who?"

I knew the answer. There was one and only one. It was Michel. He was so wise, so understanding, so strong, but also gentle. It was a happy thing to look at him. His features pleased me so, his dark brown hair, his deep blue eyes. I paused a moment then, as I had never spoken of these things.

"Who?" asked Hauviette.

"Michel," I answered.

"Michel?" She nearly shouted.

"Quiet!" I told her. "Please! I answered for your hearing. Now you tell the village!"

"Michel?" she whispered. A firefly lit so near, we could have touched it. "Does he know you like him?"

"Not in the special way. At least I never told him."

"Michel!" she said once more.

"You must not shout!"

Hauviette leaned closer to me now. "Do you know who mine is?" she asked.

"I do not."

"Do you promise not to tell?"

"If you would have it so."

"I would. Do you promise?"

"You have my word on it."

Hauviette took the reedy grass stalk from out of her mouth. She stared at me in a most serious way. Then she spoke. "You will never tell anyone in all of France the name of the boy who I like, on penalty of death and beheading."

"We had best call Simon," I joked.

"This is very serious," said Hauviette. "This is the most serious of serious subjects."

"I understand," I told her.

"Do you promise?"

"You have my word."

"Maurice," she said.

"The cousin of Mengette?"

Hauviette nodded. "From Greux," she said. She moved closer to me, pushing down the tall grass that was between us. She folded her legs beneath her, and covered them with her skirt. There had come a cool breeze. "He was here today with some of the injured," she added.

"I did not see him."

"He left before you came," she explained. "When I saw his face I felt a joyful fright as when you scared me tonight, but sweet. Inside, my stomach seemed to turn on end, my hands got cold, and then I did not know the way to speak. I just stood there with all the bleeding people and so much trouble and stared at him with a stupid look. I tried to look away, but it was hard."

"I know," I told her.

"Is that how you feel when you see Michel?"

"Somewhat."

"How is it with you?"

"I feel a special joy."

"Did he ever kiss you?"

"No."

"Do you want him to?"

"If it pleases God."

"What about you? It cannot always be God."

"It can."

"I would love to kiss Maurice," she said, "but I would be a little scared."

"Why?"

"It is something for when you grow older. I picture it sometimes before sleep. Have you ever done that?"

"I have never pictured kissing Maurice!"

"You!" she said. She reached out both her arms and gave me a shove, pushing me nearly over and into the Meuse. "You know what I mean!"

"What?"

"Do you ever picture that Michel is kissing you? At night, before you go off to sleep, do you ever picture it? I make up stories in my mind some nights. Maurice is in trouble and cut or hurt and I go to rescue him because I am the only one who can do it and then he kisses me. Do you make up stories of Michel?"

"I have."

"What are they like?"

There was one story I would sometimes see in my mind, simple and loving. I had not spoken of it, but this firefly night I shared it with Hauviette. Michel did, in truth, play the shepherd's pipe. I loved to hear him play. My story had the pipe in it.

"Tell me," Hauviette urged.

"I am walking in the fields. I come to a large, spreading tree in the faraway part of the field. Michel is there. He sits beneath the tree, his back against its trunk, and plays his pipe. The sheep are grazing near. I join him by the tree. He smiles while still he plays. The smile is in his eyes. I sit at his side. I lean my head on his shoulder."

"And then?" said Hauviette. She was ready for more!

"Sometimes he will stop his playing and put his arm around my shoulder."

"And does he kiss you?"

"Sometimes he does, but mostly my story ends here."

"What a place to end it!"

"Sometimes Michel goes back to his playing. I lie beneath the tree, just resting my head on his lap."

"How nice," said Hauviette. She liked that part.

On the way home I felt a great tiredness. I passed the church, sending a silent blessing to Pierre, alone in the tower. As I entered our yard, I thought fondly of my warm spot by the hearth, of the deep and restful sleep that was waiting. But things were not so. Much to my deepest surprise, as I lay by the hearth, I could not sleep. I could not close my eyes. I was comfortable enough. It was not that. I was well used to my place on the floor. The hardness was no trouble. And yet, this night, I could not sleep. I felt a force of life run through my body that was very strong. I did not recall such a feeling before. It seemed to me that I could run to the Island Castle, the whole way, without a stop! I felt I could reach the stars. I saw a small group of stars through the window. The moon shone brightly into the room. As I lay on the floor, this feeling of life racing through me, I watched the patterns of light cast by the moon. They fell on the stone hearth, on the strong, dark beams of the ceiling. All was still. And then.

Be good. Go to church.

The words I had heard in the garden came back to my mind. So much had happened that day since the noon hour when I had heard the voice. The fighting, the injuries, the peddler man, the tiny mouse, Pierre in the tower, the fireflies, the talk of Michel, all these had come to pass. They had caught my mind. But now, in the stillness of my hearthside bed, the only true underneath realness was filling my heart. It spilled out into my limbs, filling me wholly with life. It filled my chest, my arms, my legs. It flowed out through my fingers, my toes, through the top of my head. It filled the room, and the village, and the villages beyond. It spilled out into the whole night sky.

Be good. Go to church. Be good. Go to church.

At last I fell asleep.

12
Return

The next day was filled with our usual farm chores. I cannot remember which ones, but the day after that I shall never forget. The day began with spinning. Most often Mother and I would do our spinning in the late afternoon, or at evening time by the light of the fire, but sometimes we would have our Spinning Days. That would mean spinning all day, and sometimes into the night as well. These Spinning Days would come when Mother fell behind in the spinning work because of other tasks that came to take the evening time. Then she would say, "Spinning Day tomorrow," and we would rise with Father and Pierre and Jean and as soon as they went into the fields we would set to our spinning.

I loved our Spinning Days, so cozy and peaceful and filled with love. My hands and my arms and most especially my shoulders would tire after so many hours at the same task, but my heart would be joyful, my mind always willing to keep with the work.

Mother worked at the wheel and I had my distaff. Sometimes Mengette would join us on our Spinning Days, bringing her distaff along, but this day she did not. Mother sat at the wheel by the window. I sat on the earthen floor near her feet, by the side of the hearth, my back against the stone wall. The wall was rough in some places, so I folded a blanket and put it behind my back. This was my usual way. It made my sitting comfortable.

This day we played our Saints Game. That would always mean this. One of us would pick a saint. We would then begin the story of her life, or his life if the saint was a man. The one who started the story could stop at any time. When this happened, the other would have to go on with the story from the point where the story had stopped. You could tell as much or as little as you would want until you would stop for the other's turn. Sometimes we would go on for long stretches of time, putting in all the most wondrous parts, leading from one time of the life to the next. Sometimes we would stop in a moment. As the game went on we would each do shorter and shorter parts until often we would each take only a word before it was time for the other to begin.

This day, I remember, we chose Saint Catherine. I should say I chose, for that was how it was. I always loved Saint Catherine. She was very beautiful, as was Saint Margaret, my other special favorite. These were my favorites for as long as I can remember. I often prayed before the statue of Saint Margaret in our church. In Maxey there was the most beautiful image of Saint Catherine. I had seen it once when I was little, but now the fighting meant I could not go there.

"Saint Catherine," Mother repeated after I had chosen.

"You begin." The one who chooses must always start. That was our way.

"Saint Catherine," I began. I pinched the wool between the fingers of my right hand as I drew it through the left to twist. You need the right amount of tightness. Pull and twist, pull and twist. You take a certain rhythm. "Saint Catherine is the special protector of unmarried girls."

Mother nodded, happy to hear that part. Saint Catherine was a special favorite of hers as well. She and Father had named my sister for her.

"Saint Catherine cares for all," I went on, "but these young ones are most especially blessed by her and are never forgotten."

"Never," Mother spoke almost silently.

"When Saint Catherine was young," I continued, "she learned about our Lord Jesus. Later she saw a vision of the . . ." I stopped there for Mother to pick up.

She missed not a moment. ". . . Blessed Virgin with the Holy Child," she said. She was separating the wool with the fingers of her left hand, pinching with the right. Pinch, pull back, let go. Pinch, pull back, let go. When you work at the wheel there are some differences from the distaff, but many things are the same. For both you must be steady. You have to be simple with your fingers.

Mother continued. "After she saw the vision, from that time on, she believed deeply in the truth of God and in the goodness of Jesus, but evil ones were against the Christians. This was sad. Catherine tried to . . ." Mother stopped here.

". . . talk sense to these evil ones," I picked up. I was glad Mother let me do this part. I found it most exciting. I loved the way Saint Catherine stood up to these evil ones without a trace of fear. Oh, I know they are to be pitied. The love of God was theirs as well, but this they did not know and their unknowing made them mean. But Catherine had no fear. She spoke her mind, which was God's mind, so it could not fail, how ever it seemed.

I went on with the story, keeping a steady firmness on the wool. "Catherine tried to talk sense to these evil ones, but they would not listen. They beat her and put her in prison." I twisted the wool with the thumb and first finger of my right hand. I loved the wax feeling on my fingers. Twist and pull. Twist and pull. Steady, simple. My fingers knew the way. My ring shone as it picked up the rays of early-morning light coming in through the window. I loved my ring. It was a gift from Mother and Father when I was small. It was big for me then, so I kept it in my wooden box, the one Pierre had made for me one time. In some years I grew to be a good size to wear the ring. From that time on I was never without it. It was of shiny brass, with three crosses on it and the words "Jesus Maria."

The church bell rang. I crossed myself. Holding my distaff, I got down on my knees to pray. Mother stopped her spinning and closed her eyes. These moments of prayer added strength to our work and brought us much joy.

When our praying time was over I went on with the story. It now moved to a sad and difficult part, for as so often happens with ones of God, others do not always understand and thereby cause much suffering. It was thus with Saint Catherine.

I resumed my spinning. "Catherine was beaten and put in prison," I went on, "and sentenced to be killed on the spiked wheel. But the wheel . . ."

"Broke," said Mother.

"Exploded," I corrected.

I sounded like Simon.

"It may not have exploded," said Mother.

"Some say it did."

Mother had to agree. "Some say the wheel exploded," she went on, "but in any case it broke and many of the evil ones were hurt."

"Or killed," I added.

"I thought the turn was mine," said Mother.

"It is," I said.

"It would be hard to know."

"I am sorry," I told her. I loved the story so. Often I would get caught up in my idea of the telling and forget the game. I would forget, also, that I had given the turn to Mother. Mother never minded this, but part of the game was in Mother's pretending she did.

"Shall I continue?" she asked, "or will you be telling the story alone?"

I laughed then and told her please to continue. I adjusted my distaff under my left arm and stretched out my fingers. I was getting some finger cramps. As the cramps did not go away, I took hold of my distaff in my right hand and shook my left arm hard, swinging it from my shoulder. This helped and I returned to work. Mother took up the story. It was near the end, so we both took shorter and shorter parts, as was our way.

"After Catherine was beheaded," said Mother, "her body was . . ."

". . . carried by . . ." was all I said.

". . . angels . . ." said Mother.

". . . to the . . ." I said.

". . . mountain . . ." said Mother.

". . . where a . . ."

". . . church . . ."

". . . was . . ."

". . . built."

The day went on like this, with stories and songs, some soup, some prayers, and always the spinning. I remember at one point Mother told a funny story about how she had awakened at night wanting a drink of water. She had been dreaming of walking through a desert and thirst had overtaken her. She was half in her dream, and confused in her mind, and had stepped out of bed to the wrong side, which was not to the earthen floor but only directly on Father. He had jumped up then and been in a terrible fright thinking that she was trying to kill him since he had been dreaming of thieves in the barn. She was thinking he was a desert camel and was trying to get over him and he was trying to get free, when they both woke fully and had to laugh. I had to laugh as well when I heard the tale, as did Mother in the remembering. Then Mother began to sneeze. It was not a tiny lady sneeze, but a great big farmer sneeze, as of a worker gathering hay. This made us laugh more. Mother gave up her spinning then and laughed and sneezed and I laughed hard. It was a joyful time.

After the sneezing and the laughing Mother returned to her work. Pinch, pull back, let go. Pinch, pull back, let go. Mother never seemed to tire, but such was not with me. My shoulders would get to aching and I would have to stop my work and set down my distaff. Then I would do a thing that helped. I would stand, then bend over from the waist, hanging my arms down and my head as well. After that I would reach up as far as I could, as if to heaven, with my arms. This seemed to help.

The sun was beginning to set when Mother left the house to speak with Simon's mother on some matter. I do not recall what it was. I continued my spinning, sitting on the floor as I had been, by the side of the hearth.

Pull and twist. Pull and twist.

All at once a blazing light filled the room, a blinding, bright light as in the garden, and with it a fragrance as sweet as heaven. My heart stopped. It felt as if it grew inside my chest. My fingers ceased their work, my breathing ceased as well.

And then the voice.

Joan.

My heart pounded now, my breathing was deep.

Daughter of God.

The light was dazzling, brilliant, burning.

Be good. Go to church.

I will, I answered in my heart.

My hands were cold, my chest on fire. And all the while, the sweet fragrance, the blinding light.

Great things are expected of you.

Of me?

No answer came, only a slow fading of the light, the same dizziness I had felt in the garden, the lightness, the flush of life, the great fear, and with it the heavenly fragrance and a ringing in my ears as if a hundred distant church bells were filling me with music.

13

Saint Michael

Now I could not forget. Every waking moment, it seemed, whatever I might be doing in my daily ways, I could think of nothing but the voice. Who was it? What did it mean? There was no longer any question in my mind but that the voice was real. I knew that truth with every part of my being. It was real. It was good. It was of great importance and it would be with me forever. Even if I heard it not again, it was a part of me now, and I would not forget. These things I knew, but only these. My mind was filled with questions. Who spoke? What was the meaning? What was I to learn?

I knew it was the voice of a man, a strong man, a protecting man, a man of God. Was it Jesus? The thought would not leave my mind that it might be Jesus. The voice had all the love, all the power, all the caring, all the light of Jesus, but still I was unsure. Yet, for all my unsureness, I would not ask. I could have asked my father or my mother, or our priest, Guillaume Front. I confessed to him often, yet of this I could not speak. I cannot tell you why. Not that I would not like to, but only that I do not know.

Great things are expected of you.

The voice rang strong within my mind and heart. What things? What could I possibly do? I knew there was no mistake. I knew with every part of myself that the voice had spoken to me, had meant to speak to me and none other. But why? What did it mean?

In the days that followed I went often to the church to pray before the statue of Saint Margaret to seek understanding. I would enter our small and welcome church and go directly to the place of the statue. It was on a shelf ledge of the central pillar. I would cross myself, then kneel in prayer.

Beloved Saint Margaret, I would ask from my heart. Who has spoken? If it be God's will, may I know? Was it Jesus? What am I to understand from this? What am I to do?

Each time I did this I would feel a great sureness flood my body as I prayed before her statue of great beauty, a comforting sureness that all was in order, but no answer to my questions, at least none that I could hear.

Life's ways rushed by. Simon told Hauviette that Maurice had told Simon that Maurice thought that Hauviette made good biscuits. Hauviette had given two biscuits to Simon, who had shared them with Maurice, so that was how Maurice knew the biscuits were good. Hauviette was thrilled beyond telling and could no longer sleep at night from deep excitement. Philip Mouse disappeared for three days and was later found in Aimée's mother's wooden household chest, his little cart still attached, but broken. Nicholas was gaining weight. It was of some concern to

Simon, who felt the goose was too heavy, but Mengette saw little difference, nor did I.

These things and many others filled the days. I felt as one removed. All was felt through memory of the voice, through thoughts of wonder, of endless questions, through almost constant memory of the sound, the fragrance, and the beating of my heart. Two weeks passed, or more, in this way. The voice was as real to my heart as the moment I had heard it, my constant companion now, behind all else. Who was it? What did it mean?

It was plowing time then. Each morning Father and Jean and Pierre would rise early and begin the day's work at the plow. Sometimes, if Mother did not need me, they would let me go with them, much to my delight. We had to work especially hard with the plowing as we shared the plow horse and the plow with others in the village. We only had our turn for a small number of days. My favorite thing was to ride the plow horse as she plowed. I loved her strong, warm back, her gentle, plodding gait, her twitching ears, and the high up view of the Meuse. In summer the river was a lazy stream, only slightly bending the reeds in its shallow bed. In the season of heavy rains our Meuse was swollen by heavy torrents as it rushed along, but in summer, from high on the back of Sibelle, our kind and willing plow horse, the Meuse was always calm.

I was not truly needed on the back of Sibelle. By fact, I was not needed there at all. She could easily be driven in the straight way needed on foot from behind or led while also walking, but riding was the best. When I did not ride her I would often go behind the plow to break up the clods with a stick.

One afternoon about this time I was asked by Aimée's mother to mind Aimée while she and Simon carted some wool to be sold. We played in the front yard of my house, or more by fact, Aimée played while I sat near the woodpile by the side of the door and watched. Aimée had left Philip Mouse at home, but had brought a spade. She spent the time digging and making tiny cakes of dirt mixed with water from the Meuse. The chickens wandered about while Aimée pounded her tiny dirt cakes. I sat by the woodpile, thinking of the voice.

The next time it comes, I thought—for I was sure that there would be a next time—I must not be afraid. My fear makes the voice leave quickly, I thought. I must not be afraid.

I watched the chickens as I thought, so busy with their chicken ways. The white hen walked stiff-legged. Many chickens crowded the yard, some pecking the ground, others cleaning themselves by pecking at their feathers.

The next time I will welcome the voice, I thought. I will speak from my heart of the gladness I feel, no fear this time, only gladness.

Aimée was building a large tower of mud, with stones stuck in for windows. The chickens kept their distance.

If I do not want the voice to stay, it will not stay. It is up to me.

I slept soundly that night, a sleep without dreams, restful and deep.

Joan.

The voice woke me directly.

Joan.

My heart pounded. I turned my head and opened my eyes. The room was filled with light, a radiance far greater than the room could hold. It filled the walls, spilling out in all directions, and the fragrance, a richness beyond all imagining.

Daughter of God.

My eyes were open. I was fully awake. There in my room at the side of my bed stood an angel, and by his side two more stood, and behind them, and in the light and part of the light, and within the walls and beyond the walls, in all the brilliance, were hosts of angels, gently to be felt. The light was blinding in its radiance. The sweet smell took over my being with joy. Too much to bear was the sight of the figure, an angel, standing by my bed.

Be not afraid, I thought, through the pounding of my heart.

The angel by my bed grew more and more brilliant as the light in the room softened into purple and white, going into him and the other angels at his side. My heart was pounding so. The form was clear. In an instant I knew. It was the Archangel Michael.

Yes.

Saint Michael?

It is I.

He was tall, noble as a knight in armor, a crown for a helmet, a shield, a sword, winged, and all around the purple-white light.

Fear not.

His voice was strong. He was a figure of such unearthly beauty that I could barely contain the sight. Saint Michael, Captain of the Armies of Light, in my room, at my bedside, with all the light of heaven and the power of his goodness flowing out in all directions.

Saint Michael?

Yes, Joan. Yes.

I sat up on the bed, my feet over the side, touching the cold earthen floor. I crossed myself and put my hands together to pray.

Thank you for coming, came the words from my heart.

Joan.

The light around him glowed purple and white.

Daughter of God.

The ringing came to my ears, the heat to my chest.

You have been chosen.

For what?

Saint Catherine and Saint Margaret will be your constant companions.

I opened my eyes and saw, once more, what could not be. The Archangel Michael stood at my bed, and on either side of him Saint Catherine and Saint Margaret. They had been the figures all along, so much a part of the light, I could not make them out. I saw them clearly now, beautiful beyond all telling, with crowns of precious stones and robes of flowing softness and smiles of love beyond my wildest dreams. Tears filled my eyes.

Saint Catherine?

Yes.

A woman's voice, filled with the music of heaven.

Saint Margaret?

Yes.

And so, again.

The light began to fade.

Don't go!

And still, the light now dim.

Stay!

But they did not. And when they left me I wept, and I fain would have had them take me with them too.

Part III

"Demons, my Angels? You must be crazy."

14

Catherine

When I was very little I used to think that everyone wanted to serve God. It was always the most exciting thing to me to serve Him in any way my strength could manage, better than springtime or a picnic, better even than riding bareback by the river. Later I learned that others do not feel as I do, many others, that is. I know that some do.

Before I saw the Angels I longed to be a loving instrument of God's will. I knew that I would serve Him always, but I was asleep because I thought I knew the ways that I would serve Him. I would pray. I would go to church. I would be good. I would help others. These were my ways, and only these. The ways had edges and corners, beginnings and endings, and this is never so. Oh, we make it so with our thoughts, but this is not God's way. I sensed now that there was more, more that I could do, more ways that I could serve. I knew not what they were, but they were there. I felt this in my heart. Before I saw the Angels I had seen only a part of God's great, limitless beauty, and I set my mind to say that this was all there was. I wrongly thought that all that I held within my mind, all that I thought that I could do, was, by fact, all that could be done. By me, at any rate. But my mind is a small thing. It cannot see all of God's ways because it is only a part of God. I was asleep to this fact and thereby not truly awake. My heart saw everything, but my mind thought it knew better and in this I was asleep. The Angels came to wake me.

In the days that followed there was a gladness in my heart. The fear was gone now, only the joy and the wonder and a longing for my Angels to return. At times I would be caught up in some task or other, quietly peaceful and busy in my way, my attention to the job at hand, the sewing, the spinning, watching the flocks, preparing the food, and all at once I would remember the Angels. In my mind I could see Saint Michael and Saint Margaret and Saint Catherine at my bedside, with all the radiance and the hosts of angels and the fragrance of heaven. I would hear once more, in my mind, the strong, loving voice of Saint Michael, the gentle, sweet voices of Saint Margaret and Saint Catherine, and I would be filled with such gladness and such a sense of wonder that no words could clearly describe it. My heart would race remembering that night, so ordinary in every way except for the presence of these great ones in my tiny room, speaking to me, calling my name.

Joan. Daughter of God.

It seemed truly as a miracle. The Angels were with me at all times now. Always some inside part of me was with them, awaiting their return.

Saturday was the day for the hermitage. High up on a wooded hill slightly to the north of Greux was the tiny chapel of Notre Dame de Bermont, at the quiet and peaceful hermitage. Each Saturday I would go to the chapel with my beloved sister Catherine. Often others would go with us and sometimes we would go alone. Always it was a special day. We would take candles and light them there to burn for the precious Saints. I loved these days, partly for the special stillness to be found in the tiny chapel, partly for the long walk through God's woods, and more than all, for the time with my beloved sister.

Catherine and I had always been more than close. At the time when the Angels first came, Catherine had been married and living in Greux for close to two years, or thereabouts. I missed her still. When growing up we were as one, sharing the same room, working together in all the household tasks. Although Catherine was older, she was always kind. She never made me feel as one not needed, which sometimes happens when the sister is older.

Catherine was most beautiful and kind. Always I wanted to be as she. She was strong and gentle, always with a quick mind and a watchful eye to all that came to pass. We had many good laughs, as did Mother and I. Truly, many times the three of us would laugh, and that was something! We could go on for some long time, but then our work would start to suffer, or stop would be more to the point. Then we would try to force ourselves to take a serious way. Most often this did not work. One or the other of us would go off laughing again and soon it would be all of us.

The Saturday after the Angels first came I took some biscuits wrapped in a cloth and met Catherine by her house in Greux. Her house was small, smaller than ours by far, but it had a warm feeling of love inside so one did not mind the closeness of the quarters. This Saturday when I arrived, Catherine was sitting in front of her house, near the wood-pile, spinning with her distaff, breathing the fresh morning air. I ran to greet her and we hugged a long, loving hug.

"I miss you, Short Legs," she said, as still we hugged each other tight.

"And I miss you as well."

We broke the hug. "Biscuits?" she asked, looking to my cloth bundle. There was much hope in her voice.

"Biscuits," I answered.

"Shall we wait?"

"Until the first clearing. Would you not say?"

"We should wait."

This was always our way, as if a game, and always we would each want a biscuit at the first clearing. Once we ate them all before we left. It truly was a disappointment later.

The morning air was clear, the sky so blue. Already the heat of the summer day was strong. We headed down the dirt road toward the woods, past the mothers and fathers and children out working in the yards and in the fields beyond. All was so beautiful. At that moment one could almost forget the terrible war and the fighting and all the hardships.

"Have the boys been good to you?" asked Catherine as we moved together along the road. An orange kitten followed us.

"They are good," I answered, "though Jean is sometimes filled with the idea that he knows all things."

"No change then," said Catherine.

"Not as yet."

"Give him time."

"I will."

"One day he may ask a question."

"He did!" I said. "I should have mentioned it at once!"

"He asked a question?"

"In truth!"

"I know not what to think."

"It was a great surprise."

"What did he ask?"

"He inquired of an injured bird. He asked if it was dead."

"And was it?"

"No."

"Did you tell him?"

"Yes."

"And did he believe you?"

"No."

"That sounds like my brother."

We laughed then, enjoying our brother's special ways. The straw-colored kitten followed us still. I stopped and bent down to stroke it. It purred its deep-throated happy noise, then pushed its nose against my knee.

"Did it live?" asked Catherine.

I was thinking of the kitten then and did not know her meaning. This she sensed. "The bird," she added.

"Oh, yes," I said. "It shortly flew away." I rose then and told the kitten we must be off. It stared at us, but did not follow.

We continued on our way, growing nearer to the woods.

"And how is Pierre?" asked Catherine.

"He is well," I answered, "and always my friend."

"Tell them I miss them," she said. "And Mother and Father as well."

I told her I would.

"Colin and I will come this week to visit."

That was happy news. I loved their visits. Always we would have long and welcome meals. We would often sing together. Colin loved music. He always got us going. Father loved music too, but he would not often think to sing unless Colin was there and started the song. Then Father would sing in his deep, rich voice, the rest of us singing around him, the very center of our song. On those nights Father would stay up later than other nights, forgetting the time and the heavy chores for the following day.

When we reached the point where the two roads meet we entered the woods. I was behind Catherine. Her soft, light hair fell long and straight down her back and over her deep-blue Saturday dress. Her stride was long and eager. She was taller than I. In those days the difference was great. "I love these woods," she said.

"And I," I answered.

The trees shaded us from the hot summer sun as we

began our slow and gently winding climb. We fell silent then, the gentle silence of ones so close that words do not seem needed. The bright morning sun slanted through the trees. The birds were singing. I thought then of the Angels. I felt the sense of joy they brought me, the life in all my body, the knowing of something grand.

When will they return? What will they tell me?

I thought not to mention my Angels to Catherine. I cannot tell you why. It seemed a knowing to be kept within my heart.

As we neared the first clearing we came upon a small and questioning group of sheep. They stared at us in the funny way, as if coming to figure if they should be afraid. They stopped their grazing and stared without moving. Catherine and I stopped so as not to frighten them further. It did not help. A large ewe gave a start and then began to run. A single sheep stood in rigid fear while the others followed the ewe deep into the clearing and beyond. I sent them all a loving message from my heart to tell them not to fear, but it was too late. They would be running for some time now, as this was their way. When sheep are frightened they can run for much long a time, or else they can lose the way of moving altogether, as did the one remaining sheep. They become stiff with fear. Jean often said the sheep were stupid, but I never held this to be true. They may have had a fright locked within their minds from times gone by and things would pass to remind them. This is how I saw it, at any rate. Naught comes without a reason.

The one remaining sheep stared hard, his body stiff, unmoving. Catherine and I remained still for some time as I sent the sheep a warming message from my heart.

Be not afraid, I told him. All is well.

We moved slowly toward the sunlight and into the clearing.

"We could have one biscuit," said Catherine, stopping to take in the pure, bright rays of the sun.

I had turned to see if the sheep had gone its way. It had.

If it be Your will, may the sheep soon find the others, I asked of God.

"How is your mind on the matter?"

"The matter of the biscuit?" I asked, turning to face my sister. She was so beautiful, her soft features, her golden hair, her gentle blue eyes against the rich blue of her Saturday dress.

"Were you praying for the sheep to find its family?"

"You know me well."

We hugged then, our arms around each other, holding tight. A tear came then as I recalled the pain of letting go. We will end our embrace, I thought, and when the day is past I will go home and Catherine will not.

But then I changed my thoughts to rightful ones.

Catherine will go home, I told myself. She will go to her home and I will go to mine, but our love will keep us together always. All is one.

When we broke our embrace I dried my eyes on the sleeve of my dress, then held up the biscuits. "The time has come," I said.

We sat down on the gentle grass then. When I opened the biscuit cloth, the wonderful smell of the fresh biscuits met my sense. Mother had baked them for us with love.

"How many are there?" asked Catherine, peering into the opened cloth.

"Four," I answered. "We could each have two now and none later."

"That would not be good," said Catherine, "but I could have two now and you could have two later."

"Or I could have one now and you could have three later."

"That would not be fair," she said. "Then I could have four now, and we both could have none later."

"That is least fair!" she said. We were laughing then. In a moment Catherine most nearly attacked the biscuit cloth. She plucked out a biscuit. "I wait no longer," she said.

"Nor I," I said, reaching for my morning treat. "I will save my second for the downhill climb."

"And mine as well," she added.

Birds soared above in the brightest of blue skies as we ate the biscuits made for us with so much love. The morning sunlight slanted into the clearing through the trees to the east. Behind Catherine stood a group of white birch trees, shining the light as if lit from within. All was perfect. The stillness of the clearing held a lasting peace. It was hard to bring to mind a knowing then of war and killings, of hatred, of kings gone mad, of sons disowned, and of the terrible Black Death that had taken half of France. These things held little in sense, yet they were true.

I thought of the Angels.

And these are true as well! Saint Margaret! Saint Catherine! Saint Michael, the Chief and Lord of the Armies of Heaven! They came to my room, in the darkness of night. They brought me all the light of heaven! They spoke to me! They called my name!

"There is still no sign of a baby." Catherine's words brought me from my heavenly thoughts.

"A baby?" I asked, for I knew quickly enough of what she spoke. "For you?"

"And for Colin." She brushed the biscuit crumbs from her skirt. "It has been nearly two years of marriage."

"It is not time."

"I worry that it may never be time."

"God decides those things," I told her.

"All things," she said.

"So where is the worry?" I licked the crumbs from my fingers. That brought the biscuit taste.

"It is only that I want a child so much," she said. "I pray that it will come."

"If it is right, it will come," I told her. "If it is not right, you would not want it to come."

"That is true," she said. "My sister is so wise."

"And mine as well. Would it be wise to have a second biscuit now?"

"No," she answered.

15

Notre Dame de Bermont

When we reached the second clearing we had a surprise. Hauviette and Mengette were nowhere to be seen, but in their place, as we reached the top of the hill where the woods end suddenly and all the wild flowers stretch out before your eyes, there, on a large rock surrounded by the lavender and blue and soft yellow of the flowers, sat the straw-colored kitten.

"Kitten!" I said, so happy at the sight.

"How did it get here?" asked Catherine.

"It walked."

"It must have run. It was faster than we."

"We stopped for the biscuits," I reminded her.

"That is true," she said. "And the sheep."

The kitten opened its mouth and let out a silent cry. It stared at us as if to say, "You took too long."

"Hello, kitten," I said, moving toward the sunlit rock on which it sat. "You came such a long way."

The kitten made another silent cry, then stood up as I approached. It arched its back, waiting to be stroked. I sat on the rock and stroked her, for it was a her, from the top of her head to the tip of her tail. She rounded her back, then pushed against my hand, taking up once more her deep-throated happy sound.

"She likes you," said Catherine.

"I like her." I stroked the kitten several times then. She pushed her nose against my arm, walked away a few steps, then circled back for more.

"Will you keep her?" asked Catherine. She knew well my love of God's creatures.

"If she so wills," I answered.

The kitten pushed her nose against my hand. She walked away again, then back. She was making her loudest happy noise now, from deep within her throat. I stroked her along the back and sides. Her ribs felt thin, like sticks, too breakable it seemed, but strong. God has marvelous ways.

"Joan!" It was Hauviette calling out from the edge of the woods. Mengette was at her side. Mengette carried her distaff, as often was her way.

"Hello!" I shouted.

And Catherine, too. "Hello!"

The girls ran toward us through the wildflowers. "What do you have?" shouted Hauviette.

"A kitten," I called. I picked up the kitten and held her in my lap. She took a half-sitting, half-lying-down way, still making her happy noise. The girls gathered around the rock, falling to their knees for a close look.

"Hello, kitten," said Mengette. She held out her distaff for the kitten to sniff. The kitten sniffed it once, then had not the interest. She pulled back her nose.

"This kitten met us on the road in Greux," said Catherine. She put an arm around Hauviette's shoulder, kneeling at her side amidst the wildflowers. "We left her there and when we reached the clearing, here she was."

"She must have magic wings," said Hauviette.

I thought of the Angels.

"You say things you do not mean," said Mengette. She had placed her distaff on her lap, in the folds of her brown Saturday skirt.

"I do not say things I do not mean," said Hauviette, rubbing the kitten on the side of the nose. "Why would I bother to do that?"

"I have often wondered."

"You waste your time."

"Cats do not have magic wings," Mengette stated in her overly certain way.

"Perhaps they do," said Catherine. "We have not seen them, but even so, they may be there."

"I would doubt it," said Mengette.

"Never doubt," said Catherine. "Doubt closes the door."

"What door?"

"Any door. Any place to go through into a new place. That's what Mother used to say. 'Question, but never doubt. Doubt closes the door.' Do you remember, Joan?"

I told her I did.

"I still say that cats do not have magic wings," said Mengette.

It seemed to give her a safe feeling to have the final say in a matter. This I could understand.

We set off for the tiny chapel, Catherine in the lead with the sack of candles and the three of us after, me with the two remaining biscuits in the cloth, Mengette with her distaff, and Hauviette with a bunch of wildflowers she had picked in the clearing. The straw-colored kitten had determined to follow us, which pleased my heart. She followed at my heels, jumping over rocks and logs and all the high places, running several steps to keep pace with my one. Now and then she would look up at me to see which way we would be going next. After that she would look ahead or to the ground as she hurried along. Her tail went straight to the sky.

When we reached the tiny chapel we were out of breath from the climb. We each knelt at the entrance door, then passed inside where it was still and quiet. All was stone. There was a stone altar with candles and a statue of Jesus. I fell to my knees to pray.

Thank You for sending the Angels. I know it was You, I told Him. I pledge my devotion in all ways.

I prayed for some time.

When I came back to daily knowing, Catherine was lighting a candle at the altar. She then gave a candle to Hauviette, then one to Mengette, and one to me as well. We lit them from the ones burning and knelt to pray. It was still beyond all stillness. In our church in Domrémy God's peaceful stillness fills the walls as well, but there one hears the life sounds that come from without, the children playing, the villagers as they work or call to one another as they pass the church. One can sometimes hear a two-wheeled cart go by or a cow sending a message to her sister across the field, but in the tiny Bermont Chapel all is still. One listens for the flight of birds.

I would pray for long times at the hermitage. The others would pray as well, as I have told, but not for so long. Hauviette would say later that she liked to pray, but after some small time a stiffness would come to parts of her body and then an inside tickling that naught but movement could remove. She would have to cease her praying, jump up, and run outside to roll among the wildflowers. This was somewhat of the feeling I would get snapping the beans with Mother or after long times at the spinning, but never when I prayed. At praying times I would lose all earthly caring. There was only the flow of God's love in my veins. Pierre once poked me with a stick when I was praying to see what I would do. He later said that I did not feel it, but I did. It was of no importance to my mind, and so I did not move.

Always at the Bermont Chapel we would say special prayers for Saint Margaret. This day as we prayed I thanked her for coming and told her that if it pleased her, it would be an honor for her to return to my room.

At that time I felt a presence behind me.

An Angel? I thought. No. It is good, but it is not an Angel. I opened my eyes, turned my head, and there kneeling at the door was Michel. He carried his shepherd's pipe. My heart made another beat. Soon he rose and moved to the altar. He smiled as he passed. He looked so strong, but always in his gentle way. Catherine gave him a candle then. He lit the candle and prayed a while.

That same day we rested in the grass, among the flowers, outside the chapel. That hill was so fine, a small clearing, high up near the sky, surrounded by maples and strong oak trees and bordered by the groves of white birches. We often rested there on our Saturday outings, and always in that place we were quiet. There was a special joy in resting with others in all God's beauty, not making a sound. There was a special closeness. I lay on my back, gazing into the blue sky and thanking God for all He had given. The kitten, who had not come into the chapel, jumped on my chest then and began to make bread. That is how I called it. It was as if my chest were the dough. She worked it with her paws. Michel smiled at this.

As the afternoon came we started our downward climb. When we reached the second clearing, we still had not said a word. This was always our way, a remarkable thing for Hauviette most especially, because she did not favor quiet. I do not know what started us on this quiet way, but it was always the same. It was truly grand. Being quiet when alone is a fine thing, but being quiet with others can make all the world a church.

The clearing brought an end to our quiet, for there, running and shouting and doing turnover movements in the grass, were Simon, Aimée, and Michel's brother, Little Gérard. With them too, much to Hauviette's pleasure, was Maurice. I looked to Hauviette's face, which took the redness of a secret kept.

"Hello!" shouted Simon. "Come and roll!"

Hauviette took to his calling and ran into the clearing to join the others. The kitten, who had followed all the way, chased after, but when she got to the center of the children's rough play she turned and headed off to a more quiet spot.

We sat in the clearing then and shared the remaining biscuits. Since there were only two, we had a bite for each, a small but tasty bite. We talked and listened to the gentle music of Michel's shepherd's pipe. It carried God's love to my heart.

Aimée held the kitten under its two front legs, staring into its eyes. The kitten's rear legs hung down to nearly touch the grass. "What will you name this kitten?" she asked.

"I had not thought."

"It must have a name."

All agreed and so we set to picking a name. "Good Kitten," I said at last, and it was so.

Maurice spoke then of the war. Hauviette listened as if his were the ending words on earth.

"My father says the time is bad," said Maurice. His hair was stick straight and brown and falling in his eyes. "He says the French are broken in spirit."

"It is not just the French," said Simon, "but everyone. The Black Death did it."

"What is that?" asked Aimée.

"Please," said Mengette. She sat by Hauviette, picking wildflowers as she spoke. "Do not question him on it."

"What is Black Death?" asked Little Gérard.

"A sickness," said Michel.

"A terrible sickness," said Simon. "You get sores and soon you smell and then you die."

"Spare us," said Mengette.

"How do you get such a sickness?" asked Aimée.

"Do not question him on it," said Mengette.

"No one knows," said Simon, "but it comes. You never know until you have it. You get sores and soon you smell and then you die."

"You told us," said Mengette.

"But how do you get it?" asked Aimée.

"Do not question him on it."

"I would not worry," said Michel. "Many are spared."

Aimée thought about this. I could sense her concern. It was a hard time when first one learned of the plague. A helpless feeling overtook the mind.

"My father says the Black Death is but a part of it," said Maurice.

Hauviette moved closer to where he was sitting. She made her skirt smooth on her lap and folded her hands. I had never seen her sit so before.

"The Black Death is everywhere," Maurice went on, "but the spirit is lowest in France. Two hundred English could put to fight a thousand French. That is how my father says it."

"Why is it black?" asked Aimée.

"Do not question him on it." Mengette had stopped picking flowers.

"The sores are black," said Simon. "You get black sores and soon you smell . . ."

"And then you die," said Mengette.

"We know." Aimée began to look at her arms, checking, one could sense, for signs of death.

"Do not worry," I told her. "The sickness has not come to our village. It has been quiet in France for quite some time."

"It may start again," said Simon. "My father says that God is angry."

"God does not get angry," I told him.

"How can you be sure?" asked Mengette.

"I know it in my heart."

Good Kitten was enjoying the afternoon sun. She was sitting in its gentle rays, washing herself with her rough kitten tongue.

"The Black Death may return," said Simon. His fear made him hold the thought close.

"And it may not," said Michel. "Let us think of the good things. There are many."

"My mouse," said Aimée.

"Your mouse," said Michel, "to be sure. Where is your mouse on this fine day?"

"At home and safe," said Aimée. "Simon made him a keeping place."

"A cage," said Simon.

"A cage," said Aimée, as if it were the first for us to hear it.

Later that day, after we returned home, I took Good Kitten and climbed into the Troll Tree. We sat there for some time, looking out over the green fields to the hills beyond. Good Kitten seemed at peace. She slept in my lap as I sat, held within my favorite branches. I thought then of my Angels.

Will you come again? I asked them from my heart. I have so many questions, so much to understand. Why is there the pain and suffering of good people? You must know. From where you are you can see it all, but I cannot. Good Kitten can see it, but she says nothing. She is but a warm reminding one.

16
The Mission

Some months passed then, but my Angels did not return. The summer ended. Harvesttime came and went. The barley hung its head, the straw was left long, the crops were stacked and left afield, and still the Angels did not come.

Not a day passed I did not think of them, each time with the sense of all the grandeur of heaven, and each time I prayed if it be God's will, my Angels would return.

That year, as I recall, we kept the animals to pasture into November only, instead of the usual late December time when they were switched to grain. Father said the cold temperatures had speeded up the life of the grass, ending its usefulness to livestock a month early.

That November, toward the end of grazing time, Mengette and I had the blessed task of watching the flock. It was Father's turn that day. To my delight Father put me to the task, as Pierre and Jean were needed in Greux. Mengette's mother allowed her to join me, as often was the way. She could join me on the condition that she keep up with her spinning. This she always did.

Early that morning we headed for the common pasture where the three-field system was used. We would watch the sheep and the cows as well. To get to the pasture we had to cross the Meuse. We crossed at the narrow place to the left of Hauviette's barn. Hauviette waved to us from the door in back as we passed. She wanted to join us, but her mother needed her for work inside. Her face had a sad look.

"Look at those tiniest of fishes," said Mengette as she took her turn jumping at the narrow place.

There was a large group of the smallest fish that one would ever see in France moving up the river. It may be that there are smaller fish in France, but this I know not of. Jean always called them thus, "the smallest fish that one would ever see in France." I wondered how he knew this with sureness as he had not traveled far. I never asked him. That was not the type of question he liked to hear.

Jean and Pierre often liked to make loud noises at the side of the river when they saw the fish. They liked to watch them separate then and quickly pass in different directions. I never did this as I felt it scared the fish and that was why they parted. Mengette landed with a bit of a loud noise from her jump this day and parted the fish. Some headed toward Greux.

Later we sat beneath the large oak, with our distaffs each, spinning and watching the cows and sheep. It was cold for spinning. Our fingers soon grew stiff, slowing our time by half at least. It made us laugh wanting our fingers to move in their usual way, but finding them holding back behind our mind's telling. Pull and twist, pull and twist. So slowly they moved, without the proper tightness.

A calf was looking at me, watching me at my spinning.

An idea came to my mind then. It was a thing I often liked to do when I had the chance, and that was to put my hand in a calf's mouth. I loved the warm, sucking feeling, and warmth to my hands that day was a thing I could use.

"What are you doing?" Mengette asked when I rose to approach the calf.

"Hand warming," I answered. "I have a way."

"What way is that?" she asked. "I could use it as well."

"This way," I answered, reaching my hand out to the questioning calf.

The calf remained in her same spot wondering of my thoughts. I remained still. Soon she reached her neck out long in my direction, her nose held high.

"My hands have nearly frozen," said Mengette. She did not look at me then. She had stopped spinning and was moving her fingers many times in fast movements. "Can you lose them from a terrible coldness?"

"Lose what?" I asked. I was looking at the calf.

"Your fingers."

"I have heard tell of frostbite," I answered, for Pierre had spoken of it once, "but not in France. The temperatures are too mild."

"I hope you speak the truth," said Mengette. "I would not care to lose them. What are you doing?" She was looking at me now.

I did not answer then as not to frighten the calf who was sniffing my hand.

"What are you doing?"

I put my hand straight out, my fingers pointing to the

calf's mouth, which she opened slightly, rubbing my hand back and forth with her nose.

"What are you doing?"

The calf opened her mouth a bit more. I put my hand inside. My hand went in to my wrist as the calf began her sucking. It felt so good and warm, the sucking movement and the feel of her rough calf tongue. It pleased the calf as well, of that I had no doubt.

"You let it suck your hand?"

"Why not?" I asked.

"I have never heard of such a thing."

"Until now."

The calf was staring into my eyes, enjoying the sucking as much as I.

"You let it suck your hand?" Mengette repeated. Surprise had made her mind stay on the point without a way to move.

I felt not the need to answer for she spoke more to herself than to me. I had the thought to change hands then, for the one was warm, the other still cold. The calf did not like the idea. She knew not of my plan to give her a new hand to suck, thinking merely that I planned to take my hand away. She stared at me with a stubborn look, sucking harder than before.

"Let me change hands," I spoke. "The other will taste as good."

The calf could not guess my meaning, but felt, I sensed, that I meant her no harm. She loosened her hold, and I removed my hand, replacing it quickly with the other.

"The other hand as well?" asked Mengette. She was blowing on her own hands now, trying to warm them.

"It warms them well," I explained.

"And wets them with cow spit."

"A part of life."

"How is that for the wool we spin?"

"More than cow spit has touched our wool," I answered, "and more will touch it still."

Mengette did not bring her mind to my way. "You truly are my dearest friend," she said, "and yet, at times, I do not understand you."

"It matters not," I told her. "We have the love and that is all we need."

As afternoon approached Mengette was needed by her mother in the house. She left me then, to tend the flock alone. This I did not mind. Although I held dear the company of my darling Mengette, the time alone was also a joy. I set down my distaff and watched the creatures as they ate. The sheep bit close, with sharp, forward-set teeth, while the cows swept the grass with their rough tongues. Cows cannot bite the grass be cause they have not the upper teeth in front. A cow must tear the grass by moving its head. It later chews its cud with the teeth in back. A nearby cow was doing this, chewing with the rounded side-to-side motion, staring into the distance, thinking I know not what. I loved the cows with their heavy bodies and their long tails to keep the insects off in summer. I loved them, truly, so trusting in their way. They did not startle easy, as the sheep.

When I was small I used to name the cows, but they

would never come when called. Nor would the sheep. Only a horse will come, and a dog, and sometimes a cat. Good Kitten would always come when I called her, unless she was eating, or tracking a bird.

By the river two sheep walked toward each other, banged their heads once, and continued on their way. Why had they done that? They did not appear to be angry.

Daughter of God.

The voice.

Joan.

Yes.

Daughter of God.

On all sides there came the blazing light.

Saint Michael.

Yes.

The light blazed and then the face appeared within the light, the face so strong and loving, grander far than words can tell. The Chief and Lord of the Armies of Heaven!

Joan.

I fell to my knees.

You came back.

I was always here.

I could not see you.

Yet you were not alone.

It is you!

You must know that. Never doubt it now.

The light grew brighter still, blinding once more, once more the fragrance of heaven.

Look at me, Joan.

I raised my head to behold the figure of the Archangel Michael in all his armor, the crown, the shield, the sword, winged in the white-purple light. Tears burned my face.

There is great misery among the people of France.

Yes.

You must go to their aid.

Me?

God will help you.

What can I do?

Saint Margaret and Saint Catherine will visit you in my place.

Will you not return?

They have been appointed to guide and counsel you. Believe what they say to you and do as they direct, for such is the will of God.

Is it meant for me to pray?

Be a good child and God will help you.

To pray is all I know.

Yes.

Yes? Then that is my mission?

God will help you.

The light was fading now.

Don't go!

I am with you always.

Stay! Please! Don't leave me!

The light was gone. I put my face to the ground to kiss the place where the blessed Saint had stood.

Don't leave me.

When I sat up all was still. There was only my heart pounding, the tears on my face, the sheep and the cows, and the coldness of the winter air.

17

Joyful Counsel

From that day on I carried Saint Michael in my heart. Wherever I went, he was there, never forgotten now. And never to be forgotten for all of time.

I would pray for the people of France. This was my mission, my commission from God. I took strongly to its meaning. A child of thirteen, as I was, or thereabouts, I prayed throughout each day. I prayed upon awaking, at each ring of the church bells, before my morning meal and all the rest, before I fell asleep, while spinning, while cooking the soup, while tending the sheep, while bathing in the wooden tub, while holding Good Kitten—always, I would pray. Oh, I would put my thoughts to other things. I would play skip the stones with Hauviette, I would spend the singing times with Catherine and Colin, I would care for Aimée and mend her clay squirrel, I would race with Simon and have the sleep-over times with Mengette, I would sit with the others and listen to Michel play the shepherd's pipe, I would thrill to the blue of his eyes, all these things I would do, but it was different now. Always and through all, I would feel the Captain of the Armies of Light alive within my heart. Always, under all, I would somewhere, with a deep part of my being, pray for the people of France. And this would never change.

After Saint Michael spoke to me that day in the pasture, with all the sheep and cows, I felt a new feeling for him. Still there was the great love and the deep wonder and the joy beyond all telling at the sound of his voice, but something new was there. I sensed in him a stern side, like Father at his most serious times, but more. It almost gave me fear, as when Father would tell me a thing I must or must not do, as in the storm when I had wanted to go to the poor animals and he forbade me, as when I was but very small and wanted to play with a butterfly when Mother had need of me for the household things. Father told me I would help Mother then and leave the butterfly. I would help Mother always, before I did another thing on this earth. This I did not forget. Saint Michael made me feel the same awe and love in one moment as I had sometimes felt for Father. But with Saint Michael all was more.

After that day in the pasture when Saint Michael had come, perhaps it was two days after, I went to confession as I did each week. After confession I asked our priest, who was Guillaume Front, to tell me of Saint Michael. This he did.

"Saint Michael," he said, as if I had spoken of Christ Himself. "The Archangel Michael. The Chief and Lord of the Armies of Heaven!"

"Yes."

"He appears in apocalyptic times."

"What are they?"

"Apocalyptic times?"

I nodded.

"Times of great turmoil," he explained, "of danger. Times when darkness would threaten light itself."

"As now?" I asked.

Monsieur Front led me to a bench beneath the small cut window. Here we sat.

"Are you troubled by these times, Joan?" he asked.

"Yes," I answered. The side door was open, causing a cold draft to my feet, which did not touch the floor. "There is so much suffering of good people," I added.

Monsieur Front nodded. It seemed he knew not what to say. He felt as I did, I am sure, but did not want to frighten me further, and so he only nodded. He was quiet for a brief time. "Saint Michael is watching us even now," he said.

"Yes," I answered.

Monsieur Front nodded once more.

"What does he do when he appears?"

"He leads the faithful ones to victory over the dragon."

"How does he do that?"

"He works with Gabriel and others in destroying the wicked ones of power. He is merciful. He is always interceding for the human race."

"How does he do that?"

"He appears as the source of comfort and strength."

"What does he do?"

"He gives courage. He commands the battle." Monsieur Front uncrossed his legs one from the other then crossed them the other way. He seemed troubled. I knew not why. Perhaps he sensed he could not truly answer my questions.

I could not blame him. I wanted to know of Saint Michael's appearances and instructions to others, and yet I could not ask. I cannot tell you why. These things I kept within my heart.

Monsieur Front coughed a little then, more from lack of comfort, I could feel, than from a true need. "He is the Patron Saint of the duchy of Bar," he went on. "North of Toul, on Mount Sombar, the chapel is dedicated to him. On the pillar you can see the seal."

"What does it look like?"

"It is a round seal. In the center is Saint Michael, a handsome knight with crowned helmet, mail, a shield. He transfixes the devil with the sword."

"I would like to see that," I said.

"Perhaps someday you will."

I thanked Monsieur Front and returned home.

Three days later, Saint Margaret and Saint Catherine appeared. I was sitting in the Troll Tree with Good Kitten, waiting for the evening church bells. The churchwarden had not been ringing the bells regularly at that time. I remember I was thinking I must ask him to do so. Perhaps an offering of a cake or a piece of wool would show my good faith. Surely to be always on time with the bells, in all weathers, if one was sick or well, was not an easy thing, but more effort was needed. Perhaps if he knew there were those who cared, he would not forget. I would bring him a cake.

Joan.

The voice was filled with the music of heaven.

It is Saint Catherine.

I know.

The heavenly fragrance, the white-purple light, the ringing in my ears. And then, Saint Margaret.

Daughter of God.

The gentleness, the strength, the love of a thousand mothers.

I saw them with my bodily eyes, in a blaze of pure white light somewhere between the Troll Tree and the church. Their heads were crowned in rich and precious fashion with beautiful crowns, their faces the most beautiful that I had ever seen, not of this earth. The vision made me cease to breathe.

Saint Michael told me you would come!

Yes.

He told me I must go to the aid of the people of France.

Yes, Joan.

But how?

God will help you.

Must I pray?

Yes.

Be good.

Go to church.

How will that aid the poor people?

The light was fading now.

My Saints! Don't leave me!

Tears came now, as before.

I have so many questions!

But they were gone. All was still. I held Good Kitten tight.

I thought they would tell me more. That small part of my mind that reasons things from what it can see had made me think that they would come and tell me all. Had not Saint Michael told me? Saint Catherine and Saint Margaret will guide and counsel you. These had been his words. Guide and counsel, I had reasoned. They will answer my questions. They will tell me what to do. And this they had done, by fact, though not in the way my mind had thought. In my mind's way it went like this. The blessed Saints would come. They would tell me how to aid the poor people. They would tell me what to do first, and second, and after that. They would tell me how to pray, that my humble prayers might be of some use, that they might cause some lasting change to all the misery. For I could not see how this could be. And if my simple prayers were not enough, what more could I do, an ignorant girl, unschooled in any worldly ways?

I sat in the Troll Tree, in the soft evening light holding Good Kitten tight, recalling to mind the presence of my precious Saints. I prayed then for understanding.

Please, God, if it be Your will, show me the way. Help me to know my place.

Good Kitten stretched and began to lick her front paw with her rough tongue. She put the paw behind her ear, pressed it down, then brought it over her face. It was time to clean.

All is simple for you, Good Kitten, I thought. As so it should be for me. Saint Michael told me I must help the people of France. He told me that God will help me. He told me Saint Catherine and Saint Margaret will counsel me.

Their counsel was to be good and go to church. To be good is to be kind, and to pray. I will be kind and I will pray and I will go to church, and if I need to do more to help the poor people, my blessed Saints will tell me. I must have faith.

And so I vowed that night to have faith, and to carry, as best I could, what God had given.

In the months that followed Saint Margaret and Saint Catherine came often. Two to three times a week at least, without fail they would come. At times I would hear their voices without the sight of them I would be doing some task and hear them, or I would be sleeping and even still their voices would wake me. Be good. Be faithful. Go to church. Be not afraid. God will help you. These were the words they spoke, the sounds of their voices as clear as Mother's by the fire or Father's in the field, as clear as Hauviette's when she spoke of Maurice or Aimée's when she spoke of her mouse.

I spoke to the Saints from my heart, most often not forming the words with my lips, for there was no need. They could hear me. Sometimes, to my greatest joy, I would see them in all their glory as I had in the earlier times. Always I would weep for joy and bow down altogether at their unearthly beauty and their loving ways. Sometimes they would come as this, silent in all their splendor, not uttering a word. I would wake to find them in my tiny room, or pass through a door to find them on the other side. At these times, always, my heart would cease to beat. At other times I would sit quietly in some spot and ask my Saints a question. This I ofttimes would do silently from my heart, but sometimes I would speak the words.

That winter there was much illness in our village. To add to the dysentery and the fevers and all the rest, a terrible sickness broke out. It was called the Fire Sickness. It was first a terrible rash, as if the limb afflicted were consumed by some raging fire. It would nearly burn away the limb, which at last would drop off completely from the body. This was a horrible thing. The people were very much afraid. Henri's mother was stricken and lost an arm. When this happened I went behind the barn and sat in a quiet place to ask my Saints why this had happened, and what could be done. I saw them not that time, nor heard their voices with my ears, and yet I got my answer.

Fear not. We will ask.

I did not fully understand, but this was my answer. Later, as you will see, I found out what it meant.

Winter was long. The fogs were thick and clinging. Philip Mouse ran away. Aimée was sad beyond words, but I explained that he may have had things to do that mattered to him and that Aimée would do well to let him go. This she understood.

Nicholas did well through the winter. Simon made him a cover coat from wool, but Nicholas did not like it. When Simon put it on the goose, the goose got an angry look, grabbed it with his beak, and tossed it to the bushes. Simon would go running for the coat and place it on the goose, who would toss it once more. And so it went. And always, and through all, my precious Saints, their joyful counsel. They quickly grew to be my deepest friends.

We wintered Sibelle that year. Each family who shared

the blessed farm horse took turns caring for her in the winter. This year it was our turn. We kept her in the back pen and fed her hay and grain. That was the year she cracked a hoof. It happened toward the end of winter. Some sharp rock must have caused the crack. It went high into the hoof to where it is soft. Father had to cut away some of the hoof to help it heal. For some weeks Sibelle would not put weight on it. It was my job to soak the hoof twice a day in the bucket filled with hot water warmed in the fire. It had to be hot, but not too hot. I would lift Sibelle's leg—it was the right rear—set the bucket on the ground, then pull her hoof down into the bucket. She would stand then, with ears soft and thankful, while the heat and wetness brought comfort. I would put both my arms around her neck and hold her, my face against her soft winter coat.

One such night, as we waited for the warm water to do its healing work, the pen and Father's garden beyond were filled with blazing light.

Saint Michael, I thought, for I felt that it was he.

Daughter of God.

I fell to my knees on the cold ground, at the side of the patient horse. Once more the heavenly fragrance, the ringing sound, the force of life, the purple light, and the face, handsome, glowing, shining with power and love.

Saint Michael!

There is great sickness in your village.

Terrible sickness. Henri's mother was stricken.

Do not use rye flour kept over the winter.

I did not understand.

But why?

The light was fading now.

It is the cause.

Rye flour?

Be good.

Must you go?

Go to church.

Take me with you!

I am with you always.

My Saint!

Listen well.

And he was gone.

That night I spoke to Mother. I asked that she throw out the rye flour kept so long.

"I fear that it causes the Fire Sickness," I told her.

She did not see how this could be, but the force of my telling caused her to give her word. She would not use the flour until more could be learned.

The sickness continued in our village. Ones close were stricken. Mengette's father, Simon's aunt, my godmother, Beatrice, all suffered much pain, yet our family was spared.

The next year it came to be known. As dean of the village, Father cried the decree. "All rye flour kept over the winter must be thrown away. It holds a fungus that causes the sickness."

I fell to my knees that day in gratitude to my beloved Saint. With all he had to do, the Captain of the Armies of Light told me about the rye flour.

18

Picnic

Sibelle's hoof healed slowly. By lambing and calving time she was once more putting full weight on the leg, but there remained the deep cut-out place. In March, when we did our burning, the softness inside the hoof was only beginning to toughen. Mother made up a mixture, a paste of herbs—I do not know the kind—to place on the deep, soft spot to protect it and cause it to get hard. Sibelle would be needed for the plowing then, so the hoof demanded special care. After Pierre and Jean burned all the dead wood and branches collected from the year past, the ashes would be plowed under.

The year passed as had the others before. There was little difference, save for the presence of my blessed Saints. Every few days they would come. Saint Michael came rarely then, but Saint Catherine and Saint Margaret were my constant friends. Be good. Be faithful. Be not afraid. These were their words, so comforting, so true. Although their presence never ceased to bring deep joy to my heart, their closeness had become as expected as breathing. I wondered how I had ever lived without them. They would tell me, in truth, that I had never lived without them. I had only failed to know this.

As the year passed I grew to be at peace with the thought that praying was my mission. Who was I to say that the humble prayers of one simple soul could not help? I could not see how, but that did not change a thing. My Saints had asked me to help the people of France. They had asked me to pray. This I would do without doubting. I remembered Mother's words. "Doubt closes the door."

Everywhere the fighting continued. The danger grew worse. Again and again came the sound of the alarm, the flights in the night, the fires, the torture, the villages destroyed. By some miracle, our village had remained unharmed, but neighbors to the north and south were dying most terrible deaths.

The year was marked by many things. Sibelle's hoof was healed, which was cause for great thankfulness. Soon after, Good Kitten had kittens. Pierre thought it would be fitting to change her name to Good Cat, but this I did not do. There was no need. We kept the kittens on a warm piece of wool by the fire. Here they did well. Good Kitten spent many hours cleaning the kittens and letting them drink. They would climb on top of each other in a mixed-up way to get their milk. One was smaller than the rest. I named him Turnip. I would have to hold all the others at times to give Turnip a chance to feed.

Mengette's sister was married that year. She was not yet sixteen and did not know the boy before, which was most often the way. When Mengette met the boy she thought he was handsome. Hauviette said that Mengette wanted him for herself, but Mengette denied this in a loud voice. It would not have surprised me to learn that Hauviette was right in her thoughts. I was nearly fifteen at the time of the marriage. I could not think of marriage for myself at such an age. I had vowed to keep my virginity for as long as it pleased God. At that time, from what I could tell, it pleased Him.

Other things came to pass that year. This was one. Hauviette and Maurice went for a walk! They met in Greux where the two roads meet, completely by chance, such was the way Hauviette told it, and Maurice asked if Hauviette would like to go for a walk. As you can imagine, Hauviette said yes, and then it happened! They went for a walk! She told me later that she thought for some time that he was going to kiss her, but he did not. She told the story many times.

Another thing that happened that year was Simon's Animal Day. He planned it to his mind's idea, telling us what to do. Everyone would make a costume for their favorite animal. Then we would put the animals in the costumes and bring them to the place where the two roads meet. Here food would be served, and a contest would take place. There would be a judge who would pick the best costume. After that, everyone would dance.

There were many questions. What will the animals do while we dance? Who will make the food? Who will be the judge? What if the animals do not like their costumes? What if they eat them?

Simon had answers for all. The small animals could be carried while we danced. The larger animals could watch. Mengette and Hauviette and I would make the food. Pierre would be the judge. Most of the animals would not mind wearing the costumes for a short time, others would not even notice. The ones who did not like the costumes would not eat them because they would be well fed with other things and would not be hungry. As it came to be, the day was quite merry. All accepted the plans, even Pierre, who agreed to be the judge. Normally Pierre did not play with the younger children, so it was a welcome surprise when he joined in that day. Nicholas was the winner. He was dressed as a court jester. I dressed Good Kitten in a tiny colored vest and a wool cap, with holes cut for the ears. She cared not for the cap.

The year passed. I was now fifteen or thereabouts. It was a beautiful spring. The first sign was always the tiny flowers that would come out around the bottoms of the trees on the side of our house by the church. I never saw them on the other side, but always on the church side they came, telling of the coming of spring. For this I was most grateful. The winter was so much without color. Oh, there were the pines, and all year long the ivy vines would stay on the Grandfather Tree so it looked green, but elsewhere all was gray. Springtime brought such life, such color. It was a welcome time.

Some days after receiving the Sacrament of the Eucharist at Easter, it was our custom to have our first of-the-season picnic. This was always a blessed event. The whole family would go, Catherine and Colin as well. This year I took Good Kitten. Her kittens were grown now and slept in the barn. Most often they were off and doing, but Good Kitten remained in my shadow. This picnic day I gathered her under my arm and joined the others on our walk to the picnic hill.

Each year it was the same spot, the hill at the edge of the woods near the Bois Chenu. It was so beautiful on those first warm days of April. Sometimes we would try to rush picnic time and go in March, but it was too cold. In April it was perfect. The birds were happy, and we were as well. There was great joy in the family being together, excepting Jacquémin, of course, who was in Vouthon. We always spoke of him on our picnic days and sent him the love of our hearts.

We reached our picnic hill in short time, Catherine and Good Kitten and I in the lead. As we walked, getting higher and higher still, the valley on our left stretched out beneath us. It always seemed to me that our valley must surely be the most beautiful place on earth, the green rolling hills, the patterns of trees—a row so straight in some places, then at ease in small groups—just resting in God's beauty, the river winding through the green, green grass, the rocks, the blue sky, the mountains on the far side, so big, but rounded and friendly, the cattle grazing, at peace with their lot, the sheep so still, at peace as well, the birds soaring through the air, singing, chirping, resting on a branch or in a nest, then off again. God must have made other places like this, but truly I have never seen them. Whenever I looked at our valley it was none other than heaven on earth, God's sign that all was well.

Good Kitten was fussing. She wanted to be set down. This I did. She followed along then, running her small steps to keep apace.

"Here we are!" shouted Pierre. He passed us, running at fast speed, then threw himself on the soft grass. In April there was always the mossy undergrowth beneath the grass on the picnic hill. It looked moist, but it was not when you touched it.

Jean passed us then as well, running as Pierre, and threw himself on his brother. They rolled in the grass then, laughing and playing the fight. Mother and I set out the meal.

Father loved our picnics. He would always sit farthest up on the hill, facing the valley squarely, looking every once in a while to the left and then to the right. As always he ate more than usual on Picnic Days. He was so happy, so filled with the vision of God's beauty. Indoors, in colder months, he would, it seemed to me, always be partly thinking about the war and the safety of the village. Up on the hill at picnic time, it seemed that nothing ever could be wrong.

Good Kitten asked for some fish. She made her loud wanting sound, her mouth open wide, the part beneath her whiskers folding back.

"She may have one bite," said Mother, "but that is all. People before animals."

I did not like to hear that, but I supposed it was true. The fish from the Meuse were small, and Mother and Father and my brothers and sister were hungry. I gave Good Kitten the largest bite I could manage. She chewed it with her side teeth, on the one side only.

After we ate I lay back with my head on my beloved sister's lap. She stroked my hair back from my forehead in the soothing way. She had done this since I was very small, since ever I could remember. Always when she did this my joy was full. I watched the few white clouds floating in the bright sky. Hawks were circling over head, high up. I liked to think they noticed us and wanted to share our lunch. I felt this was most likely not the truth, because they were so very high. Still, I liked the thought. They looked as tiny spots of dust. I doubted they could sense our lunch. They may have sensed us though. Hauviette often used to say that my thoughts went their own way at times like that. I knew this was so, but it did not matter, I pray God. The hawks moved into a noisy, low, circling clump. Some thing needed doing. It was a glorious day, a day so far from war and sickness and pain that one forgot them nearly.

I sat up next to Father. I felt such love for him as he sat, so straight, so trusting in that moment as a boy of ten. I followed his gaze from the edge of the hill, looking down into the gentle valley, to the village of Domrémy to the left, to the church, to our house by the church near the edge of the village, to the Meuse running through the fields, to the gentle rolling hills, to the sometimes straightest rows of straightest trees. You see God clearly in the quiet places. Why make difficulties when all is one?

19

Another Place

Not long after our picnic it began. I could be at any task, awake or asleep, alone or in company, in silence or amid the noisy times at play, and still it would come.

Daughter of God.

The words alone, as whispered in my ear.

Daughter of God.

And yet again and again, and soon it would be many times a day.

Daughter of God.

It was, of course, my blessed Saints who spoke thus. First, Saint Michael.

Daughter of God.

And Saint Catherine.

Daughter of God.

And Saint Margaret.

Daughter of God.

And so it went.

At the sound of these words, when alone, I would fall to my knees. "Yes?" I would ask. "Yes, my beloved Saint? What is it you would have me know? Speak more, I pray, that I may know your will. Let me see the blessed vision of your face." But this they did not do. For the past two weeks it was but the phrase sounded once, no more, and gone.

Daughter of God.

No sight of my blessed Saints, only the sweet fragrance, always the fragrance, and the simple words.

Daughter of God.

And then, no more.

There was something different behind the words than such as there had been before, a pulling, a thing I was supposed to learn, to grow toward, a getting ready. This I strongly felt, and yet I knew not what it was. I felt at times as I were being called away to another place where I would receive something, or was in truth receiving something then, and still I knew not what it was. I would ofttimes awake and feel that I had been working in another world where the light was brighter than the world I knew, and still I knew not truly where it was. I wondered at this, but kept it in my heart.

It was a busy time. Father had returned recently from a trip to Vaucouleurs, where he had met with the commander of the town, the king's captain and provost, Robert de Baudricourt. I would know more of this man soon enough, but at that time he was but a name—Robert de Baudricourt, the big captain Father met with at the castle in Vaucouleurs, five leagues north of Domrémy. Father had gone to speak for our village and the village of Greux, in a lawsuit involving taxes. I do not remember the small facts, but it was in some way about our village and Greux paying taxes for protection and being too poor to pay in full.

Father spoke of the event one night soon after his return. We had finished our evening meal. I was with my distaff in my sewing corner, Mother was at the spinning wheel, Pierre and Jean were in the barn attending to some work, and Good Kitten was at my side. She had just had another litter of kittens. Their eyes were shut, their ears tiny and down. They slept in a jumbled heap close to their mother. Father was at the table that night. He had his papers and was reading by the light of the fire. He had remaining the toast, which he dipped in the watered wine. He often enjoyed this added part to his mealtime, a return to some earlier part of the meal when the cake or the pudding was done. "Four years of misunderstanding," he was saying. "We offer taxes for protection, we pay what we can, and more. They take his wool, they take his grain, they take his horses."

"Whose horses?" I asked. The idea of stealing someone's innocent horses appealed to me not.

Father told me then, but I cannot remember the name. It was a wealthy villager, who had pledged security. Now nothing seemed to satisfy the one in charge.

"We put together all we have," Father went on, "both villages, and still it is not enough. These are difficult times. Goodwill is needed."

"As always," I agreed.

"Yes," said Father.

"Was the captain helpful?" I asked.

"De Baudricourt?"

"Yes."

"He did what he could. He had little time to put to the matter. He is loyal to the Dauphin, with few to aid him."

I looked up from my spinning to see Father make his tiny spot-hole for reading. It was a thing he came to do as he grew older. When tired and in need to read, he would round in his first finger tight, closing thumb around. His three end fingers would be raised high, and he would always close one eye. With the other eye he would peer through the tiniest of holes made inside his circled finger, moving hand and head to one side and the next, across the page. This was the first time I had seen him do this.

"What are you doing, Father?" I asked. I did not stop my spinning as there was no need.

Father did not at first answer. He was deep in mind of his reading.

"Let him be," Mother told me.

"What?" said Father. He had heard us then.

"Joan had a question for you, Jacques," said Mother. "I told her it could wait."

"And why should it wait?"

"You have much work tonight, and the shearing tomorrow. Joan can save her questions."

But Father did not mind. "What is your question?" he asked. He looked away from his tiny seeing hole, but kept his hand raised still. "I need not bother you," I told him, for I was feeling very much the bother then, Mother having called my mind to its selfish way.

"You never bother me, my own," he said. "What would you know?"

"Why do you look through the tiny hole? Is it not hard to see?"

"Without the hole I cannot see at all, not to read in any case, not at my age, in this light, at this hour."

"Does it help you, truly?" asked Mother.

"It does," said Father, still reading. "I would have told you of it, Isabelle, for your sake, but you need both hands for your spinning."

"I need not see for spinning after all the years," Mother explained.

"In truth?" Father was surprised, one could tell, and also quite amazed and proud. "You could spin with eyes closed," he added, thinking the matter over as he spoke.

"Joan can do the same," Mother told him.

"That is well done," said Father.

I set down my distaff and did as Father was doing, with thumb and first finger rounded, looking through. It worked! If one made the hole small enough one could see quite clearly, but then I could see quite clearly with out the tiny hole, so I had but to take my father's word.

Daughter of God.

And so it came once more, the voice, Saint Michael, my blessed Saint, calling to me from everywhere and nowhere, whispering in my ear as I sat by the fire with Mother and Father and all their love around me, and Pierre and Jean in the room next, and Good Kitten and the kittens so warm at my side.

The shearing started early. I had not the knowing until just before that I would be allowed to join in the work.

Mother might have needed me inside, as so often was the case, but no. This time I could help.

When first we rose the sky looked as rain would come. Rain was not welcome at shearing time. One needed the dryness. But two days was the extent of time between washing and shearing, so this sometimes caused a wondering concern.

Father had to make the choice. He stood in front of the house, looking at the thick clouds and thinking. The day before it had rained and shearing could not be done, so this was the needful day. Pierre and Jean stood by his side, thinking also, checking the clouds in all directions. This I could see from the window as I cleared the breakfast things. I could see Pierre and Jean nod their heads. They had agreed on something. Father came inside.

"Come, Joan," he said from just inside the door. "We will shear the sheep."

I looked to Mother, who smiled a smile that said all is well. This brought joy to my heart.

The early hour and heavy clouds made it cool, even in summer, as Father and Pierre and Jean and I went to join the sheep in the far field, to the east of the house. The cooler weather would be nice for the sheep. It would afford protection from sunburn. Father and Jean carried the shears, while Pierre carried the box of dressing for the tender places or any broken skin. I carried the sacks.

It was always my joy to see the sheep in all their peaceful ways. This day it was the usual sight. Many stood, facing in different directions. An ewe lay down by folding her front legs, then falling to the ground. A ram was lifting a back leg to scratch behind an ear. The lambs stared up with questions.

Once, when I was six or thereabouts, I tried to get the sheep to pray. I thought of it that day as we neared the sheep. It went like this. Every time the church bells rang I loved to get down on my knees and pray and give thanks to God for all His goodness and blessings and the love in His heart for all His children. The ground was sometimes rough, but always welcome beneath my knees.

This one time, when I was six, it was autumn. I was in the far field to the east that day as well as I watched the sheep. The church bells rang. I tried to get the sheep to stop eating and look to the church tower, but they would not do it. This upset me, but I was only six. The sheep meant no harm. God did not give them the understanding of certain things, but still they knew Him. They knew Him in the grass, and in the warmth of the barn in the winter months, and in the sureness of the flock. It was my lack of understanding to ask this thing of them, but the bells gave me such joy. I felt such gratitude. I wanted the sheep to know this. I was only six.

Daughter of God.

The voice brought me back from my remembering, so clear, so strong, the whisper in my ear, the calling. Saint Michael, my beloved.

"I had better take this one!"

It was Jean shouting to the rest of us. He wanted us to know that only he could handle the largest ram.

20

Daughter of God

Pierre set down the box of dressing. A ram moved forward and pushed it with his nose.

"Get away!" shouted Pierre.

The ram appeared not to hear. He tipped the wooden box over on its side. Father handed Pierre the shears. "You take that one," he told him, pointing to a nearby ewe.

The ram was still nosing at the dressing box.

"The dressing is soon to disappear," said Jean. He already had his ram tipped back in the half-sitting position, one hand beneath the jaw, the other at the tail. This half-sitting way will make the sheep sleepy.

"Get the dressing box, Joan," said Father.

I liked to watch the ram nose about the box, but surely Father was right. Sheep will eat anything. I moved to the box and took it from the ground. The ram stared at me with a sad and puzzled look.

"I doubt the mixture would taste good," I said. He did not understand.

It was not my job to do the shearing itself. That was for the men. In ways, I would have taken well to the job, as a shorter person has more ease. In shearing the sheep one must bend over for many long hours. This is hurtful to the back. The shorter men had not so far to bend, and thereby had the ease. I often felt I could have managed with the ewes. They most often take the shearing calmly. The rams are active and require strong handling.

My jobs were thus. First, I helped to sort the sheep. The young lambs we let go. The ewes still suckling were done separately. Some of the old ewes had the fleece dropping loose. These we did not shear as they were near lambing time. They could do with the extra warmth, and also the lack of handling. These ewes I would find and move to a place a bit away, where Jean had built the pen. I would also apply the dressing from the box to any broken skin or tender place.

I loved to watch the shearing. Mostly the sheep would take it well and be not afraid. Often I could sense their pleasure at being rid of the heavy fleece, so deep and thick. Father was the finest at the work. His hands were sure. His touch could always feel where the fleece was fine, close to the skin, but not too close, and there he would clip. Pierre and Jean were always careful, but sometimes they would cut. Then I would apply the dressing.

When the sun was overhot Father always left a ridge to the wool to protect the sheep from sunburn. Jean and Pierre were learning how to do this as well. All three looked so strong and able. They were firm, but always kind with the sheep, a hand beneath the jaw, a hand beneath the tail, the flip, the cut like a jacket coat down the front, and then the folding back. Hauviette's father tied the legs of the sheep at shearing time, but this was never Father's way, and so he taught the boys.

We worked without a stop as all the sheep needed shearing while the sun was full. Later Pierre and Jean would go back for the two-wheeled cart to load the fleece. These Mother and I would lay flat, the close to-the-skin part up, to remove the soiled or matted wool. We always folded the four leg pieces in. Some times we began the rolling the next day, but not always. It depended on the other chores.

I was most tired that afternoon after the shearing. I know not why, but this I remember. This was not my usual way. When I reached the house, Mother told me the fleece rolling would be left to the next day. This was welcome news. I had some soup from the pot and a piece of bread, gathered my distaff, and returned to the sheep. There I would do my spinning.

When I entered the field Pierre and Jean were starting home with the fleece in the cart. "Short Legs!" Jean called, as he saw me approach. "Have you had not enough of sheep?"

"No," I answered, for truly it was so. I always loved their company, but why I had returned that day I did not know. I wondered in my own mind why I had come. Most usually after a long morning outside with the sheep I would have remained in the house helping Mother with the inside things. She did not ask my help inside, or surely I would have stayed. But why did I, that day, choose to spend all day with the sheep? I wondered this as I sat beneath the large oak tree and set about to spin. I wondered this, and other things as well. Why had I not asked Hauviette or Mengette to join me? This, too, was unlike my usual way. I had not been in their company for many days. That afternoon would have seemed a fitting time to join with them in spinning together. But no. I came alone.

"And so, farewell!" shouted Jean as he and Pierre left with the cart. Jean played the joke as if he were going off to war, or to some far-off land, not merely to the barn behind the house.

"Farewell, my brother. Keep you safe!" I called, playing his game.

A beautiful stillness settled then, as I sat beneath the oak in God's beauty, the sheep so peaceful, the quiet grass, the trees that rustled in the gentle wind, the terraced vineyards on the hills behind.

Daughter of God.

Saint Michael, my Saint, my own.

The voice and only that. Tears filled my eyes.

Yes?

All was still.

Yes! Where are you?

More tears now, hot and burning. Silence.

Oh, my blessed Saint, I have not seen you in so long. Where are you? Why do you not come?

A lamb came near to me beneath the tree and stood, his black face questioning. His mother was near, the fullness of her fleece gone now, only the narrow look with the tiny ridges of wool to protect her from burn. Did they see my tears? Did they wonder at their reason? I felt so.

I had then a strange and far-off feeling. In some way the place my eyes could see did not seem real. Tears came still.

Where are you? Why do you not come? Have I offended thee?

No answer still.

I felt that time a deep concern. I felt in my heart there was something I needed to do, yet I knew not what it was. Some time passed then, with tears as well.

Daughter of God.

The voice, the fragrance of a thousand flowers, the blazing light, and then Saint Michael was before me. All flooded purple before my eyes, great blazes of purple light, deep purple, blazing first here, then there, by the sheep, near the bush, by my feet, and brighter than all, amidst all the purple, in blinding white, Saint Michael, the Captain of the Armies of Light. I fell to my knees, embracing him as to never let him go.

My beloved Saint!

He felt so very much alive. It was as embracing a loved one's breath, a web of cool yet, at the same time, warm light. How could it be both? And yet it was.

Daughter of God.

The pounding of my heart, the ringing in my ears once more, the same, and everywhere the blinding light.

I missed you so.

I was with you.

I asked to see you, but you would not come.

I could not.

Why?

It was not time.

I love you.

I love you, Daughter of God.

I held him thus, not wanting ever to let go. Some time passed. I sat back to gaze at him.

Have I displeased you?

You could not. You, Joan, are pure light, pure goodness. Others will come to know this.

Tears flowed beyond my help. I knew not what he meant.

Others will know you as I know you, as Saint Catherine and Saint Margaret know you. They will see your beauty. They will feel your powerful truth. They will be changed.

I am a poor farm girl. I know nothing.

Daughter of God.

Yes.

You must go into France. You must go to the aid of the Dauphin. No one can do it save you.

I understood not his meaning.

I, go into France?

Yes, Joan. It is for you to do, if you will have it.

Am I not in France?

In your heart.

In my heart and soul! I have always lived in France! It is my home!

Yes.

Then where do I go?

You must ride into France to meet the Dauphin. You must help him.

His words were as lightning, as thunderbolts, striking my mind, pushing it back I knew not where, 'til all I could feel was my heart and the tears burning my face.

How can I help the Dauphin?

No one can do it save you.

I am no one.

Daughter of God.

I know nothing.

God will do the work.

What must be done?

You must ride into France.

I know not how to ride. Not well.

You will learn.

All was purple-white now, my Saint, the sheep, the field, and all the sky. My heart pounded so hard in my chest that I feared it would burst. My Saint, the truest of true, spoke words my mind could not hold. Could he mean what he said? It could not be so! And yet he always meant what he said. Never was a false word given, never an untrue thought. Always he would give pure mind, pure reason. I must reach. I must reach!

Daughter of God.

My heart was filled with questions. I must ride into France to aid the Dauphin? How can I aid him? I thought I was in France? How can I go to where I am already? Where is the Dauphin? Who will take me there? What will I say?

Who will listen? How could what I do make any difference?
I must ride into France and save the Dauphin? How? How?
Who am I to do this?

Daughter of God.

And he was gone.

21

Hauviette's Plan

I slept soundly that night and well into the next day. When I awoke the sun was no longer high in the sky, but low behind the trees in back of the house. I did not immediately know where I was.

I could see the slanting rays of the sun on the brook outside my narrow window, an unusual sight for morning.

"What time is it, Good Kitten?" I asked, but got no answer. I sat up then to look more clearly through my window. It was afternoon.

Why did I sleep this day? I asked myself. Then I remembered. Saint Michael.

I felt a tightness in my chest, a quickening of my heart, as I tried to remember my beloved Saint's words. My mind held back from knowing, while all was sounding loudly in my heart.

He spoke of something grand. Grand and fearful. But what? What did he tell me?

Good Kitten pushed her nose against my arm, then flopped down hard on the bed and stretched. I forced my mind to think. My heart pounded louder than before, and then his words, resounding in my mind.

You must ride into France.

Dear God. That was it. I must ride into France! Those words he spoke to me, and more! I must aid the Dauphin! No one could do it save I! What else? There was more. Others would see my light, and be changed. What could he have meant by that?

My mind could not contain the sense.

I must ride into France and aid the Dauphin!

The questions returned. I must ride into France and aid the Dauphin? How can I aid him? I can pray. But I am praying now. Why must I go into France? Am I not in France already? Where is the Dauphin? Who will take me there? I must ride into France? I know not how to ride!

I remembered his words.

You will learn.

I thought of Sibelle, of sitting high on her straight, broad back. She was with another family now. They would need her for the work. I could not use her for riding. And she was not a fast horse. She merely moved in a steady way with the plow. She merely walked. Surely one does not walk to France, if indeed one is not there already. I must learn to ride a fast horse. I thought of Hauviette's horse, the big gray one. I had seen Hauviette's oldest brother, Charles, ride The Gray at quite a pace. This would be a good horse to learn on.

I lay back on my bed. My eyes closed to rest a while. I fell asleep. When I woke again the sun was nearly down. Mother was at my side. "Are you not well, Joan?" she asked.

She put her hand to my head. "I feared you had a fever, but you are cool."

"Yes," I answered. "I think I am well. Forgive me for sleeping so."

"Your body had good reason."

"Were you rolling the fleece?" I asked, my mind slowly returning to the tasks of life.

"Yes," said Mother.

"I will help you."

"If you are able."

We worked in the front room, with Good Kitten and the kittens watching. My mind felt relief to work at the simple task, letting the other thoughts go. I would figure all that out later. For the moment I would bask in the light of my mother's love. We would roll the fleece.

We worked at the table, laying the fleece flat. The neck wool we pulled out, ropewise. Then we rolled the fleece from the tail end, making a neat bundle. This we tied with the rope of the neck wool. Each roll had to be even. We then put the rolls on the clean, swept floor of Pierre and Jean's room. The rolls were white and quiet. If we rolled the day of shearing, the fleece was always live and warm. If the night was cool after the warmth of the day, a mist would come around the wool and the cooling fleeces would stir in the night. This caused great fear to Pierre when he was small. He would try to sleep, and hear the stirring of the cooling fleeces and also the faint sound like soft breathing. He could never sleep those nights. He would sit by the fire and tell

Mother and Father of the dragon in his room. They would always tell him it was but the cooling of the fleeces, but this he could never believe. Jean told me of this. Many things Jean told of Pierre were made up or stretched to a foolish point, but this, I felt, was true.

We worked quietly, Mother and I, saying little. With Mother it was possible to be at peace, without the need of talk. This was especially welcome that day. I felt awkward, I remember, and made mistakes in the work that usually I would not have made. Quite often the words of my blessed Saint would sound in my mind.

You must ride into France. You must go to the aid of the Dauphin. No one can do it save you.

I was very much afraid. Not so much afraid of riding into France itself, though this caused worry to my heart, but there was something else. I was afraid because the words of my beloved Saint had no sense to my mind. When the surest of the sure seems a strange thing, it is a fearful time.

I did not think to tell Mother of the words that were spoken. I knew in my heart that one day she would know. This did not feel the time. We worked thus until we began to prepare for the evening meal. I left then to fetch the water.

Each thing in its time, I told myself as I crossed the road and headed for the Meuse.

The sun was very low, warming on my back. I must take each telling, and do it fully. Then I will be given more. All in time, as with the rye flour. One day I will understand. When I need to know, all will be given. For now I must learn to ride. That simple thing. That I can do, and gladly! I will ask Hauviette if I can ride the big gray horse.

"Joan Romée, 'tis time for play!"

It was Hauviette, running from her house. I stopped, holding the bucket.

"Joan Romée, come play today!"

She made the rhyme from my mother's surname, which I held, as was the custom.

"I cannot," I told her, "for I must help with the supper."

Hauviette fell in a heap at my feet. She was nearly out of breath. "Oh, Joan, my truest friend," she said, "I have not seen you for days, and now you say we cannot play. That is too cruel!"

"I would like to," I said, "truly, but this is not the time."

She got on her knees then and begged. "Tomorrow you must come!" she said. "Charles has agreed to hitch the pony cart. Simon is coming, and Mengette and . . ." She paused to add suspense, then whispered in a most important way. "Who would you say?"

"Maurice."

"How did you know?" It seemed to please her not that I had guessed.

"It could only be, the way you put the words. Maurice, or the King of France."

"The King of France in a pony cart?"

"I think not," I answered, "and so that leaves Maurice."

"And so it is!" said Hauviette. She tipped back in the evening grass, putting her legs out straight before her. "You must come," she said. "I have a plan."

[173]

"What is it?" I asked. I thought of Mother, waiting for the water, wondering where I was.

"I have planned this all in my mind," she went on. "Are you listening?"

"Yes," I said. I set down my bucket.

"Good. Now, here it is. I will get in the cart before Maurice, and before you, and you will get in after me. Do you have that in your mind?"

"I have it."

"Good. You will get in after me, but you must let no one in between. First I will get in the cart, and then you will get in the cart."

"With no one in between."

"Just so. You will follow me into the cart, I will sit down, and you must sit next to me."

"On which side?"

"It matters not."

"In truth?"

"In truth. But you must sit next to me."

"I sit next to you."

"Yes. You sit next to me until . . . and here is the special part."

"Until . . ."

"Until Maurice gets into the cart. Just before Maurice is ready to sit, you will get up, as if there were a certain reason in your mind. You must decide what the reason will be, but you will get up, leaving the seat next to me empty, and Maurice will sit in it." She smiled then, thinking, I believe, of how it would be. "Is it clear to your mind?"

"'Tis clear."

"You must be sure he thinks you have a reason."

"I will make a reason."

"What will it be?"

"I will think on it."

"What will it be?"

"I have not thought."

"Think."

I paused then. I took a breath to clear my mind. This was of great importance to my friend. I must be kind. I must think through this matter of Maurice and the pony cart. I must put from my mind all thoughts of riding into France, of aiding the Dauphin. I forced my mind to consider Maurice and the cart. "I will get up to go inside to tell my mother an important fact before we leave."

"What will you tell her?"

"It matters not."

"It should be real."

"Maurice will not be there!"

"That is true," she said, accepting the thought. "But there is something else!"

"And what is that?"

"What if they do not wait for you?"

"Then I will miss the ride."

"But you cannot!"

"I need not ride in the cart."

She looked troubled for a time, until she had a thought. "That will be my job," she said. "I will make sure we do not leave without you."

"As you wish."

"So you agree?"

"I agree."

"We go shortly after noon. Charles will hitch the cart."

"That is well."

"You will be there?"

"If God wills."

"Must you always speak of God?"

"Yes," I answered.

"I know," she said. "I love you, Joan." She had gotten up from the grass and held me in a hug.

"I love you," I said, holding her tight.

As we parted I reached down for my bucket.

"I will come with you to get the water," she said.

When we reached the river's edge I bent, tipping the wooden bucket to receive the water's flow. Then I told her. "I want to ride the big gray horse," I said.

She had a puzzled look. "Why?" she asked.

I answered with a certain part of truth, withholding some, as she could not contain it. "I love to ride Sibelle at the plow," I said, "but she is only slow. I want to learn the fast way."

Hauviette agreed that sounded good and, best of all, she agreed to ask Charles to teach me.

That night as I lay on my bed, the questions returned. My thoughts came, one upon the next, and I was very much afraid. I could not sleep, my mind and heart racing in the dark, empty stillness of my room.

I must ride into France and aid the Dauphin!

What did my blessed Saint mean by these words? I thought of it many ways. Perhaps Father was to go on some business near where the Dauphin was. Perhaps I would go along with Pierre and Jean, but why would they take me? Mother would need me at home. And she would fear for me, too. She would not let me go. And with all that, what would be the reason? Perhaps a girl in the group would make us clearly a family, less threat to the enemies. Perhaps if I went, our group would be safer. But no. Women and children were being murdered every day in France. There must be another answer. My mind raced on.

Somehow I will be near the Dauphin, I thought, and as I pray for him at such a close distance this will help. But why would I need to be near him to pray? A prayer at any distance will help, if it is true. I must ride into France. How? On a horse? In a cart? Perhaps a cart. But Saint Michael said I would learn how to ride. He must have meant a horse. I know how to ride in a cart. Why would he tell me to learn something I already know? And why would he tell me to go somewhere I already am?

The questions only made new questions, with not an answer.

I sat up then on my bed, my feet on the cold, earthen door, and prayed. I prayed with all my heart to my blessed Saint that he would reveal what was asked of me. I spoke the prayer out loud.

Very sweet Lord, in honor of thy holy passion, I beseech thee, if thou lovest me, to reveal to me how I am to understand. How may I ride into France, and how may I aid the

Dauphin? I am a poor farm girl and know nothing. In this it may please you to instruct me. What did you mean when you spoke thus, my beloved? How am I to understand the words?

As they were spoken.

The voice and only that, with all the power and love and majesty of the heavens. Saint Michael, Captain of the Armies of Light, slayer of darkness, simply let me know.

As they were spoken.

22

Pony Cart

Shortly before noon the next day I asked Mother if I might be spared from the inside work for a time. I explained that Hauviette had need of my help with the children in the pony cart. Mother agreed. She would be spinning that afternoon and I could join her when I returned. I thanked her, took a nice piece of bread, and left the house. Good Kitten followed.

The sun was high and strong as I crossed our yard. The church bells rang. I fell to my knees, grasping my bread, and prayed, giving thanks to God for all His goodness. Good Kitten walked in circles around me as I prayed. She was eager to be on with the day.

When we reached the road I could see Hauviette in front of her house, and her brother Charles with the pony. I remember not the pony's name. It may have been Acorn, but I cannot swear to that. He was small and brown and very strong, that I can recall, and seemed to love to pull the cart. As I approached I could see Simon as well, sitting on a large rock, his goose nearby. Charles was hitching the pony to the cart.

Hauviette called out when she saw me. "You came!" she shouted, running to meet me. "I was so worried!"

"I am not late," I answered.

"Not yet." We hugged a greeting. "Do you remember the plan?" she asked.

"I remember."

"I slept not last night," she said in a whisper as we made our way to where Charles was hitching up the cart. "Not one minute did I sleep." She sounded pleased to tell me. "Do you have a question?" she added.

I told her I did not.

"Good," she said. "We must speak no more of it now. The others might suspect something."

"That is well," I answered.

"How does it go with the cart?" Hauviette put the question to Charles in a very loud voice, with more interest than the question could bear.

"Fine," said Charles, without looking up. He did not greet me, which was the usual thing to expect. He spoke few words to others. It was not a friendly way, and yet he meant no harm. He always seemed to be busy, never of a mind to interrupt his tasks. I did not expect a greeting. I felt thankful only that he hitched the cart. It had such meaning to Hauviette.

"Hello," I said.

"Hello," said Simon. He sat on the rock still, staring at some stones in the road. Aimée was nearby, sitting in the road watching Nicholas, who was resting on one leg, the other folded back into his feathers.

"Look at this goose," said Aimée. "He has only one leg, and sleeps and sleeps and never falls."

"He has two legs," said Simon. "The one is folded back."

"I know," said Aimée. "I have eyes."

"Then why do you say he has only one leg?"

"I say what I say."

"We hear that."

Something troubled Simon that day, one could tell. I spoke of it as we waited for Charles to finish the hitching. "What bothers you?" I asked.

"Nothing," Simon answered.

"It seems not so."

Nicholas kicked out his folded leg without warning, a kick, and another, and another, then folded the leg back into his feathers. His neck was bent around, with head facing behind, resting on the top of his body. He appeared to be dreaming. Simon stared at the stones in the road.

"What troubles you?" I asked once more.

"I will never go to school," he said.

I sat on the grass by his side. "Perhaps you will," I said.

"Never," he said with sadness. "I wanted to, but soon I will be too old. The fighting will never stop."

"One day it will."

"I will be too old."

It was a sad thing. The boys of our village would go to school in Maxey, but now it was too dangerous. Pierre and Jean had wanted to go as well, but Father would not let them.

"You can learn apart from school," I told Simon. "Pierre can read, and so can Jean. Father taught them."

"My father is too busy."

"I will ask Jean to teach you. He loves to teach people things."

"Would he teach me?" Simon looked at me for the first time that day.

"Perhaps he would."

Aimée was trying to stand on one leg, like Nicholas. She did well until she closed her eyes. Then she fell to the ground.

"How does it go with the cart?" Hauviette loudly asked once more of Charles.

"Fine," said Charles.

"Where are the others?" I asked.

"What others?" said Simon.

"Oh, Mengette, and Henri," said Hauviette, "and was there someone else?"

"Maurice," I said.

"Oh, yes," said Hauviette, as if it mattered not at all. "Maurice. I had forgotten."

I wanted to say, "You had not forgotten! That is all that fills your mind." But I did not.

Then I heard the music. A minstrel was coming down the road, playing a lute, and at his side was Michel, who played his shepherd's pipe. My heart went as turned on end, my breath grew short. My knees felt a weakness. Michel laughed then. I know not why. He stopped his playing for a moment, then picked up the tune once more. His joy could be felt at a long distance.

"Oh, here comes Michel," said Hauviette in a certain tone for my ears only. "Perhaps he would like to ride in the cart. What would you say, Joan?"

"Perhaps he would," I said.

Would he sit next to me? I thought.

Michel saw us and waved. My heart beat loudly. Nicholas woke up, made two questioning squawks, and poked out his long neck. The music had brought him from his sleep.

"Squawk, squawk!" and again, "Squawk!"

Good Kitten cared for this not. She ran across the road and into our yard.

"Squawk, squawk!" The goose stared at Michel and the minstrel as they came near. The song ended then. Michel smiled at the minstrel, who smiled back, saying something I could not hear. The minstrel was thin and carried a cymbal tied to his back with a rope. He pointed off in the direction of Greux, from where they had come. Michel nodded, then the minstrel went off.

Let Michel join us on the ride! I thought. Let him sit at my side!

I had to laugh at myself then, as I sounded so much like Hauviette.

Michel approached the cart. "Are you going for a ride?" he asked.

"We are," said Hauviette. "Would you like to come?"

"If there is room," he said. "Hello, Joan."

"Hello," I said. "I liked your song."

"Thank you," he said. His eyes were so blue.

"There is room," said Hauviette.

"That is well," said Michel. He sat on the rock by Simon.

Aimée was chasing Nicholas, trying to pick him up. Nicholas ran, head down and level with his body, squawking all the time.

"Let him be," said Simon.

"How does it go with the cart?" Hauviette said once more to Charles, who was working with the harness.

"Fine," said Charles.

Hauviette looked down the road in both directions. "Not everyone is here," she said in a worried way.

"They will come," I told her, and it was true. Soon Mengette had joined our group and Henri, to my dismay, and at last, Maurice.

Hauviette's face was suddenly red as she saw him approach. "Everyone is here," she said.

Charles was soon finished with the harness and it was time to get into the cart. I felt at that moment a feeling I would come to know well. It was this. I was with my friends, talking and listening to their words, and yet, in some way, I was not there at all. Saint Michael had brought me to a new place, far more real than anything before my seeing eyes. This new place was now my truest home. I had not asked for this with my knowing mind, yet it was so. All about me was seen and felt and heard as from a distance. My new home was open, with light and air and soft colors. This I did not see, but felt only in my heart, and this I would feel always as I walked the earth.

23

Knowing

Charles had important chores to do and could not drive the cart, so Henri took the job.

"Let me handle this," Henri said, climbing in and taking the reins before a decision could be made in the matter.

I did not like the idea, as Henri was so stupid with the animals. He was sure to drive the pony too hard, but I said nothing. It was Hauviette's cart. She should say who took the reins. Her mind was elsewhere though, as you would think. She noticed not. "Everyone in," she said, climbing into the cart. Then she took a seat. She gave me a strong look then to be sure I remembered my part.

I climbed into the cart and sat by her side. Henri glanced our way. "All the pretty girls together," he said, for no reason that I could tell. Mengette was still out of the cart, and so was Aimée. There were pretty girls throughout France and all about the world, but Henri always said the stupid thing, the thing that made no sense, and smiled to himself while he said it.

It was Mengette's turn to climb into the cart then. She sat by Hauviette on the other side. "My sister is having a baby," she whispered in a low voice, so Henri could not hear.

Hauviette did not appear to be listening. She was staring at Maurice. He was with Michel and Simon. They were chasing Nicholas, who did not want to ride in the cart.

"Everyone in," shouted Hauviette.

"As soon as we get the goose," shouted Michel.

"She shows the signs," continued Mengette.

"That is well," I said. I thought of Catherine, hoping she would soon be with child. She wished it so.

Simon grabbed Nicholas, who squawked loudly.

"Get that goose!" shouted Aimée. She was standing up in the front of the cart by Henri.

The time was at hand! Simon, Michel, and Maurice approached the cart. Hauviette poked me hard in the side and kicked my leg. "Get ready!" she whispered.

"For what?" asked Mengette, smoothing her skirt down over her knees and folding her hands.

"You soon will see," whispered Hauviette.

And then it happened. Maurice climbed up into the cart, I got up, and Aimée sat in my seat!

Hauviette looked as if she had seen the dead. "Not here!" she whispered in a very strong voice to Aimée. Hauviette kept her mouth nearly shut, speaking through closed teeth. "Not here!"

"I need a sitting place," said Aimée.

"Not here!"

"Why not?"

Maurice sat on the far side of the cart.

I felt unsure of what to do next. Should I sit in some other seat, or leave the cart as I had planned, to go in to Mother. It seemed to matter not. Hauviette stood then and brushed her skirt with both her hands. "Crumbs," she said. There was naught on it.

"Where?" said Aimée.

I was standing in the cart as Michel passed me.

"Why does everyone stand?" asked Aimée.

Michel sat by Maurice. I looked at Hauviette, who had lost all color in her face. She stared before her with a curious look.

"Shall we sit?" I asked.

"Sit, ladies," said Henri. "Do not stand for this ride. It will surely be a rough one."

"You might ask if all would like a rough ride," I told him. "The pony would not. I can tell you that."

"Sit down," said Hauviette. She pulled my sleeve.

Simon got into the cart with Nicholas, a most angry looking goose, and we were off.

The ride began at an even pace. The pony's ears were straight up in the happy way, the sun was bright and the breeze welcome. Simon held Nicholas tight. The goose seemed slowly to accept the ride and began to doze. Maurice smiled at Hauviette. Hauviette returned the smile, then looked out at the country as it passed. I could feel her heart beat in her chest from where I sat.

We had a way with the pony rides. When a hill would come we would all get out so the pony did not have such a load to pull. When we came to a down hill we would get out also, as the added weight in the cart would cause the cart to bang into the rear of the pony.

When we got to the first down hill Henri did not stop the cart.

"Stop to let us out," I said as the cart banged into the pony. Henri paid no mind.

"You heard Joan," said Michel. "Stop the cart."

"The hill is small," said Henri. "There is no need."

"We always stop," said Aimée, "or this pony gets banged."

"Not this time," said Henri.

"He was," said Aimée. "He was banged and banged."

"The road is flat now," said Henri. "Enjoy the ride." Flat or not at the moment, there had been a hill. Henri had been unfair. "You do that once more and you will live to regret it," I told him.

"Joan the serious," said Henri. "You have no fun."

"Neither will you if you do not listen."

"Tell him, Joan," said Maurice.

"Tell him, Joan," said Hauviette, who liked to echo her friend.

"And what of the pony?" I went on. "What of his fun?"

"Joan is right," said Maurice.

"Joan is right," said Hauviette.

"And you are wrong," said Aimée.

Up ahead was the hill before the Bois Chenu. It stretched up high before us.

"Stop the cart," said Michel.

Henri did not stop, but only hit the pony with the reins.

The pony pulled on slowly, breathing in a heavy way, panting and scared.

I stood up. "Stop this cart!" I shouted.

"What?" said Henri, pretending not to hear.

"You shall know what soon enough," I shouted. "Now, stop this cart!"

Henri pulled back on the reins. The pony gratefully stopped.

"How dare you be cruel to that pony?" I went on. I was standing still. "You must have God in you somewhere! You would do well to show it!"

"I stopped," said Henri. "What more is on your mind?"

"More than you would care to know."

"Get out and walk if that is what you want."

"We always do," said Aimée, climbing out of the cart. "You must be stupid."

God help me, she had it right.

From that time on the ride was more peaceful. There were not many hills, but always when we came to one Henri would stop the cart and we would get out. We would walk the hill and then return to the cart. No one minded. This had always been our way.

We turned shortly after the Bois Chenu, retracing our way through Domrémy once more, then on through Greux toward Burey. Nicholas slept. We were quiet for a time, just feeling the wind on our faces, watching God's beauty on all sides. There was joy in my heart, my beloved Hauviette on one side, Mengette on the other, my loving friends so near,

Michel so fine of feature, his thick brown hair blown by the wind. His arm was around Simon as it rested on the side of the cart. I wished then that I was Simon. It was not a sad and lonely wish, but just a sweet imagining.

The way home through Greux is flat and straight. The pony picked up a good pace. Nicholas was awake now, content it seemed to rest in Simon's arms. He stared ahead, thinking, perhaps, of supper.

"I want to ride more," said Aimée.

"Charles needs the cart," said Hauviette. "We must return."

"Can we ride tomorrow?"

"Soon," said Hauviette. She glanced at Maurice. "Did you enjoy the ride?" she asked.

"I did," he said.

Her day was fine.

"Will you ask Jean if he will teach me how to read?" asked Simon, looking to me from across the cart.

"I will."

"If the fighting would stop I could go to school."

"I know," I said.

"If only the prophecy would happen."

"What is that?" asked Aimée.

"A prophecy is when it is said that a thing will happen," said Simon.

"What thing?" asked Aimée.

"It can be anything," said Simon.

"Not the burning death prophecy with witches, let us

hope," said Mengette. The cloth from her head had loosened in the wind. She held it in her hands.

"No," said Simon. "Why would I want that to happen?"

"I have never understood you," said Mengette, in her over grown-up way.

"He means the maiden from Lorraine," said Hauviette. "The prophecy says that she will save France. Then there will be no more fighting, and when there is no more fighting, Simon can go to school."

For one moment it was as all the other times I had heard it, the old familiar saying, nothing new. Then in an instant all shifted, as if sliding off the side of a slanted roof without warning. Saint Michael's words filled my mind and heart.

You must ride into France. You must help the Dauphin.

I saw my life until that time pass before my eyes, swift, like an arrow. I was moved wholly to another place, out of France, out of the pony cart, away from my friends, never to be the same.

The girl from Lorraine was me.

I felt a gentle slice through my heart. My head was light. I held the rough wooden side of the wagon for fear of falling I knew not where. I would leave these dear ones, Hauviette, my treasured friend, a part of my own self surely, Mengette and her sweet mother ways, Simon with all his worry and his dear, beloved goose, tiny Aimée in all her childhood thoughts, and Michel. Michel, so gentle, so strong, so wise. I would not know his embrace. I would leave them all. I would not return. I gripped the cart tightly as it pulled to a stop.

Part IV

"I must go and I must do this thing,
for the Lord wills that I do so."

24
The Walk

The summer was especially hot, and felt, most certainly, long. Two or three times each week Saint Michael would return, sometimes with Saint Catherine and Saint Margaret and sometimes alone. Once the Angel Gabriel was with them. I knew this as Saint Michael told me it was he. The Angel appeared with the others, radiant and true, the Annunciation Angel, at my side, in all his majesty, but silent. What would he have me know?

Always Saint Michael and Saint Catherine and Saint Margaret would speak of going into France.

Daughter of God. You must leave your native village and go to the aid of your king.

This they would say and little more. Their visits were brief. When I begged them to remain, to tell me all that I must know, this they did not do. They would appear, radiant, blinding in the power of their light, all loving, all kind, the winged Saint Michael, Saint Catherine and Saint Margaret, their heads crowned in most precious fashion, the Angel Gabriel, all golden fire, and others. For a brief moment they were there, in the church, in the yard, in the field, in my room. They would speak their chosen words, like arrows of light, and be gone. Saint Michael would always end as this.

It is your job, if you wish to accept. There is no commanding.

What is my job? I would ask. How may I aid my king?

God will help you.

And the light would dim.

Stay, please! I would beg. I wish only to serve you! Tell me how I may do this!

God will do the work.

And they would go, leaving me to the haymaking and the spinning and the flax, to the long days and the hot July sun, to Good Kitten, to the tiny, new kittens underfoot, and all the rest.

The knowing that had pierced my heart when hearing of the prophecy was gone. I know not why this was so. It was as if somewhere the truth of it was in my heart, but it was gone from my mind. I think perhaps the knowing left my mind as it was too much for me to carry then. At times I would think, Me, the maiden from Lorraine? Oh, yes. I remember how I thought that in the cart.

I did not think to ask my Saints if it was so. I know not how they would have answered.

A month passed before Charles could begin to teach me to ride. July is haying time. All haymaking must be completed before August, so it is perhaps the busiest of months. The hay has to be cut with the scythe while it is still full of growth, the sap strong, but one must harvest dry. Damp hay can heat until it takes fire, and is also in danger of mold. Throughout the fields in July one can see the farmers moving forward, swinging the scythe from the right to the left, in almost a half circle. This I did not do, but sometimes I joined with the other women in turning the swathes to allow for better drying.

The month passed. I spoke twice of Henri in confession. I knew there was God in him, but I could not see it. I had great trouble forgiving him for the way he had treated the pony, and this was not right. All deserve our forgiveness, even the enemy.

It was a time of great devastation. Several lost their lives in Coussey to the south, and a fearful attack was made on Sionne. Twice we fled to the Island Castle. Our village was heavy with fear.

The month seemed to have no end. Charles said I must wait until haying was done before he could teach me to ride, Jean said Simon must wait until haying was done before he could teach him to read, and Catherine was waiting and waiting and still no sign of a baby. The month was long.

Troubling my mind was the question of going into France. When I asked my Saints if I was not in France already, they told me I was. When I asked them how I was to go there, they said that God would help me. What did my blessed Saints mean?

I decided to speak to Father. I had my chance one evening, just at the end of haying time. Mother and I were by the hearth, spinning the flax. It had already been soaked and beaten and combed. It now was shining and smooth. It looked as Catherine's hair. Supper was ready in the iron pots—hot porridge and beans. The meal cakes were warming.

Father came in early. He had been meeting that day on town matters in Greux and had stopped in the fields on his way home to check on the haying. He was concerned that night, I recall, as the rams, he suspected, had not been fertile. He was quiet when he came in, which was not his usual way. He took his drink of water, then sat on the stool near the window, his back against the wall.

"Was all well at the meeting?" Mother asked. She knew at once that he was troubled.

"Well enough," said Father.

There was a silence then as Mother and I worked on with the spinning. We had the flax on our laps, gathering the strands with our distaffs. In some moments, Mother spoke again. "How was it in the field?" she asked.

"The ewes will not bring forth," Father answered. "The month was too warm."

"Can you not wait the days and mate again?"

"One cannot be sure."

It had happened before. When July is overhot the rams do not have the power to bring forth the lambs. They mate, as is their way, but it does not bear fruit. One must wait then, until the ewes are once again in their time and mate again. This causes much wasted time, and sometimes no success.

"I am sorry about the rams, Father," I said. I was working my distaff in the way for the flax, gathering the strands on my lap at the center, my distaff bringing them away from my body.

"There is nothing to be done," said Father.

"They may still bring forth."

"They may."

There was another silence then.

"I know!" said Father, sitting up high on the stool.

"What," said Mother.

"A walk."

"A walk?" said Mother.

"A walk."

"A walk?"

"You know how it goes," said Father, playing a bit of a joke. "One foot and then the next?"

Mother smiled. "I know how to walk," she said as she spun. She picked up the strands on her lap, tipping the distaff first to one side, then the other. "I know how it is done, but why would we walk now?"

"Why not?" said Father. "I was all day inside. One needs the air."

"The door is open."

"One needs to be with trees."

Mother laughed. "We are working. The supper is cooking, and soon to be served. Where are the boys?"

"Stacking the hay."

"Soon we will eat."

"Joan will walk with me. What do you say, Joan?" asked Father.

"If it is well with Mother."

Father stood up from the stool. "Would it trouble you, Isabelle? Just a short walk? Before the boys come in?"

"As you like," said Mother.

"Are you sure you do not mind?" I asked.

"Go, my baby."

I could tell she truly liked the thought. I got up, setting my spinning work on the low wooden chest near Pierre and Jean's room, then went to hug Mother. "Thank you," I said.

As we parted I noticed the gray hair that was new at the sides of her face. She looked beautiful, as always, but all at once older. I had not thought of it before.

The sun was just setting behind the birches on the near hill. All was pink and gold and softest deep blue in the evening light. Father and I walked together up the path behind the house, toward the setting sun. Good Kitten followed. Birds returned to their favorite trees for the night, as the breeze rustled through the leaves, turning them underside and back. The leaves of the aspens picked up the light and shone it out like tiny stars. There was much joy in my heart to be alone with Father. I rarely had the chance.

"This is good," said Father. He smiled at me, then breathed in deep, looking all about at God's beauty.

As we crossed the road behind the rear field and started up the gentle hill in back, I had at once the thought to speak of France. Perhaps Father could somehow end the questions in my mind. But how to say it so as not to cause him to wonder why I asked. It did not feel the time to speak of my Saints to Father. I did not know if it ever would. Talk of my Saints would have been hard for him to bear. His mind was always on a thing that he could see. This gave him comfort, and this I could understand.

"Are there some parts of France that are more French

than others?" I asked, as we started our gentle climb. The question was strange to my ears, yet I had already asked it. It could not be taken back.

"All of France is French," said Father, "all equal in the eyes of God."

"Oh, yes," I said. I could see that I would have to put it more plainly. "What would you say if someone told you to go into France?"

"Why do you ask?"

"I was thinking of it."

"Of going into France?"

My heart felt a fear. I could not lie to Father, and yet I sensed he would not understand. I did not understand myself. I asked quickly for God's help to put the words truly and for the best for all.

"I was not thinking so much of going to where I am," I said, "as of being asked to do so. If someone asked me to go to where I was already, I would not know what to do."

"That is well put," said Father.

We passed the group of large maples to the left that marks the halfway place to the top. Father stopped then and stood, listening. I stopped as well. We neither spoke for minutes. I knew he was listening for a wild creature. I knew not what. My mind had been taken up with my thoughts. I had heard nothing.

"A deer," said Father. But it had gone, and with it, for the moment, all of Father's wondering of my going into France. God had intervened in the form of a deer.

As we continued on our way I dared to return to the

matter. "I spoke of those things," I said, "as I had heard we were not in France. I liked to hear that not."

"I understand," said Father. "We are in France. Have no fear about it."

We walked some steps in silence before he told me.

"We are French," he said, "and always we will be. It matters not, but as the courts would have it, Lorraine is not part of France. It belongs to the duchy of Bar, and has its own court in Nancy."

I felt a shiver then.

25

The Gray

At last the day came when I could ride The Gray. The hay was cut and stacked. It was time to harvest the wheat, but Charles kept his word. He took time from the harvest to teach me.

Early one morning Hauviette and Charles and I gathered behind Hauviette's barn. I had asked Mother if I might spend the morning with Hauviette, and she agreed.

"I will get The Gray," said Charles, for that was what we called the horse. It suited him well.

Charles held the bridle in his left hand, the reins in his right. He started off toward the fenced-in field where the horse was grazing.

"Come along," said Hauviette. "He wants to show you how to catch The Gray."

Hauviette knew her brother well. It was hard for me to know his wishes. He spoke so little.

When we neared the field, The Gray stopped eating all at once. He stared at us, watching our approach. He was handsome indeed, so tall and straight, his gray coat shining in the sun.

We reached the fence. Charles climbed over it, heading into the field.

"Go with him," said Hauviette.

Again I knew not what Charles wanted, but followed Hauviette's lead and climbed the fence. The Gray watched us with a steady gaze. Charles moved slowly forward. He had a good and quiet way with horses. Horses do not like loud noises or quick movements or a lot of jumping around. They prefer the peaceful ways.

When we got quite close, The Gray turned his head and began to walk away. He was playing a game. We followed him slowly, not rushing the matter. Soon The Gray glanced back to see what we were doing. He stopped, then moved off in the direction of some low trees by the river. I followed Charles in a steady, even way as he changed direction, going around behind The Gray, approaching him from the other side. The Gray sensed us there and turned away, walking still. We followed, slow and steady. For some reason, The Gray stopped then and stared at us. We moved slowly and gently forward, approaching The Gray on his left side. Charles reached out and slid the reins over The Gray's high neck, grabbing them underneath. The Gray stared ahead, not at us, but at Hauviette by the fence. Charles patted The Gray on the neck. Then, holding the reins and the top of the bridle in his right hand, the snaffle in his left, he eased the snaffle in between The Gray's teeth. There were six teeth on top and six on the bottom in the front, all flat and even where they met as if cut with a straight blade. The snaffle bit was of two joined pieces of metal. It was softer on the horse's mouth than the straight curb bits used in battle.

The Gray reached his nose high in the air, curling his lips back in a strange way, as if unsure of the pleasure of the snaffle. After a moment, he lowered his head, seeming to have forgotten the whole matter. He waited patiently as Charles fastened the bridle, then followed along as Charles led us to a place where the ground was more flat. Here we stopped. Charles let the reins rest over The Gray's neck. Then he bent over, joining his two hands, with fingers laced together. I put my foot within his hands, grabbed The Gray's thick mane, then swung my leg up over the horse as Charles lifted me up. The Gray's back was not as broad as Sibelle's, but just as high from the ground. I liked it well. His coat felt warm and soft on my legs beneath my skirt.

Charles gave me the reins to hold. "Keep them in one hand," he said.

"Which hand?"

"It matters not."

The Gray's ears were half up and half back, in the wondering way. When the horse's ears are up, it is good. When they are down, it is a sign of trouble. Halfway most often means a questioning mind. The horse is none too sure of a matter. This I could understand in The Gray at that time. He had a new rider on his back, one who had much to learn. I loved being astride The Gray, so high, so safe. I always felt safe on a horse. I know not why.

Charles told me then the first things that I must know. Sit high, with a straight back. Reins right, if I wanted to go right, left if I wanted to go left. To back up, pull back on both reins. He told me also to be gentle on the reins. A horse's mouth is tender. Too much forcing on the reins will annoy and confuse the horse, and even hurt him. This I would not do. Charles told me also to sit well down and to grip with my knees. The command for faster would be to squeeze the lower part of the legs, or even kick with the heels. A gentle pressure with the lower leg on one side will direct the horse to lead with the front leg on the opposite side. In turns, the horse should lead on the inside leg for better balance.

"Walk him," said Charles.

I gave a squeeze with my lower legs. The Gray began to walk. His ears were up, which I took to be a good sign.

"May I run?" I asked from my spot high up on the back of The Gray.

"If you like," said Charles.

My heart began to pound. I felt much joy. I squeezed The Gray with my legs, gave a kick with my heels, and we were off. We started at the slower bumpy way, which was a trot. I bounced a bit then.

"Faster," said Charles.

I kicked again and The Gray broke into a heavenly gallop. I held tight with my knees, taking a big piece of his mane in my hands, along with the reins. My heart pounded, the wind blew in my face. It was as flying. I rode for some long time.

Charles was pleased. He said I had done well as we walked, Charles at The Gray's side, along the row of trees by the river.

"May I ride again?" I asked.

"If you like," said Charles.

I bent down to give The Gray a hug. He was breathing hard. Behind his ears and on his neck he was full of sweat. It had a fine, rich smell.

"Good horse," I said.

"Cool him down," said Charles.

"How do I do that?"

"Walk him some, then let him drink."

"Can he stand in the river?"

"If he likes."

"Will it be too cold for him?"

"No."

I was hugging The Gray still. I felt I could stay that way forever.

"I have to go," said Charles.

I sat up then. "What must I do with the bridle?"

"Give it to Hauviette," he said, and started off.

"Thank you," I called.

He raised a hand in a kind of half wave, but did not turn or answer. He did but what was needed.

When I had walked The Gray and there was no more sweat, I urged him into the shallow Meuse. He liked it well, putting his head down instantly to drink. I loved the gentle sucking sounds he made, bringing the water up through his nearly closed mouth. This I could see by hanging over his neck, my arms around him in an other hug. He drank for some long while.

As we turned and headed for the fence, I could see Hauviette had been joined by others. I could not make out who. When we got closer I could tell. It was dear Simon, without his goose for once, and none else but Henri.

"God is in him," I told myself, repeating it several times.

"That was great," said Simon.

"It was," said Henri. "You ride well."

A nice word from his mouth. That was a surprise!

"You were wonderful," said Hauviette. "You went so fast. I could hardly see you."

I knew it was time to leave The Gray, but I could not. Not yet. He put his head down to eat the grass. I made the reins long so he could reach.

Simon put his hand through the fence to pat The Gray's nose.

"Where is your goose?" I asked.

"At home," said Simon.

"Why is that?"

"Aimée was lonesome. She is sick and has to rest."

"Is she very sick?" I asked.

"Just a little," said Simon, "but Mother will not let her play."

"I see," I said. I felt another reason still for the goose remaining at home, but could not tell what it was.

"You look good on The Gray," said Henri. He held a hand above his eyes to keep out the sun as he looked at me.

Nice words spoken twice! I thought. What can have happened?

"Shall I take the bridle?" asked Hauviette.

"Very well," I said. I did not want to leave The Gray, but it was time. Mother would need my help. I slipped down off his strong welcoming back, landing hard on the ground. My legs felt weak. I felt at first that they would not hold me up, but they did.

The Gray did a funny thing then. He leaned his big head down and rubbed my back, nearly knocking me to the ground. It was a surprise to be sure, but such a friendly feeling. He did it several times. After the first time I held my body tight so as not to fall. When he stopped, I scratched him behind the ears.

"Take off the bridle," said Hauviette.

I reached up and pulled the top part of the bridle over The Gray's ears and forward, letting the snaffle leave his mouth. He was well pleased then and turned, walking off to eat the grass.

"May I speak to you, Joan?" asked Henri, as we went along with Hauviette to put the bridle in the barn.

I paused, unable quickly to answer.

What did he mean? I thought. He was already speaking to me. Why did he then need my permission?

"I must speak to you," he added.

"Very well," I said.

"Alone?"

"Why alone?" said Hauviette.

"I would like to," said Henri.

The thought troubled me. I wanted to hurt him not, but to be alone with Henri was not a welcome thought. The exchange was sure to be stupid, at best.

"Why must you be alone?" said Simon. "Do you want to kiss her?"

God forbid, I thought.

"Of course not," said Henri.

"Then why?"

"It is not your concern."

"Yes, it is," said Simon. "You want me to go away."

"Joan and I will step apart," said Henri. "You can stay."

"I can stay without your permission," said Simon.

"That is true," I said.

"May we step apart?" asked Henri.

"You may speak to me here," I told him. "We are all friends."

"Please?" he said.

"Speak to me here, or not at all," I said. I was beginning to lose patience.

Henri stared at the ground. He seemed uncertain. His manner was different than ever I had seen it. At last he spoke. "I am sorry for how I acted in the cart," he said.

"You should be," said Hauviette.

Henri answered her not, but looked to me.

"I forgive you," I said.

"Thank you," he said.

"Is that it?" asked Simon. "Is that why we had to leave?"

"Good-bye," said Henri, and he was off.

"I will tell you something later," Hauviette told me, as we continued toward the barn.

"What?" said Simon.

"Something," said Hauviette.

"What?" said Simon.

"It is not your concern."

"Nothing is my concern this day," said Simon.

"It happens to all of us," said Hauviette.

We had reached the barn then. It was cooler there, and dark at first, as our eyes were not used to the lack of sun.

"I heard a bad thing," said Simon.

"What was that?" I asked.

"Maurice told me."

"Maurice?" said Hauviette. Her voice was high and pinched together, as tight stitches in a cloth.

"What did he tell you?" I asked.

Simon paused for a long moment, his thoughts within. "There are wolves in Paris," he said.

"Wolves?" said Hauviette.

"Wolves," said Simon. His eyes were wide and fearful.

"In the city?" said Hauviette.

"In the city," said Simon. "Wolves."

Hauviette hung the bridle on the wooden peg. "And so?" she said.

"And so?" said Simon. "Wolves are in Paris! Great packs of wolves, hungry wolves with sharp teeth, roaming, prowling, stealing food, eating babies!"

"Maurice told you that?" I asked.

"Not about the babies," said Simon, "but he said there are wolves, and what would they do?"

"Who knows?" said Hauviette.

"Well, what do you think?" asked Simon.

"There may be wolves in Paris," I said, "but you take it too far."

"How far would you like me to take it?"

"To the point of reason only."

"Will they come here?"

"Who?" said Hauviette. Her mind, I think, was on Maurice.

"The wolves," said Simon. "Will they come here?"

"From Paris?"

"From anywhere."

"I doubt it," said Hauviette.

"If they are in Paris they are after the garbage," I said. "The place is none too clean."

"We have garbage."

"The pigs eat it," said Hauviette.

"And we use it for compost," I added.

"Wolves would eat Nicholas," said Simon, in a most worried way.

"Is that why you left him home?" I asked.

"Maybe," said Simon.

"I would not worry," I told him. "Wolves have not been seen in Domrémy, not that I know of. And should one come, the news would travel fast."

Simon's face brightened then. "That is true," he said. "And if wolves came from Paris, there would be many towns for them to pass through first. We would hear of that for sure, unless everyone was eaten, or had their tongues ripped out."

"That is most unlikely," I told him.

Simon paused a moment, then he spoke. "Nicholas may want a walk," he said, and he was gone.

When we were alone Hauviette told me what was on her mind.

"Henri likes you," she said. "I thought it before, but now I know. Beware!"

26
Father's Dream

In the months that followed, thoughts of the prophecy returned strongly to my mind. I practiced riding, which was a joy to my heart, but there built beneath the wondering of why. What would I need this riding for? Would I truly ride into France? When would I do this? What would I do when I got there? And then the prophecy would come full to my mind. "France will be ruined by a woman and saved by a maiden from the oak forests of Lorraine." It could not be, and yet I knew within my heart that it was so. The maiden was me.

Saint Michael was silent that fall. I did not see him once, nor hear his voice. I prayed for him to come, but still he did not. He was with me in all the real ways, this I knew, but the sight of him, the sound of his loving voice, these I would not know, not for some time.

Several times each week my blessed Saint Catherine and my blessed Saint Margaret would speak to me. I saw them rarely in those months, but always the sweet fragrance, and always their gentle voices I would hear. Always they would speak the same.

Daughter of France. You must go to the aid of the

Dauphin. You must restore his kingdom to him.

And always they would close thus.

This is your work. You must decide if you will take it.

They spoke often, but always then it was brief. No answers to my questions. Only . . .

Have faith. God will help you.

And I would hear no more.

They spoke to me at all times now, alone or in company. When there were many others near, when at play with my loving friends, at home with Mother and Father, Pierre and Jean, or with Good Kitten screaming, at these times when my Saints would speak, there would be too much noise and I would fail to understand.

During these months I spent more time alone. I needed the quiet for my mind to rest. Always I loved my dear friends, Hauviette, Mengette, Simon, and all, but the noise of our play was unwelcome to me then.

There were other concerns as well. Catherine was with child and not feeling well. There was a worry that she would lose the baby. I went to the Wish-Fulfilling Tree that fall, when all was golden and orange, to pray that if it be God's will, the baby and my beloved sister be spared. We would have to wait and see.

Often those months I would spend long hours in the church before the statue of Saint Margaret. Her living, her dying filled my mind and heart, all that Mother had taught me. I saw her as a child. I felt her love of Christ. I saw her father, too, the pagan priest. I saw her driven from his house. I saw her as a shepherdess. I saw her refuse the evil prefect who would have her for his own. I saw her charged as a Christian. I saw her holding to her love of Christ. I saw her thrown in prison. I saw her with the dragon. I saw them try to drown her. I saw them try to burn her. I saw her in the flames and dying not! Dear God! I saw the beheading! Why did she have to suffer so? How did she bear it? One day I would ask.

The fall passed. Mengette's sister gave birth. The baby was strong and well, a girl. Mengette was well pleased to be an aunt. She longed for a baby of her own one day. This she told me. I prayed this would be so, if it be God's will.

Jean taught Simon his reading. This pleased Simon full well. Often of an evening they would sit by the fire while Simon learned the letters. Some evenings Pierre would join in as well. Once Simon brought Nicholas, but this was not well, as the goose was restless and went about squawking and poking people with his beak.

"Leave the goose at home," Jean told Simon, and this he did.

The evenings were warm and friendly. Father would doze or read his papers by the fire. Mother and I would be spinning or sewing nearby, Good Kitten at my side, some-times quiet, sometimes screaming. The kittens were growing quickly. They stayed in the barn with Turnip, the runt, and the older ones. A squirrel would be in the window. He had taken to coming inside. I fed him morning and night from my hand. Acorns were his special treat.

Hauviette had the biggest news. Maurice had kissed her in the barn! They had gone inside to be out of the rain one day, and it happened! He said nothing before or after, as Hauviette told it, nor did she. One quick kiss, and that was it. It was as though it had not happened. In the weeks that followed she waited for the next one, but as yet it had not come. Hauviette confessed to me that each night in bed she would retell the event in her mind from when the rain started to going into the barn, to the kiss, to the quiet time watching the rainfall after. She spoke daily of the event, and of what the future might bring. She also spoke often of getting her monthly sickness, which had not yet arrived. Mine had not come either.

Henri continued to be well spoken, if no less the fool. The few times in which I saw him, he seemed to be watching me. He would sometimes smile oddly, and often said he liked the way I looked. I felt he was just as stupid as before, though making an effort to be nice. I could not help but feel that Hauviette was right in her thoughts. He had found cause to like me in the special way, or so he thought, as Hauviette liked Maurice, as I liked Michel.

I saw little of Michel in those months, as he and Little Gérard were much of the time in Vouthon on family matters there. I remember not what the matters were, only that he was gone, only that I missed him.

Time passed, as the days grew colder. I rode The Gray, worked with Mother by the hearth, and thought without end about my mission. Could it truly be that I was the maiden from Lorraine? My Saints had told me that I would restore the kingdom to the Dauphin, if I so chose. Then it was I. It must be! But how? When? Why would my Saints not tell me more? They said only that this was my job, if I chose it, and to trust in God. Why would they not tell me more?

I was thinking these thoughts one morning as I spun. I had just fed the squirrel, who sat in the window. Good Kitten slept at my feet. Mother was spinning as well. I noticed that day that she was not keeping an even pace as was her way, but stopped for long times, gazing into the fire.

"Are you well, Mother?" I asked, as this I saw her do.

"I am well," she said, and returned to her spinning. But soon she had stopped once more.

"Does something trouble you?" I asked.

She shook her head. "No," she said, but this was untrue. She tried to return to her work, but could not. Tears came into her eyes.

I felt pain in my heart when I saw the tears. "You are crying," I said.

She said nothing.

"What troubles you?"

Mother stopped her spinning then. Her hands in her lap, she stared into the fire.

"What is it?" I asked. I set down my distaff.

"Your father had a dream."

"What was it?"

Mother looked not at me, but only to the fire. "He had it last night."

"Did he tell you what it was?"

"He told me in the morning. The sun was not fully up."

"What was it?"

"It had no reason."

"What was it still?"

"You went off with soldiers."

"With soldiers?"

"That is what he said."

I did not understand. "What happened?" I asked.

"He did not say."

"That is a strange dream."

"I told him as much." Mother stared into the fire still, hands in her lap, her spinning work forgotten.

"What is it, Mother?" I asked.

She did not answer.

"Why are you troubled?"

"Father was troubled by the dream."

"Why is that?"

"I told him it was but a dream."

"And so it was."

"And so it was," Mother echoed. She rose then, and poked at the fire, as it was going out. She looked not my way, but went on speaking still. "He told me that if such a thing were ever to be talked of, and he were not here, to tell your brothers to drown you in the river rather than to let you go."

I felt a numbness then.

"He said if he were here he would do it himself."

A dread overtook me. It was sudden, like a knife in my heart, unexpected, terrible. I thought of riding into France, of aiding the Dauphin, of restoring his kingdom. Was I to go with soldiers? Is that how it would be? Not praying in a nearby church, but riding with soldiers? Surely not. It could not be. Yet if it were, by some strange chance, if that were asked of me, would Father want me dead?

Mother sat once more. She wiped her eyes on her sleeve. I had this feeling then that all was unreal, happening to someone else, not to me, or not at all. Mother shook her head. She spoke quietly, to herself almost. "I know not what I would do," she said. "My baby."

I went to hold her then. My tears had come as well.

Later that same day I went out into the field. Far from all, save the grass and the trees and the birds in the air, I fell to my knees.

"Oh, sweet God," I prayed. "What am I to do? Saint Michael! Saint Catherine! Saint Margaret! Help me! I beg our lord and lady to send their counsel now! I pray with all my soul!"

The fragrance, the blinding light, and then Saint Catherine and Saint Margaret at my side, their love pouring forth, their heads crowned with all the jewels of heaven.

Daughter of God.

Oh, my blessed Saints, what is to become of me? I have great fear! Father dreams I will go off with soldiers. He would have me drowned, drown me himself if that were needed. Was the dream a foretelling? Will I go off with soldiers? Would Father want me dead? I love him so. I could not bear to hurt him. I want to do right. Help me!

Your Father loves you.

Yet he would want me dead.

Never.

Why does he speak so?

He is fearful.

The light glowed white-purple and in the very center of this light my Saints in all their heavenly beauty, their robes so soft, glorious, spun of air. Saint Catherine spoke not, but raised a blessing hand from which streams of light poured forth. I reached out to touch her robe. It felt as the breath of life. Saint Margaret spoke.

Be not afraid.

Am I the maiden from Lorraine?

You are.

Will I restore the kingdom?

If you so wish.

I wish only to be with you always.

Have you another wish?

To serve God.

And?

The salvation of my soul.

These are yours.

I sat up then, my hands clasped, gazing at their heavenly faces. My tears were coming strong.

How can I save France? I am a poor farm girl. I know nothing. God will grant the victory.

What must I do?

You must decide if you will have it so. You must make up your own mind. There is no commanding.

I am no one.

Daughter of God.

I know nothing.

It is your destiny, if you will have it so.

And if not?

It will not be.

But Father will be angry!

It will be hard, but he will come to understand.

And Mother?

It will be hard for her as well.

And yet I must do this thing?

If you so wish.

When must I go?

It will be a difficult mission. There will be great struggle.

I do not mind.

It will be painful.

Not if I am with you.

I moved to them, and reaching out my arms, I held them about the legs. The heavenly softness, the fragrance of paradise! I did not let them go. Saint Margaret spoke once more.

There will be pain.

You suffered pain.

Yes.

Would you do it again?

Yes.

I love you so. I feel such sadness for your pain and torture.

It was not a big thing.

It seems so to me.

Yet still, it was not so. Fire into fire does not burn.

You felt no pain in the fire?

It was as it were happening elsewhere.

Surely there was pain.

Only in the fear. And that was brief.

The light was fading then.

Don't go!

It is the Lord who goes before you. He will be with you. He will not forsake you. Do not fear or be dismayed.

And they were gone.

27

Uncle Durand

Father did not speak of the dream. Always, from that time on, he took great care to know where I was, but never did he mention why. Mother was quiet on the matter as well. I sometimes saw a worried look in her eyes after that time. I felt it was her concern that Father could even speak of drowning their daughter. I think she believed not that he could ever do this, yet still there was the worry. My brothers never mentioned Father's dream. I can only guess he never told them. Surely, they would have spoken of it if he had, if only to show that I could be in trouble with Father too, that they were not the only ones.

It was a sorry winter. The fighting grew worse. In many neighbor towns the poor people were losing their houses, their livestock, and their lives. Villages were destroyed, burned to the ground, families split apart, some murdered, some left to live ungratefully alone. When I heard these things I would think of the Dauphin. If only I could reach him, that might somehow help to make the horrors stop. How, I could not tell, but why then would my blessed Saints request it? These thoughts would lead to thoughts of Father and his dream. How could I leave and cause him pain? I did not know. And still the awful war! Simon's uncle was killed in Soulosse, along with his baby daughter. The wife was spared, but cared to live no longer. She came to stay with Simon's family, but would not come out of doors. I went to see her once, to bring her a tiny cake, but this she did not want. I left it by her chair.

Many times that winter we escaped to the Island Castle, returning to find our village still there. One time it would not be. I think we all feared this, and lived with heavy hearts.

Catherine lost the baby. I knew it was only as God would have it, some blessing in it to be found, yet my sadness was great. Catherine had hoped so much for the child. I felt a pity for her in her time of loss. Mother and I visited her every day for a fortnight or more, until she regained her strength and was able, once more, to laugh.

One day at lambing time I went to the Bermont Chapel to think. My mind and heart were pulled in many ways. I needed the stillness, the time alone, to understand my way. My Saints had told me all that I must know. Surely it was up to me.

Mother gave me permission to go. She was spinning that day with friends. Henri's mother and Gérardin D'Epinal's wife, Zabillet, were there. Gérardin was a Burgundian, but this troubled Mother not. With them was one of my godparents, Beatrice, the widow of d'Estelin. She had a round and friendly face. I bid them good-bye and set off.

Good Kitten followed me on the climb. We hurried on our way as the day was cold and the swiftness of walking brought on needed warmth. When we reached the chapel, Good Kitten did not follow me inside but remained in the meadow, as was her way.

Inside it was cold. The stones held a certain dampness, yet, with all, it was restful, safe, still beyond my telling. I fell to my knees before the stone altar and the statue of Jesus, then sat to pray and think. These were my thoughts, as I recall.

There is so much suffering of good people. I want to help, but what must I do? Father is worried now. I will cause him pain. My Saints have told me this. There will be pain. For myself I do not mind, but not for Father. It will be hard, they said, but he will come to understand. Mother as well. It will be hard. I cannot bear to cause them pain. Yet they will come to understand. In understanding the pain will ease. This is always so. My Voices say I must decide. There is nothing to decide. I want only to serve God. There is no deciding. The matter is only, can I do what is asked? Am I able? I am a poor farm girl. I know nothing. Yet my Saints would ask this thing of me. I must only say that they know better. Better than I know. Better in all things. They are in the very center of God's reason. I am no one. There is no deciding. Only a prayer to serve God, to be a fitting instrument. This fitness I may question, but never doubt. Doubt closes the door. Mother told me this. I will not doubt. I love you, Mother. I love you, Father. I love you Catherine, without your tiny baby. May God grant you another.

I sat then in prayer for some long time, not minding the cold. I prayed that I be in God's grace. I prayed with all my heart that if I was not, God might put me there, that if I was, He might keep me there.

When I had finished praying my mind was no more torn. I would serve God as best I ever could. This was all I could do, and it would have to be enough. If this I did truly, God would see to the rest.

When I returned home I had a nice surprise. Uncle Durand was there with Mother, sitting by the fire, drinking the warm cider. He looked tired, as he had traveled hard, but was at peace and happy to see us. His eyes shone with an inner gladness.

"How is my girl?" he asked, giving me a good, strong hug.

"Well to see you," I answered, then sat by his chair.

Durand was not truly my uncle, but this I called him. He was my cousin by marriage, being the husband of my mother's niece, Jeanne, daughter of my mother's sister, Aveline. This was told me as a child, but was truly hard to understand, and so I called him Uncle. This he did not mind. He seemed more an uncle than a cousin as he was older than I by many years. He was my special friend. Often, as a child, I had visited Uncle and Jeanne in Burey. I would help them with the chores. I loved these special times. There was a tiny waterfall in back of their house and a willow tree as well.

Good Kitten screamed a greeting then, and jumped on Uncle's lap, moving as to make bread with her paws. Uncle patted Good Kitten on the head, then ran his hand several times down her back. This she liked well. She made the happy rumble noise. Uncle looked my way. "When will you come to spend some time with us again?" he asked. "You are strongly missed."

"I will come when you say," I answered, "if it is well with Mother and Father."

"What do you say, Isabelle?" asked Uncle.

Mother was mixing the flour. She looked up from her task. "In spring if you like," she said. "I know the chores are many then, and Joan is much help in the work."

"She is indeed," said Uncle, "but I want not to take her from you. You need her as well."

"We can spare her for a short while," said Mother. "I will speak of it to Jacques."

Father and Pierre and Jean came in then. They had been carting manure to the field in the cart, and smelled not well. Uncle did not seem to mind. He greeted them in a friendly way, hugging each.

"A change of clothing would be nice for all," said Mother, looking up from her dough. She smiled, making the joke, but hoping, I am sure, that they would hurry to follow her thought.

"Oh, yes!" said Father. "Boys!" and they went off to change their clothes.

Uncle had to leave shortly as he needed to reach Burey that evening. I gave him some biscuits and a large bit of cheese for his journey. I was sad to see him go.

That night I helped with the lambing. This was most often done by Father and Pierre and Jean, but Pierre had injured his arm that day in the field and could not do the work. Some sprain had been caused to the wrist. It swelled to two times the size. Mother applied some herbs, making him soak the arm to bring down the swelling. Pierre did not want to sit the long time for the soaking, but this he had to do.

When Jean went out to check on the ewes before supper, he found one ready to bring forth. Father joined him in the lambing pen behind the barn, refusing his supper. Mother was not pleased, yet this she was well used to. Lambs could be born at any time, but they most often chose the coldest nights. Why, I do not know. With many births the ewes do well on their own and need no help, but often there are the troubled ones. One must check on each birth to see if help is needed, day or night. Often at lambing time Father and Pierre and Jean would not sleep for days. Many meals were missed as well. This year lambing time lasted two months, as many of the rams had had to be mated twice.

This night there was trouble with a birth. Jean came running in to get me. "Father needs you, Short Legs," he said. "Let's go!"

This pleased me well.

"I can help," said Pierre from where he sat near the fire. His sleeve was rolled high, his arm stuck in the iron pot with the warm water and herbs that Mother had prepared.

"Not tonight," said Mother.

"I can, truly."

"Sit where you are and let Joan do it."

I headed for the door.

"Come on, Short Legs," repeated Jean as I followed him out.

It was dark outside, and very cold. When we reached the pens Father was helping an ewe. She was bringing forth a lamb whose feet had come first.

"Help me," Father said to Jean. "Joan, see to the ewe by the barn."

The ewe was backing into the side of the barn. This they would sometimes do for comfort of mind, I believe, yet it was never best for the lamb. I pulled the ewe to the center of the pen. She seemed to be confused.

All is well, I told her from my heart. You are here in this pen for a reason.

The ewes must be kept in pens, and not inside, as dampness is the worst for the newborns. Lambs can die of too much cold or too much dampness, but dampness is worst and more often the cause. There must be proper airflow. The pens can have no sides, but must allow the wind.

My ewe had a fine birth, in little time—twins, as often was the case. I prayed it would go as this, according to God's will. Sometimes the lambs are born dead from disease, and this is sad. Other times the ewe will die. This is sadder still as it is hard to get another ewe to take the motherless lamb. There are ways, but they do not often work.

That night all births were well. Father and Jean had much trouble with their ewe, who dropped a single lamb, but at last all was well, the new babies joining their grateful and tired mothers. I did not like leaving the baby lambs at all, especially in such a bitter cold, but Father insisted. They could not be brought into the house. This Father knew to be my thought on the matter before I spoke the words. "The lambs cannot be brought inside, Joan," he said. "They cannot be parted from the ewes. They need to drink."

This I knew full well. They needed to drink often, for at least sixty days, yet it pained me to leave them.

"Why not sleep in the pens," Jean teased. "This way you can care for them. Unless you freeze to death."

"It is not that cold," I told him.

"Then the lambs will not freeze either."

"That may be."

We started toward the house.

God has made the cold, I told myself. God has made the cold, and God has made the lambs to come forth on this night. God will care for them all.

"I knew Short Legs would want to bring the lambs inside," Jean said to Father as we neared the house.

"Leave her be," said Father.

But Jean could not. "Think of this," he said. He turned my way. "Why not bring the lambs *and* the ewes inside. That way they will not be parted. Bring them all in. Let them take your bed. You can have the floor."

That had been my wish, but I had mentioned it not.

Mother had warm soup waiting for us. We sat by the fire, eating the soup, with bread to dip.

"Short Legs wants to bring them all inside," said Jean, drinking from his bowl.

"All who?" asked Pierre.

"Let her be," said Father.

"The lambs," said Jean.

"That is all we need," said Mother.

"And the ewes as well," said Jean.

"It is not surprising," said Pierre, his arm still soaking in the iron pot. "She would have us all in the barn, the lambs in our beds."

"And the ewes as well," I added.

"That is all we need," Mother repeated.

I stayed awake long that night, thinking of the tiny lambs, placing them each in God's care.

I must name them, I thought. I will watch them grow. Perhaps I can bring them inside to sit by the fire one time later, when they do not need their mother's milk.

Daughter of God.

Saint Michael!

It was his voice, the voice I loved with all my heart. The voice I had not heard these many months.

Daughter of God.

The blinding light, the heavenly fragrance.

Daughter of God.

And there he stood, noble, winged, in full armor, with sword, in all the blazing light, and all about the purple flashes, by the door, on the ceiling, at the end of my bed.

Joan.

You have come!

I sat up, my feet on the earthen floor, my hands clasped before my heart.

Sweet light.

I missed you so.

I am with you always.

I did not see you.

I was here.
I did not hear your voice.
There is much suffering.
Yes.
You must raise the siege.
I did not understand.
What siege?
You must raise the siege of Orléans.
The city?
Yes.
What is a siege?
You will know.
How?
The light was fading now.
Don't leave me!
Sweet light.
How will I know?
Trust in God.
I know not what a siege is! How can I raise it?
Have faith.
I want only to serve you!
And so you do.
Don't leave me!
But he was gone.

28

Simon's Fear

For days I thought only of the words.

    You must raise the siege of Orléans.

There was room for nothing else. All life seemed a dream. It was as I was not there, but once again far off, in a different place, watching the things of earth, not really a part of them.

You must raise the siege of Orléans.

The words echoed in my mind and heart, drowning out near all else.

The squirrel wanted nuts. As I fed him . . .

You must raise the siege of Orléans.

Mother needed the water. As I fetched it . . .

You must raise the siege of Orléans.

Hauviette told of Maurice. As I listened . . .

You must raise the siege of Orléans.

On waking, on sleeping, always it was the same.

You must raise the siege of Orléans.

My mind was filled with questions. What was a siege, and how could I raise it? Where was Orléans, and how could I get there? I struggled, but could find no answers.

Must I go? I thought. Must I pray? I must pray, surely,

but how can I pray to raise a siege if I know not what it means? I must have the sense of my prayer in my heart. It must have meaning to my mind and soul, not words merely. I must come to understand.

I asked in prayer for my Saints to tell me more, yet this they did not do. When Saint Catherine and Saint Margaret spoke, it was of simple things.

Have faith. God will help you.

This I knew to be true, yet still I was troubled.

In Vouthon there was a bloody attack. We had much fear when we heard of this as Jacquémin was there on Mother's land. I went to the Wish-Fulfilling Tree to pray for his well-being, for Mother's peace of mind, and Father's too. Many days later, when we received word that Jacquémin was safe, I returned to the Wish-Fulfilling Tree to offer my thanks to God.

Simon was very much afraid. The death of his cousin and of the tiny baby had brought much fear to his heart. He kept Nicholas in the house. There he would stay as well, seldom to come out. Simon's cousin, who had lost both husband and child, would sometimes venture out as far as the front yard, but never down the road. Some days when the sun was full, she would sit in the yard, but never would she speak.

One day soon after Saint Michael had come and spoken of raising the siege, Father cut the first furrow of the year. This was always cause for celebration. Spring planting would soon begin. Once the first open furrows were cut, the plow went up one side and down the other, going between the open furrows and making a ridge. This was done in the same way as the furrow, save for the fact that the soil was turned inward instead of outward. This I knew, as sometimes I would help. I loved to watch the soil turning.

As Father and Pierre and Jean worked in the field, Mother and I finished the household tasks, then began to prepare the special meal for our celebration. It was this. Soup, oak-bark bread, which was Father's favorite, beans with special herbs, biscuits, which were my favorite, white wine, and a bit of smoked fish. The fish was Good Kitten's favorite, although she rarely had more than a thimbleful. We had dried fruits for dessert.

The meal was ready long before Father and the boys came in from the fields, so Mother let me go outside. Good Kitten and I visited Simon.

We stopped first to check on the lambs. They were still being kept with their mothers in the pens behind the house. As we reached their holding place Good Kitten ran as if to charge them all. No fear. I know not what was in her mind, but tail straight up, she charged. The sheep took little notice.

The lambs were growing fast. I wanted so to carry them off to my room, to rest with them on my bed, but this would have to wait. They were drinking still.

Good Kitten left the pen, as none were paying her mind. She rubbed about my legs, suggesting we be on our way. The lambs stared at me with their wondering look, which Jean called their stupid look. Jean was stupid to call it that. When I was little and Jean spoke thus, before I reached the age of understanding, I would punch him in the stomach.

"Good-bye," I told the lambs. "Drink well."

Good Kitten and I set off. It was a warm day for March. There was a wind, but the sun was strong. Hints of spring were all about. Simon's cousin was seated on a stool in the front yard. Her eyes had a faraway look.

"Hello," I said as I neared her. "The day is fine."

She did not answer, but looked off down the road.

I sent her a blessing from my heart.

Simon was in the house with Nicholas. They sat on the floor near the hearth, Simon tossing small stones against the wall, Nicholas dozing. All was quiet.

"Where is everyone?" I asked as I came in.

"*We* are here," said Simon.

"I mean the others, your mother and Aimée. The house is quiet."

"They went to Greux."

"Would you like to walk?" I asked, not moving from the door.

"No," said Simon.

"You must stop being afraid."

"I am not afraid."

"You must come out sometimes."

"I do."

"When?"

"Sometimes."

"I see you not."

Simon tossed more stones.

"We all have fear," I told him.

"I am fine."

"It seems not so."

More stones.

"What game is that with the stones?" I asked.

"No game."

"You toss them merely?"

"Sometimes."

"Enough!" I said. I moved in from the door to where he and Nicholas were sitting. "Get up!"

"Why?"

"Get up!" I was speaking loudly now. Good Kitten's ears moved forward and back, one side and the other, sensing the excitement. She nosed into the table leg, pushing hard as she rubbed the side of her nose on the sharp wooden corner.

"I like it here," said Simon.

"You do not!" I told him. "Speak the truth! You do not like it here, and Nicholas does not like it here! There is no sun, no wind, no trees, no sky, and there is nothing to pass the time! You hate being inside all the while, and yet here you stay because you are afraid!"

Simon stopped tossing the stones. He stared at his hands.

"Get up!" I said.

Nicholas woke. He pulled his head off his rear feathers, then turned to look at me. He blinked in the light from the doorway.

"Think of your goose," I went on. "You keep him as a prisoner, with never a trip to the river, because you are too afraid to live with the rest of us! We all may die at any time, and that is up to God! We all have fear! In the village, in all of France, good people have fear! What of it?"

Simon spoke then, his voice small and full of tears. "My cousin was killed, and the baby. Next it will be me."

I knelt at his side and held him then. We were quiet for a while. Then I spoke. "We know not when it will come," I said. "That is only up to God. But now is time for sunlight and spring. Now is time for taking Nicholas to the river. Think how happy he will be."

"I give him water."

"From a bucket! It is not the same! Think of your goose. He knows nothing of wars, and of the English, and the dying that will come. He wants only to wade in the river, to feel its rush on his legs and his beak, to walk among the reeds. Let us take him!"

"We may be killed."

"Yes."

"You cannot say we will not."

"I cannot. Yet better to be in the light."

Nicholas splashed and flapped and waded in the river with much joy. He hurried about, putting his beak in the water, then bringing it out, raising his head high, shaking it from side to side, as Simon and I sat nearby. Good Kitten was off chasing some wild animal that had caught her eye, a field mouse perhaps, or maybe a squirrel. She was most calm with our house squirrel, but other squirrels caused her much excitement. Something wild had moved in the distance, and she had run into the woods, leaving Simon and Nicholas and me to care for ourselves.

The day was most beautiful. The sun was bright, the sky, a soft blue. The leaves had not yet come to the trees, but tiny buds were beginning to show themselves, and the flowering bushes were showing the early signs of spring. From where we sat I could see The Gray, head down, grazing, at peace, the pony as well.

"Thank you," said Simon. He was digging in the earth at his side with a small, pointed stick. He looked not my way.

"For what do you thank me?" I asked.

"For making me come out."

"I did not make you come."

"You did."

"You came by your own mind."

"It was because of you."

"Perhaps."

"It was."

"Perhaps."

"You were right."

"It was time."

"I know."

"Have you heard of a siege?"

I had not expected to ask that. I know not where it came from. If I had chosen words to speak, they would have been simple, less worrying—words of Nicholas, of summer coming, of picnics, or of wading in the Meuse. Yet of these I spoke not. "Have you heard of a siege?" These were my words.

"A siege?" asked Simon.

"Yes," I said, watching to see if my question had upset him. I could not tell.

Why had I spoken thus? Was it because I knew I could not ask Father? Father was worried already for fear of my going off with soldiers. A siege sounded as something to do with battle, a subject never to be touched with Father or Mother or Pierre or Jean. They might tell Father I had been asking strange questions, questions to do with war. This Father could not bear. Had I asked Simon as I had none other to ask?

Michel, I thought. He would have been the one to ask. So wise. He would have known, and had no fear.

29

The Siege

"A siege," said Simon, turning his thoughts to the past. He had stopped digging. "Why do you ask me that?"

My heart stopped.

I must answer with care, I thought. In truth, but with care.

"I heard it somewhere," I answered. "I knew not what it meant, and wondered."

"Something bad," said Simon. "A siege is something bad that lasts for a long time."

"Like what?"

"Like anything."

"Like anything?"

"Anything bad."

"Anything bad."

"Very bad. Anything very bad that lasts for a long time."

"Like the war?"

"It could be the war."

"What else could it be?"

"Joan, Joan, Joan, Joan, Joan!" It was Hauviette racing toward us, her arms outstretched, with the biggest smile.

"Hauviette!" I ran to meet her, my arms as hers, my

smile as well. We met with much force, knocking each other down and rolling over and over.

Hauviette joined us by the river, and soon Aimée was there. She had been looking for Simon. Others followed—Mengette, who had been looking for Hauviette, Little Gérard, who had been looking for Michel, and then Henri, who had been looking for me, God help me!

"So, Joan, you are looking well today," Henri said in a tone that made me wonder what he wanted.

Hauviette told me later what she thought he wanted, which caused me to feel sick in the stomach.

"You are looking very well," he repeated.

"We all look well," I answered, "thanks to God."

I knew the mention of God would cause him unrest and so I put a special weight to the words. Henri merely looked out over the river and praised the gentle breeze. I did not feel his heart was in the telling.

"And where might Maurice be today?" asked Mengette. She looked directly at Hauviette, whose face went all at once to red.

"I know not," said Hauviette, her voice higher in sound than was usual to hear. She was trying to sound as if it mattered little to her where Maurice might be, but as one would guess, she did not manage. Henri noticed this. In his stupid way, he took to making the joke of Hauviette.

"You know not, do you?" he said. "What do you know?"

"Nothing."

"Do you know who he has kissed?"

"Who?" asked Hauviette. She turned at once quite pale.

"I know not," said Henri, smiling a twisted half smile. "I thought you might know." He put much weight to the word "you."

"Why would I know?" asked Hauviette. She was angry now, one could tell.

"I merely thought you might."

"I do not."

"What do you think, Joan?" asked Henri.

"Of what?" I asked.

"Of anything."

"That is not a question one can answer."

"What do you think of me?"

"Nothing much," said Hauviette.

"Nicholas, you big one!" shouted Aimée. She ran toward the goose, causing him to flap his wings in alarm. He hurried off to a place farther down the river.

"Let him be!" shouted Simon.

Aimée put her head down then and began doing turn over movements in the rough winter-spring grass. Her legs went up over her head. Then she tumbled on her back. "Over and over," she shouted.

"Stop before you get sick," called Simon.

"If I want to," said Aimée, as she rolled.

My mind left then, pulled to the faraway place. All about me seemed unreal. I heard only the words "You must raise the siege of Orléans."

I heard Simon speak as from a distance. "She got sick from doing that once," he said.

"Must you speak of it?" said Mengette. She lay in the grass at my side, holding my hand.

"It went everywhere," said Simon.

"He always does this," said Mengette.

"It smelled."

"Please."

"It did."

Mengette sat up. "If you do not stop speaking of this I am leaving," she said.

"I am finished," said Simon.

"Fine," said Mengette. She lay back in the grass.

"Joan wants to know what a siege is." Simon's words brought me back from the faraway place.

"Why do you want to know that?" said Mengette.

My heart took an extra beat. "I heard mention of it," I said. "I knew not what it was and wondered."

"A siege is any terrible thing that happens for a long time," said Mengette.

"Like what?"

"Like anything," said Mengette. She still lay on her back, looking up at the clouds in the soft blue sky.

Something terrible is happening in Orléans, and I must stop it, I reasoned. Raise it must be as stop it or take it away.

The others went on offering many thoughts of what a siege could and could not be. I was pulled once more away. I heard them speak as from some great distance.

"A drawbridge," said Little Gérard.

"What?" said Hauviette.

"A siege is like a drawbridge."

A drawbridge? I thought.

"I never heard that," said Hauviette.

"You did now," said Aimée.

"How can a siege be like a drawbridge?" asked Mengette. "That makes no sense."

"Some way," said Little Gérard. "I forget exactly how."

Must I raise a drawbridge in Orléans? I thought with a small, top part of my mind. Surely there are others who can do that. And how can it be of great importance?

"A siege is a bad thing that happens for a long time," said Mengette. "That cannot be a drawbridge."

"A drawbridge can stop you for a long time," said Little Gérard.

"Which could be bad," said Henri.

"It makes no sense," said Mengette.

"So a siege is any bad thing that happens for a long time," said Hauviette, as if it had just come to her mind.

"As I said," said Mengette.

You must raise the siege of Orléans.

Once more, the words filled my being. I saw Saint Michael in my mind as he had been those few nights past, there, in my humble room, radiant, all-knowing, in the blazing, purple-white light. A stillness came over me, and a tingling throughout my body. There was also a whistle sound in my ears that grew louder as the moments passed. My loving friends continued their talk. I heard them faintly now.

"A long torture," Simon was saying.

"Or someone dying," said Little Gérard.

"It would have to be a lot of people," said Mengette. "For . . ."

"A long time," said Hauviette.

"It could be one person," said Little Gérard, "if you are taking care of that person, and they are sick, and then they die."

"Or if they live," said Simon. "It could still be long and terrible. Maybe they would lose an arm."

"Please," said Mengette.

The whistling in my ears continued, as did the talk of my friends.

"It could be a snake," said Aimée.

"What?" said Simon.

"A siege could be a snake," said Aimée. "A snake is long and terrible, so a siege could be a snake."

"You are so wrong," said Simon.

"Why?" said Aimée. She was upset, one could tell. Her lower lip began to tremble.

Simon spoke too harshly, I thought. It was not needed.

"A siege is something terrible that happens for a long time," said Simon, "not a long and terrible thing."

"Oh," said Aimée.

"You have to listen."

"I listen."

"A long time without any food," said Henri.

"A long time without any water," said Simon.

"A long time with too many rats," said Hauviette.

[247]

"That would do it," said Mengette.

All at once, coming toward us was Michel, strong and tall and gentle, with the warmest of smiles. "Hello," he said.

I returned from the faraway place. The whistling ceased. My heart pounded loudly.

"Is a siege a terrible thing that happens for a long time?" Little Gérard called out to his brother.

"You could say that," said Michel. "Mother wants you in the house."

"Could it be anything?" asked Little Gérard .

"I suppose it could," answered Michel. "You had best go in."

"Joan wants to know," said Little Gérard .

Michel sat at my side. It was my turn to blush. It was as no one else was there, just he and I alone.

"You want to know of a siege?" he asked. His eyes were the deepest blue, so true, so understanding.

"Yes," I answered.

"What kind of siege?"

"Perhaps a siege that happens in a city."

"In a city," he said, thinking the matter over. "A siege that happens in a city."

"It has to be long and bad," said Aimée, "but not a snake."

"He knows," said Little Gérard.

"You should be in the house," said Michel. He looked into my eyes. I felt as I would melt. "A city held in siege," he said, "in time of war, would mean the enemy had sur-rounded the city. No one could go in, or out."

"I see."

"The people soon would starve."

"Is there a siege in Orléans?" I asked.

"I have not heard it."

"There must be!"

I should not have said that, I thought.

But it was too late.

"Why must there be a siege in Orléans?" he asked.

I wanted so to tell him, to open my heart to him, to pour out all that was inside, but that was not as God would have it. This I knew. Michel's eyes were wise and blue and filled with understanding, yet still I must contain within all that had been given. It was not Michel's to carry. It was mine, until God told me otherwise.

"I feel there must be cities in siege throughout all of France," I answered merely.

"This may be so."

"There is so much suffering. Yet here, by our Meuse, with the trees and the birds and all God's beauty, we cannot truly know."

"My cousin has a siege," said Simon. "Her husband and her baby died and now she has to live."

We all were quiet then.

30

God's Choice

The time is now.

The voice struck at my heart. It was lightning and thunder all at once. I was weeding in Father's garden. The afternoon sun slanted, but was hot.

Again the words, full and strong.

The time is now.

Beloved Saint.

Sweet light. The time is now.

For what?

You must go.

I am not ready. My hands are filled with dirt.

You can no longer stay at home.

My dress is soaked with sweat.

You must go into France.

I felt as I would faint, hot and cold at once. All around the light was blazing, blinding, searing white, and everywhere the scent of roses.

How will I go? I know nothing. I am no one.

Daughter of God.

I want only to serve you. Help me. I am ignorant. Tell me what to do.

And he was there, in all his armor, shining out unearthly brilliance, touching all, blazing, in endless streams of pure, white light. He carried his sword and with him, too, a banner of untelling beauty, its cloth floating in the gentle air of light.

I rose, unsure my legs could carry me. I moved to the Grandfather Tree, placing my hand on its trunk to steady myself, as I thought I might faint. Saint Michael was so near to me then. I could have touched him, though I did not. I saw on either side of my Saint, and some small way behind, my beloved Saint Catherine and beloved Saint Margaret, their gentle robes as soft as the light around them. I felt their silent rays of love, sent to ease the pounding in my heart. Saint Michael spoke once more.

Daughter of God.

Yes.

Listen well.

With all my soul.

Go to Robert de Baudricourt at the stronghold of Vaucouleurs. He will give you men-at-arms to take you to the Dauphin.

A terrible fear was with me then. My heart felt as it would leap from my chest. My eyes burned with the wish to face him full, to drink in all the precious light, to know what could not be known. My mind was far too small.

I, go to Vaucouleurs? To the Dauphin? With men-at-arms?

The time is now.

I am no one.

You will lead the Dauphin to be anointed and crowned.

I have no way.

You will drive the English out of France.

I know nothing of war.

Saint Margaret and Saint Catherine will guide you.

I am ignorant.

This work is yours, if you will have it.

I am no one!

Daughter of God.

I know nothing of war and fighting!

No one can do it save you.

No one?

It is yours, if you so will.

It is *your* will, not mine!

You must decide.

There is no deciding. I wish only to serve!

What else do you wish?

I wish to be with you always! I wish the salvation of my soul!

These are yours.

I wept then. Saint Michael touched my brow. I felt the light streaming from his gentle hand to warm my soul.

Sweet light.

How will I get to Vaucouleurs? I know not the way.

Your uncle will take you.

Uncle Durand?

The same.

Must I tell Mother and Father?

That is as you wish.

It would cause them pain.

Yes.

They would try and stop me.

Yes.

I must not tell them.

As you wish.

And then my tears came full. I fell to my knees.

Mother and Father . . .

Yes.

Will I see them again?

You will.

I love them so.

Be not afraid.

The light was fading now.

Don't leave me!

I am with you always.

Yet stay!

Have faith.

Don't leave me!

Have faith. Robert de Baudricourt will not yield until asked three times.

I need you!

Have faith.

The light was gone.

I sat then so still. I knew not fully where I was. I was staring at the daisies and the buttercups all around. The buttercups were of the brightest yellow, with the soft middle part. I counted the leaves. There were five rounded leaves, so shiny.

"Here you are." It was Mengette, coming into the

garden. She carried her baby niece. "Look at this baby," she said. "Have you ever seen a thing as cute?"

I felt so far away. I knew not words to speak.

Mengette knelt at my side. "I have cared for her this whole day through since breakfast," she said. "Look at her tiny fingers."

I looked, but could not speak. Good Kitten came and rubbed against my arm.

"I want so to be a mother," Mengette went on. "One day we shall both have such a one as this for all our very own."

"If it pleases God."

"Oh, it will."

I thought then of my vow on the very first day I heard the voice in Father's garden, to remain pure and in service for as long as it pleased God.

"We will have babies and care for them together," Mengette continued. "We shall sit in this very garden with babies of our own."

Saint Michael's words came strong to my mind.

You must drive the English out of France.

I think I knew in that moment that I would not have a child, or husband either. My way would be different.

To my great surprise, life went on with all the simple things. The flowering tree to the left of the house grew full with the bright pink blossoms. Father began the haying, Mother worked at the wheel, Pierre and Jean mended the pens, while I was as one struck with a blow to the head. I carried on with my chores as always, yet my mind was dull.

Saint Michael had spoken words to change my life, but they were words whose meaning could not be held.

In the days that followed I forced myself to bring the words to mind. It was not an easy thing.

I must go to Vaucouleurs. I must ask Robert de Baudricourt for men-at-arms to take me to the Dauphin. I recalled Father speaking of de Baudricourt. They had met about the taxes. Father had made the tiny spot hole for reading, then he had told me. Robert de Baudricourt was the captain of the town. He was loyal to the Dauphin. If that were so, the Dauphin would listen to him. If Robert de Baudricourt gave me men-at-arms they would protect me from the English, from the Burgundians, too. My precious Saints had all these things in mind. And more! I must raise the siege of Orléans. I must lead the Dauphin to be anointed and crowned. I must drive the English out of France.

The words struck terror to my heart.

These things were given me to do by my Lord, yet I can never do them. This was my thought. I am ignorant. I am no one. I felt the awful fear that always comes when the truest of the true has ceased to hold a meaning, and there is nothing left.

Days were spent in such a sorry state. Then one night, all was changed. It happened thus.

It was some short time after Saint Michael had come to the garden. I was not able to sleep, as had been the way for many nights. Good Kitten slept well, at the foot of my bed or by my ear, yet I remained awake. I was deeply tired of body, and of mind as well, but sleep was not a friend. I asked that night for help, a call from my heart to my beloved Voices.

Saint Catherine! Saint Margaret! Help me! Saint Michael has told me to have faith, but mine is small now. Help me! He said you would guide me always. I need you. Saint Michael has told me to do things I know not how to do. He said they would be done by me, and no one else, if I would have them, yet I cannot! I do not see the way. I am no one. I know nothing. All I know is the truth of my Lord. Now He speaks, and makes no sense to my mind. What is left for me? Help me! Tell me what to do!

The answer came, swift and clear. My blessed Saints spoke the words together, as if one were speaking only, or all of life. I saw them not with my eyes that night. It was not needed. The words alone were sent, perfect, simple, straight, three words breaking through the stillness of my darkened room.

Honor God's choice.

All was clear. God had chosen me as an instrument. I must honor His choice. It did not matter how it seemed to me. How it was with God was all there was. I must defend God's choice in all. Who was I to argue? I knew this well, but when it came to what I could do, I challenged God. This was wrong. Did I know better than God in the matter? Was God right in all things except this one? No. Never. God had chosen this humble servant. Who was I to say He should have chosen another? God had chosen me. That should be good enough.

And there was something else. I would not do these

things. God would do them. And God would choose the instrument. What care that it was me? I would honor His choice no matter who it was. Even myself! God help me.

From that night on I was of a different mind. I feel it was more of God's mind. I pray this to be true.

It was a few short days before Uncle would come to take me to Burey, as had all been arranged in winter. It had been agreed that I would stay for a week. That would give time enough for me to help with the chores there, and still not leave Mother without help for too long. Burey is near to Vaucouleurs. There I would go with Uncle, but only I knew this. Oh, yes. I told Good Kitten, but she, of course, was silent on the matter. Well, that is not full with truth. In the days before I left she screamed more than was her usual way. I asked Mother to give her special concern while I was with Uncle. This Mother agreed to do. But still Good Kitten screamed. Father was not pleased. Pierre told him to put some small pieces of rolled-up cloth in his ears that he would not hear the screams, but Father said if he did that, he would not hear anything else either, and that would not be well. Pierre had to agree.

Father was having more dreams. These he told me of. I feel he knew, somehow, of what I was to do, and when he slept this knowing filled his mind. Three nights he dreamed I was away with large and rough men. In one dream he went looking for me in a field and found me talking with them. In another I was on a large white horse, the men on horses too. And in one more Father was walking on a road. I was with the men just ahead, but Father could not catch up. When Father told me of the dreams, he said they caused his heart to ache.

Mother said Father's dreams were his way of missing me when I was with Uncle. Jean said they were from overdone cider. Father laughed, but held me tight those days, often in the wonderful big bear hugs I loved so well. I wanted never to let go.

I rode The Gray as many times as I could manage in those days before leaving. I knew not when the day to ride into France would come. I wanted to be ready. I loved my times on The Gray. We became, it seemed, as one, racing through the high grass. I felt as I could know his mind, and he knew mine as well. I could think a thing for him to do, and he would do it. A sudden turn, a new direction, a slowing down, a quickening, these he always knew. I had great comfort now at fast speeds. More than comfort, I would say. It was a love.

The days passed quickly. Saint Margaret and Saint Catherine came often then to guide me. Never had their counsel been so frequent. They told me many things. I should speak boldly. I was to tell Robert de Baudricourt to send word to the Dauphin that he should remain ready, but not engage his enemies. I must say as well that the kingdom did not belong to the Dauphin. The Lord wished the Dauphin to become king and hold the realm in trust, and that the Dauphin would be made king in spite of his enemies. I prayed that I could hold these many points in mind, that they might be carried purely to that place where God had meant them to be heard.

Saint Margaret and Saint Catherine repeated my need

for faith. Robert de Baudricourt would not yield until asked three times. I asked if I would return to Domrémy. They told me I would. This brought great joy to my heart. I had been told by Saint Michael that I would see Mother and Father again. This I knew, and this brought comfort to my mind, but I could not bear to say good-bye to my home and my dear friends forever. I was grateful it would not be so. Still, I did not know when I would return. This I did not ask, and it was never told. I prayed it would be soon.

It was not an easy thing to say good-bye. This I did as best I could. My friends knew of my plans to go to Uncle's for a week. I said good-bye to each as if, truly, this were all. I wanted them not to worry. However long I might be gone, they must sense the truth that I would return. To each I said farewell, but in an easy voice, as easy as I could manage. Hauviette was hardest, and Mengette as well. To each I gave my love, to Simon, he was doing well with his reading, to Aimée, she had found a new mouse, to Henri, that was easy, to Maurice, to Little Gérard, and of course to Michel. Once more I felt the wish to tell him all. He would understand. He might stroke my hair and kiss me once. He would pray for me when I was gone. But I did not tell him. I merely said, "Good-bye. I am going to Uncle's for a visit."

"Good-bye," he said. "Be well." And that was all.

31

Burey

It was late of an afternoon when Uncle arrived. I was on The Gray when I saw him. My heart stopped at the sight.

It begins, I thought.

Uncle was coming down the road from Greux with Catherine at his side. They were talking, enjoying each other's company. They did not see me.

I rode to the near field, where I always left The Gray. I hugged him fast about the neck, enjoying the rich horse smell. "I will see you again," I said, "if God wills. I pray it will be so." I slid from his back, then moved to his head. "Thank you for the rides," I said. I stroked him in the soft spot beneath the ear. Then I took off the bridle and went to hang it in the barn. The tall grass tickled my legs as I walked.

Catherine stayed that night for supper, and Colin came as well. It was a merry time. Catherine told of the night I had been born in that very room, and how happy she had been, at last to have a sister. Pierre remembered not the event, but Jean did. He had wanted a boy. After that Uncle told stories of funny things that had happened in times past. He told of a time when Catherine and I had been small. It seems we made up a story of pigs and played out all the parts, each one a pig. Uncle and his wife, Mother and Father, and Pierre and Jean and Jacquémin all had to watch. Pierre and Jean had wanted to be pigs as well, but we had not let them. All the pigs were girls. This was our reason.

The story lasted well into the night, Uncle said. Everyone tired of so many pigs, except Catherine and I. Father fell asleep and went right off his chair with a crash. I had some sense of the event in a far-off place in my mind. Catherine remembered it well, as she was older.

It was late when Catherine and Colin headed back to Greux. It was planned that Uncle would stay the night. We would leave for Burey at dawn. I offered him my bed, but he refused. He would sleep with Pierre and Jean.

All that night I did not sleep. I could think only of my leaving, of the trip to Vaucouleurs. And then? I knew not what. I asked my Saints when I should tell Uncle of the plan to go to Robert de Baudricourt. They told me merely . . . Not as yet.

I would wait.

Good Kitten was restless that night as if she knew I was leaving. I held her close to quiet her, watching the moon from my window. It was so large, a wide and flat pink-orange circle, low near the horizon, over the hills, across the Meuse. As the night went on the moon grew higher, turning pale. It grew yellow-white and not so large, but still was flat and still above the hills to the east.

Good Kitten slept at last, but I did not. I held her merely, and prayed and watched the night. I thought of Mother and Father sleeping in the next room. If I were to be long away, I would have a letter sent, to tell them where

I was, that I was well. This I had decided. I felt such love for them. I missed them, though they were so close.

Dawn came slowly. At last the sky turned its light blue. The mist was thick. Good Kitten rose and stretched. I set her down, then leaned my head full out my tiny window. The moon shone still. It was high above Mengette's house, glowing rich yellow, not yet white.

We ate breakfast all together. Then it was time to go. I wore my red patched dress. Mother packed me some other small things to take. She tied them with a cloth, and said her love was in the bundle too. I knew this to be true.

I hugged Mother and Father, and kissed them good-bye. Then I hugged Pierre and Jean, and Good Kitten last. I could not make too much of the matter as it was understood by them to be a short and easy trip. Good Kitten sensed the rest. Perhaps the others did as well, but no one spoke of it.

The mist was heavy on the ground as Uncle and I made our way along the road, through Greux, past the little road that leads up to the Saturday Chapel in the woods. You are halfway up the hill on the west side of the valley as you travel this road. It is very beautiful. The wooded hill continues some way on the left, the valley on the right, where the mist lay on the ground. The tops of the trees came through it as coming through clouds.

Uncle and I were quiet then, just enjoying the walk and God's beauty. The sun was low above the mountains. The Meuse was making steam. On we went in the cool morning air, past a straight row of trees on the right, past the cows lying in a clump looking in different directions, past the brown plowed fields with rows of tiny shoots, through Goussaincourt, to where all opens to a fine view of rolling hills. Next came the wooded hill straight in front before Maxey-sur-Vaise, then through the town, winding, and past the tall trees in a row. The mist had risen here and all was bright. Everywhere were fields of bright yellow. The sheep in a far field all faced the Meuse. Heads down, they ate.

It was a morning's walk to Burey. After some time we stopped a while near some cows resting in the tall grass. It had grown hot. Uncle wiped his brow with a cloth. "I have always loved cows," he said.

"And I as well."

"They are so gentle."

"I have found them so."

I was quiet then. I asked my Saints silently, from my heart, if now was the time to ask Uncle to take me to Robert de Baudricourt. To me it seemed the time, but the answer came . . . Wait. And so I waited.

Uncle watched the cows. "They are hot," he said.

"They have no shade."

"They must manage somehow."

"With God's help."

We rested a while, sitting on a large rock by the side of the road, near the cows. Some lay in the grass among the yellow and white flowers so high that only the very tops of the cows' heads could be seen and the upper parts of their backs. One stood, the high grass touching her belly. She stared at me with a question. After some time she lay down.

When we reached Burey, Uncle's wife, Jeanne, had a fine

meal ready. She stood so straight and simple, with brown hair to her waist. We ate, sharing a loving time. I asked Jeanne how best I could help her during my stay. She said with spinning and sewing mainly, and caring for the garden. I told them I would be happy to help with the animals and other outside work as well. With this they were pleased.

It was a joy to return to Burey, where I had not been in some years. After we ate, I went to look around. The tiny waterfall in the brook behind the house was my first stop. It rushed and tumbled as I had remembered. I placed a small stick in the brook just before the waterfall. I pictured, in my mind, it was a boat. It was carried swiftly over the falls, on its way to the Meuse.

I moved to the large willow tree so sheltering, then, walking all about, I saw the old familiar things from my visits as a child. The stone drinking trough, with walls so thick, was still by the side of the house. The ladder leaned against the wall in front. The moss on the stones around the small garden in back, the wood stacked by the door, all was as I had remembered, as I had hoped.

I stayed for nearly a week, working and enjoying the company of my dear Uncle and Jeanne. Uncle was busy with the haying. He took the first cut, as many did at that time. Everywhere was the fresh hay smell.

I worked most often in the house with Jeanne. She was gentle and sweet, a quiet soul with a loving voice and way. It was cool in the house, a welcome change from outside. A breeze came through the open doors and windows.

One day I worked in the fields with Uncle. He was

preparing a new part of the field. We took the stones and stacked them beneath the tree. I worked also in the garden. I pulled each weed high, shaking it clear of soil, as I had so often done in Father's garden.

Each day I would ask my Saints if it was time to speak to Uncle. Always they would tell me . . . Soon. It seemed the time would never come.

After five days, or maybe six, I was weeding the lettuce in the small garden to the side of the house. It was planted in a circle. I was weeding when all at once I heard . . .

Tell him today.

It was Saint Catherine's voice.

Today?

Speak boldly.

That was all she said.

I found Uncle with the sheep.

"Uncle," I said as I approached.

"Sweet Joan."

I sat beside him under the tree. "I have something to ask."

"Dear one," he said. "Whatever I can do for you, I do it gladly."

"I want to go to France."

"To France?" he asked.

"I must go to the Dauphin, and have him crowned."

Uncle was surprised at that, as you would guess. He looked at me in an unknowing way. It seemed he feared he had missed a most important point. "You, crown the Dauphin?" He spoke not to make the joke, merely to understand.

"Yes," I told him.

Tell him about the prophecy.

It was Saint Margaret, speaking in my ear.

Speak boldly.

"Has it not been said that France would be ruined by a woman, and afterward saved by a maiden from Lorraine?" I asked.

"It has."

"That is me."

"You?"

"You must take me to Robert de Baudricourt, that he may give me men-at-arms to take me to the place where the Dauphin is to be found."

Uncle stared at me, unable to speak.

"I have word that he must hear."

"You are the maiden?"

"I am."

"How do you know?"

"God has told me."

Moments passed. Uncle was quiet. I watched him closely, pleading with my eyes, with all my soul, that he would understand.

Speak boldly.

Again the voice. This time Saint Catherine and Saint Margaret spoke as one.

"You must take me!" I cried out. "I have no other way!"

"You are the maiden?"

"Have I not always been truthful?"

"More than any I have known."

"So I am now!"

"Forgive me," he said. "This is more than I can understand."

"I must do this thing!" I cried. "I would a million times rather stay at home with Mother and Father, and care for the sheep, and rest in God's beauty, but this I cannot do! I must go and I must do this thing, for the Lord wills that I do so!"

"Do your parents know of this?" he asked.

"It would only cause them pain."

"They would be angered with me."

"They will understand."

"De Baudricourt will not believe you."

"I know."

"He will not grant permission."

"I know."

"Then why go to Vaucouleurs?"

"It is commanded. Later he will agree."

"I think not."

Speak boldly.

"It will be so! Take me! You must!"

"When would you go?"

"Better today than tomorrow. Better tomorrow than later."

"I know not what to think."

"Take me, please! I beg you! I have no other way!"

Moments passed before he spoke, great ages of time. He looked off at the sheep. When at last he did speak it was quiet, as barely to be heard. "If God speaks to any, it would be you."

"God speaks to all," I said, "but not everyone listens."

And he agreed. The next morning we left.

32

Vaucouleurs

It is a short walk to Vaucouleurs from Burey. We set out early, up the hill that leads from the town, past the cows waiting on the right. The sun was hot. Uncle was quiet, as I was as well. I was thinking of all I would say to Robert de Baudricourt, praying I would carry God's words. Uncle seemed to be feeling some worry of how we would be received. I had no worry for that as I knew we would be refused twice, and then accepted. Uncle had not the sureness of this as I had, and so he had the worry. I sent him a loving message from my heart.

The road from Burey leads by the Meuse, through the village of Neuville-les-Vaucouleurs. Just outside the village we passed five sheep huddled beneath a tree, crisscrossed, resting on each other. It was a loving sight. Beyond we could see the small group of village houses, and beyond these, far up to the left, the walls of Vaucouleurs!

I had not seen Vaucouleurs in all my life before that day. It was a fine sight, the walled fortress high on the hill. There was a castle too, and many towers. Never had I seen such a sight. I quickened my steps. Uncle followed.

When we reached the top I had a surprise. The fortress

gates were open. People moved freely in and out, which was not as I had thought. In my mind there were men-at-arms waiting at the gates, questioning all who would pass. I had thought out what to say to such a guard. I would tell him that he must send word to the place where Robert de Baudricourt was, that we would speak with him on a most important matter. If this did not move him to respond, I would be of a stronger way. I would say that Uncle and I insisted on being taken to the Captain, and would not leave until this was arranged. It was a matter of importance to the kingdom of France. Robert de Baudricourt would not be pleased to learn that it had been disregarded. These thoughts were racing through my mind as we climbed. When we reached the top, there was the happy sight.

"The gate is open!" I said to Uncle.

"Yes," he said, his mind elsewhere it seemed.

Above the stone gate was a beautiful carving. It was of the Holy Mother and Child. The Mother was of simple feature, with a crown and cape. The Infant was held in Her loving arms. He looked so wise. I bowed before the carving. After that, we passed through the gate and into the town. Many people moved about.

"Let us rest a moment," said Uncle.

I did not care for the idea, as I wanted to get on with it, but Uncle needed the rest. We moved a short way to a quiet spot near the east wall. There was grass here. Tiny lavender-pink flowers grew out of the wall where it had crumbled and there was moss on top. A large tree spread out by the edge of the wall, with the valley to be seen on either side, the unsuspecting cows grazing in the fields below. Here we sat, resting from the long climb, looking out on the green, rolling hills. There were small clumps of thick woods in some places, but mostly there was open country, with blue sky overhead and the small towns in the distance. One could see several towns in different spots across the hills. No one bothered us here.

"Would you have some bread?" Uncle asked.

"Thank you, not as yet," I answered.

The food will delay our meeting yet more, I thought. It is not to my liking, yet Uncle needs the food. I must wait.

Uncle opened the sack, which Jeanne had packed. "I feel the need of something," he said. He pulled out some bread and a piece of cheese. Then he closed the sack.

I watched the people moving this way and that, hurrying about with the daily tasks. They moved quickly here. In Domrémy all was at a slower pace. I looked out at the fields of yellow buttercups. Cows and sheep were as dots of white and tan on the faraway hills.

Uncle ate slowly. It was hard to sit still, so near to Robert de Baudricourt, so close to the place where I would bring God's words. I felt as when I sat too long to snap the beans, but more strongly of that feeling still. I wished to jump up and run to find the man, that there be no delay. But Uncle needed time. More than the food, it seemed he needed the moments to ready himself for what was to come. I sensed his growing fear of how we would be treated. He spoke of it not, but this I could feel.

Be patient, I told myself. You must wait.

I looked about.

Here we are, by the wall in Vaucouleurs, overlooking the valley, on a glorious day!

I could hardly believe it was real. The time had truly come!

Let me speak as God would have it, I prayed silently, and let Uncle finish his cheese! We have to go!

Uncle took more bread.

"Where will we find him?" I asked.

"In the main hall, I would say," said Uncle. Then he took another piece of cheese.

Again he was silent. "Are you certain, Joan?" he said at last.

"Of what?" I asked.

"That you would do this thing?"

"I must."

Uncle nodded then, and looked out over the valley as he ate.

No one stopped us as we entered the hall. It was the largest room I had ever seen, dark and cool with tall and thin windows at the far end and a stone floor. Shafts of light came through the windows in giant streaks, but all the rest was dim. Most all the room was empty, but facing the entrance, far to the other side beneath the windows, was a raised-up place. Two steps up, and there, a large table. Around the table were several men. Four were sitting, others, maybe two or three, stood about near the table. One looked out the window, one slept, another wrote on papers, while another spoke some words. Another listened. Most appeared as knights, most with large boots and huge swords. Uncle touched my arm. "They are busy," he whispered.

"It matters not," I said.

"We best wait."

"We cannot." I moved toward the windows and the big table and all the men. One man was larger than the rest, with boots above his knees. He was the one looking out the window.

That is he.

Saint Catherine and Saint Margaret spoke together, clear to my ear.

I moved forward.

Uncle stayed behind. I carried his cloak.

"What do you want?" It was one of the knights at the table who spoke. It was not the listening one, nor the writing one, but the one who spoke the words to the writing one who spoke. His voice was deep and stern.

"I would speak to Robert de Baudricourt," I said.

"By what authority?"

"By my Lord's."

"We are engaged."

I moved directly to Robert de Baudricourt. He turned to regard me. His face was stern. He looked so tall, as sure he was, and up the two steps as well. I felt a rush of fiery heat.

Speak boldly.

The Voices came once more.

I stopped and, rooted there, I spoke. "My Lord has sent me to tell you to send word to the Dauphin that he should remain ready, but not engage his enemies."

"Who gave you leave to enter?" It was the man with the writing papers who spoke. The others stared in silence.

"My Lord has given it," I spoke. "And there is more."

"We are busy here."

I looked still at Robert de Baudricourt, not moving my gaze. He stared at me as he could not believe I was there.

"The kingdom does not belong to the Dauphin," I told him, "but my Lord wishes the Dauphin to become king and to hold the realm in trust. The Dauphin will be made king in spite of his enemies. I myself will lead him to be anointed and crowned."

Robert de Baudricourt looked down at me from all his height and high on the raised steps. He looked not pleased. "Who is this lord you speak of?"

"The King of Heaven."

"Is that a fact?"

"It is. I have come to you on His behalf to be sent to the Dauphin so that he will be all right."

"The Dauphin is in need of you?"

"Just so. I must go to him, and you must give me men-at-arms to take me there."

"Who are you?"

"Joan, the maid."

Robert de Baudricourt called past me then to Uncle, far behind. "Is this your daughter?" he called.

"No, sir," said Uncle. "She is my cousin."

The men were watching me, except the sleeping one. A standing knight sat down. He spoke not but seemed somehow friendly, familiar to my eye. I knew not why.

He will help you.

Again, my Voices spoke. I knew not what they meant.

"Take her home to her father," said Robert de Baudricourt.

Speak boldly.

"I shall drive the English out of France!"

"You are a child!"

"I am appointed nonetheless."

"Take her home to her father! And box her ears as well!"

"The Dauphin must place his kingdom at my command!"

"Cuff her roundly!"

"And not only that!" Up the steps I went to face him squarely. "I shall raise the siege of Orléans!"

"There is no siege in Orléans!"

"Then there will be! And I shall raise it!"

"Enough!" he bellowed. "Take her home!"

"In the name of God you take too much time to send me!"

"Enough!"

I sensed I would get no farther. His mind was set.

"I shall come again, and again, and then I shall have the men-at-arms," I said. "You would do well to give them now."

"Take her home!"

I turned to Uncle. "Let us go back now," I said, handing Uncle his cloak.

"And box her ears!"

Uncle and I walked silently from that place, through the gate and down the hill. When we reached the road, we turned and headed for Burey. I felt the rush of fiery heat that was not of the weather. I felt ready then to do the thing, to reach the Dauphin, to bring him aid. Yet all must wait. All would come in time, as had been told.

Uncle was quiet still. I knew not what he thought.

33

Friendship Stone

I remained another day in Burey before Uncle brought me home. Jeanne and I churned the butter. We used the wooden plunge churn, which Jeanne shared with others in the town. This was her time. We took turns with the task. One spun while one churned, and then we changed our jobs. This was a better way than keeping to the same job, as the churning took many hours. The arms would tire and badly need rest. The spinning was a change. For this, one did not need the strength.

Uncle was in the fields. He had told me the night before, as we sat by the fire, that after seeing me with Robert de Baudricourt, he no longer had a doubt that God had put me to this task. He knew that truly I must be the maiden. I told him this was well. He seemed more quiet with me thereafter, but no less loving. God bless Uncle for his kindness.

That same night I asked Uncle to speak to me of the listening knight, the one I felt I knew. This was Bertrand de Poulengy, Uncle told me. The knight had been in my home several times, when I was but a tiny child. Uncle had heard he was a good man, and close to God. This was fine to hear.

My Voices had said that he would help me. One day I would learn how.

While Uncle was busy with the haying, Jeanne and I kept to our churning work inside. Jeanne asked not of our time in Vaucouleurs. Uncle had told her he had need to go on "some small business." This was all she knew. It seemed enough.

I worked first with the churning. One has to force the long handle up and down. At first it moves with ease, but as the mixture changes, one needs more strength. This is when the tired time comes. Up and down, up and down. The over and over of the task served to calm my mind. I had slept little in the night after our meeting in Vaucouleurs. I felt a restlessness. Now I must wait. How long? I had asked this of my Voices, but they had said only this.

All will come in time.

"Thank you for your help these many days," said Jeanne, breaking in upon my thoughts. "It was so good of you."

"It was my joy."

"Will you come again?"

"Gladly."

"Soon you will have a husband. It will not be easy then."

A husband? I thought. Not soon. Not soon, if ever.

"I pray you will return."

"That would be well."

"You must bring your husband."

I thought of Michel.

"As God will have it," I answered.

Jeanne took her turn with the churning then as I spun.

We worked in gentle silence. When I returned to the churn it was not long before there came the uneven feel of the loose butter lumps floating inside. It was time to cease churning and open the churn. This we did. Then we scraped down the sides and the plunger to collect the soft butter. Our work was done.

Uncle took me home the next day, in the early after noon. I was grateful to see my beloved Domrémy once more. Hauviette was in her yard as we approached from Greux. When she saw us she shouted for joy and ran to greet us. We hugged a welcome hug.

"I have so much to tell you," she said, in a most excited way. "Ask your mother if we can play a while."

I told her I would.

When Uncle and I reached the house, Mother greeted us each with a loving embrace. Good Kitten was curled up by the fire. When she heard us come in, she lifted her head. Then she reached out her front legs, first one and then the other, stretching them with furry toes spread, then hurried to meet me. I picked her up, holding her close. She made her loudest happy, rumbling sound.

Mother gave us cider and cakes. We sat together eating, Good Kitten on my lap. A squirrel watched from the window as Uncle spoke to Mother of our week. He spoke of the butter churning, of the spinning, of my work in the garden, of gathering the stones, but nothing did he say of Vaucouleurs. For this I was most grateful. I hugged him long before he left. "Thank you, Uncle," I told him from the deepest part of my heart.

"God bless you, Joan," he said. "My sweet."

"God bless you, Uncle."

And so he took his leave.

Hauviette had much to tell. We sat by the Meuse, behind her barn, Good Kitten at my side. The Gray was grazing in the field beyond. The tall grass touched his belly, making him look shorter than he was.

"Where to begin!" said Hauviette. Her face was flushed with excitement. "Where to begin! That is the question!"

"Begin where you like," I said. "What happened with Maurice?"

"This you will not believe!"

Good Kitten rubbed against my leg. With my open hand I pounded her with a gentle force upon her side. This she liked.

"Close your eyes," said Hauviette.

"And why is that?"

"Close them merely!"

I closed my eyes.

"Hold out your hand."

This I did. I felt an object placed there, a stone it seemed. I was not sure.

"Now open them," she said.

I opened my eyes. In my hand was a small gray-white stone.

"What do you think?"

"Maurice gave you this?" I asked, for I sensed it was so.

"A friendship stone," said Hauviette. "He told me to keep it forever!"

I touched the precious stone, which had been held, for days surely, in the hand of my loving friend.

"It leaves me not," she said.

"It is a loving gift."

"He would not have thought to give me such a thing if he did not like me. Would you say?"

"He would not."

"Never."

"No."

"Would you say?"

"I would not."

"He told me to keep it forever!"

"He cares well."

"Would you say?"

"I would."

I returned the stone to Hauviette, who held it tightly in her hand. "I sleep with it," she added.

"I should expect as much."

"And!" she said, pausing to give a greater interest. "There is more!"

"About Maurice?"

"About Mengette!"

"And what is that?"

"Guess."

"I cannot."

"You can!"

"I cannot!"

"She is betrothed!"

"In truth?"

"In truth!"

"To whom?"

"I know not the boy, and she does not. It all has been arranged!"

"Mengette is betrothed!"

"He comes from Coussey."

"Is she well pleased?"

"What would you say?"

"I would say she is."

"You would be right! 'Well pleased' does not full tell it. She is more than well pleased."

"As I would think."

"I should have let her tell you for herself, but I could not."

"I understand," I told her. I was thinking then of Michel. The talk of boys and marriage had caused my mind to picture his eyes, the gentleness of his strength, the simple wisdom in the way he spoke. I felt a sadness then, that I would never be his wife, for this I felt was not to be.

Later that evening I went to gather the water for Mother. On the way I stopped to find Mengette, but she was not at home. Aimée and Marguerite were playing by the house. I waved to them as they tumbled in the May grass.

"I have a new mouse!" shouted Aimée.

"What is his name?" I called.

"He does not want a name."

"And why is that?"

"He is a hiding mouse."

"I see."

"He hides, and when you find him, you know not who he is."

"I see."

"And so he has no name."

"That suits him, I suppose," I called across the field. I waved again and moved off to the Meuse to collect the water. Good Kitten was with me still. She moved carefully through the tall grass.

When we reached the river I knelt, tipping the bucket to get the water. There were tiny white flowers on long marshy stems, coming out of the Meuse at the wider part before you get to Hauviette's barn. The stems were swept along by the flow of the river, in gentle shapes. On the far bank were the lavender, pink, and yellow flowers. The long straw weeds came out of the green, leafy weed cover.

I filled the bucket and rose to leave. All about was filled with peace and beauty. I gave my thanks to God for returning me safely to my beloved home. Then I had a rude surprise. Henri had crept up from behind. "Boo!" he said.

I nearly dropped the bucket.

"Did I scare you?" he asked. As always, he had posed a stupid question. He had seen me jump. He knew of my surprise.

"You scared me," I told him merely.

"I wanted to."

"Why?"

"For no reason."

Once more, he made no sense. I started off with the water.

"Where are you going?" he asked.

"Home," I answered.

"May I walk with you?"

"If you choose."

Along he came. Good Kitten hurried ahead, escaping the path of his careless footsteps. Henri reached out his hand. "May I carry the bucket?" he asked.

"There is no need."

"You are a girl."

This I knew!

"And so?" I asked.

"So I should carry the bucket."

"There is no need."

"I am stronger."

"It matters not."

"So I should carry the bucket."

"Then carry it," I said. Anything to quiet him on the matter!

He took the bucket. "Do you like me, Joan?" he asked, as we moved through the high, scratching grass.

"I like you well enough."

"How well is that?"

"I see God in you."

"Must you always speak of God?"

"Yes."

He was quiet for a moment. Talk of God most always stopped his tongue.

We reached the road. "I like you as well," he said.

"I must go in."

"So soon?"

He stopped then, as did I. "Give me the bucket," I said. "I will carry it in."

"There is no need." I reached out my hand, but he gave me not the bucket.

"So," he said, as if the word alone had sense.

What does he want? I thought, unsure I cared to hear the answer.

"Give me the bucket," I repeated.

"So," he said.

"Give me the bucket."

"I like you, and you like me."

"Mother needs the water," I said. I took the bucket and hurried inside.

Supper was a loving time. It was so good to see Father again, Pierre and Jean as well. The haying had gone well for them, as the weather had been dry. They were in grand spirits.

There was much talk of Mengette's betrothal. It was the important news of the village. Mother said Mengette's parents had planned the match carefully, and were well pleased.

Tomorrow I will see her, I thought, early, before my chores.

At bedtime Father gave me the longest hug. "Thank God you are home," he said.

"Thank God," I echoed, holding him tight.

The brook outside my window was most loud, as it

always was in spring. I remembered then how often in times past it would send me to sleep. But not this night. All was different now. I had the bigger thing to think of. I would drive the English out of France.

34

Ungiven Vow

Mengette was well pleased indeed. We sat beneath the alder tree by the stream to the side of her house, speaking of the betrothal and all that was to come. Soon she would meet the boy. Her sister had seen him in Coussey, and had liked him well. They would live in Domrémy, as Mengette had always hoped. Soon she would have a house of her own and a husband and then, if God would grant, a child. I felt a joy in my heart, that all should be as was desired by my true and loving friend.

The fighting grew still worse. From the south and from the east as well came news of bloody battles, of villages burned to the ground. It would merely be a matter of time before Domrémy would be destroyed. This we knew. The knowledge caused an awful fear.

Not long after my return from Burey, rumor was heard that Vaucouleurs had been threatened. The governor of Champagne, and a Burgundian as well, was said to be making a dreadful plan. Some did not believe this, but others did for sure. Father was one who believed it. He said we must be ready. When I heard this I asked my Saints if the threat was true. They told me yes, but that I must be unafraid. There was fear enough to go around. I must have faith. I must see the village well and strong.

Look into the face of fear and it will vanish.

This they said to me.

I asked if it was time to return to Robert de Baudricourt, as all of France was in a sorry state and growing worse. Not as yet, they answered. They said no more on the matter, and so I waited.

Another rumor came to Domrémy. It was that a maid, of tender age, had gone to Robert de Baudricourt, telling him that she was chosen by God to take over the kingdom of France. She would rule in place of the Dauphin and everyone should listen to her, as only she knew the truth.

They had it somewhat wrong!

Hauviette had heard of this rumor, and Simon and Mengette as well. Hauviette thought a maid could rule far better than the Dauphin, who was a "stupid idiot," to take her phrase. I told her this was far from true, but she said that whether the Dauphin was a stupid idiot or not, he was not doing a very good job of running things, and the maid should be let to try. I said this made some sense.

Simon felt it would be too dangerous for a young girl to rule France, and that she better not try it. Mengette felt the story had been made up.

The rumor caused me great concern, as Father must not know. Oh, he knew of the rumor, but he must not know the maid was I. Thoughts of worry filled my mind. Had the listening knight known who I was? He had seen me as a child. Did he remember? Would he tell Robert de Baudricourt?

Would Robert de Baudricourt tell Father? They had met on one occasion, maybe more. What if they should meet again? And what of Uncle? Had he been known to someone there? Durand Laxart, with cousin Joan. Surely that would point to me!

Father must not know! I thought. It would cause him too much pain. And then, I must return! Surely he would try to stop me! Father must not know!

I watched his face those days, when talk of the rumor was heard. He was uneasy over the whole matter, this I could tell, yet he spoke of it not. Surely he worried it was I, and yet he did not ask. Perhaps he did not truly want to know.

Father's worry on this matter may well have caused what was to come. It happened thus.

Some weeks after my return, Father asked me to sit with him and Mother in quiet, apart from Pierre and Jean. There was a matter of importance to discuss. I wondered what it could be, as matters of importance were most always discussed as a family. But this was different.

We three sat of an evening by the hearth. Outside there was a gentle rain. I sat upon the stool, Good Kitten at my feet. Mother sat by her wheel, but busied herself not with the spinning. Father stood at the window. They both had a serious way about them, but with that an excitement and a sense of joy. There were tears in Mother's eyes.

Of what must we speak? I wondered.

My mind gave no answer.

For a time there was quiet. I looked to Father, and next

to Mother, but nothing did they say. I waited. Before me was the wooden beam to the side of the fireplace where Mother kept the candlestick in the flat holder. The wax was dripping down.

"Joan," said Father, by the window, still. His hands were deep inside his belt. "Henri has told us of your vow to give yourself to him in marriage. With this we are well pleased."

It was as all blood stopped within my body. I could not move. I could not speak. I could not see. All was dim before my eyes.

Mother spoke as from a far-off place. "Henri's mother is so pleased," she said. "She loves you well. For this she has always hoped."

I felt a lightness in my head. My hands were cold.

Father spoke again. "To think the time has come for marriage."

And Mother then, "Our baby."

"Yet it is well." Father's voice was deep and firm, yet distant to my ear. "The time is right," he said, "just right. We are well pleased."

Mother's voice came stronger then. "He is a good young man. He will be a worthy husband."

"No!" It was my voice, my own voice, surprising to my ear. And loud! "No!" I cried. "It cannot be!"

"What?" asked Father.

The dimness in the room had gone. I was standing by my stool. "It cannot be! I cannot marry!"

"But why?" asked Father.

And Mother, too. "But why?"

"I cannot! I never said I would! Why would he tell you that?"

"He assured me this was true," said Father. "You gave your promise as a child. This is what he said."

"I never promised!"

"Joan, baby." It was Mother now who spoke, the tears falling down her face. "We thought you would be pleased."

"I am not! I cannot marry him! I never said I would! You must believe me!" I was crying then as well, my life in pieces all about. I could marry no one! Not then! It was not possible! And Henri! It seemed a dreadful dream, more horrible than could be real. "You must believe me!" I cried. "I never told him so!"

Father came to me then. He wrapped me in his arms. I felt so small. I was shaking, sobbing, blinded by my tears. He held me tight to comfort me. "We believe you, Joan," he said.

All in me let go. I held him fast, not speaking. In time my crying ceased.

Later that night Mother made warm milk. She hugged me and stroked my hair back from my face. We rested then, sipping the milk and speaking of Henri. Mother and Father believed me well, that I had never promised. They said I always spoke the truth, that this they knew. They added still that Henri would make a fine husband. Mother felt he may have wrongly thought some kind words of mine had suggested a promise. Perhaps, she felt, his care for me had caused his mind to go too far on the point. For this I should not hate him.

I did not hate him, I told her. I merely did not wish him for my husband.

Father thought I would do well to marry. It was time for marriage. Henri was a fine young man. Our mothers were true friends. I would be well cared for.

I made a silent prayer.

Help me, God, I prayed.

All was quiet then. I held my milk strong between my hands, the steam still rising from my cup.

Help me, God.

I looked to Father, deep within his eyes. "I love you, Father," I said.

"I love you, Joan."

"Do not force me. I beg you. I cannot do this."

"As you will," he said.

The days passed. Henri spoke to me not, which was a welcome change. I sent him a blessing from my heart, a blessing of forgiveness for his lie. I asked that God grant him peace. But at a distance! I prayed it would be so.

News of the fighting continued. Fires could be seen nightly now, mostly to the south and to the east as villages were burned to the ground. A terror was rising.

My Saints said little. I saw them not at this time. I asked often when I would return to Vaucouleurs, when I would receive the men-at-arms. The answer was always the same.

Not yet.

Why? I would ask. There is so much suffering of good people. Why must I wait?

Have faith.

This was their answer.

On the day before the feast of John the Baptist there was a special afternoon, with bright strong sun and clear blue sky. I was returning from the fields where I had been watching the sheep. Pierre and Jean had been needed elsewhere. When I reached the west field, not far from the Meuse, beside a spreading oak, who should be going there but Michel! My heart stopped for sure.

"Hello," he said, his eyes as blue as the sky.

"Hello."

"Was your time well in Burey?"

I told him it was.

"Would you sit a moment here?"

My heart thundered in my chest. "Yes," I said. And so we sat beneath the tree. I felt sure it was a dream.

"Were you working in the field?" he asked.

"Yes," I said. "And you?"

"I am going to check on a calf. She seems not strong. I thought to bring her near the house."

"That would be well."

"I think it would." He leaned his back against the tree.

What shall I say now? I thought. Can he hear my pounding heart?

"The sky is blue today," I said. As if he did not know!

"It is," he said. He looked up through the leaves of the oak, then turned his head to gaze across the fields. "What a beautiful valley," he said.

"Oh, yes."

"I pray it will be safe."

"And I as well."

There was a stiffness to my back. I thought to lean against the tree as he did, yet I felt this might cause my arm to touch him. I remained still.

"Have you heard tell of the maid?" His question brought a flush of life.

"The maid?" I asked.

"They say a maid has sworn to rule in France. They say she went to Vaucouleurs, at God's command, to take over the kingdom."

"I have heard that too."

"I pray it may be so," he said. "Perhaps she will bring peace."

I longed to tell him then, as I had never longed to before. But I could not. It was not mine to tell. It was God's thought. It was His command, my work to do, to carry in my heart.

May I tell him something? I asked my Saints silently as we sat beneath the oak. May I tell him some small thing?

It is not needed.

Surely this is true. But he is wise. He is good. He will not betray me.

He will not.

May I tell him anything at all?

Yes, but not of you.

I looked at Michel, so loving, so strong. I looked straight into the blueness of his eyes. He returned my gaze, and smiled.

"I know not if what they say is true," I said, "but I tell you one thing. Between Coussey and Vaucouleurs is a girl who, in less than a year from now, will cause the Dauphin to be anointed King of France."

"How do you know?" he asked.

"I feel it in my heart."

"I believe you," he said, "and it is good to hear." He smiled again, a warm and loving smile, and then he rose. "I must go now to the calf."

As summer reached its middle part, there came the awful news. Vaucouleurs had indeed been threatened. The governor of Champagne, whose name was Antoine de Vergy, had set out with many hundred men-at-arms, all Burgundians, to capture Vaucouleurs. They were marching now, burning every village in their path. Domrémy was in that path.

Father held a village meeting, a two-village meeting in truth. The people of Domrémy and Greux gathered to make plans. It was decided that the Island Castle would not be safe. All would have to seek refuge in the fortified town of Neufchâteau.

At home that night we made our family plans. We would leave the following day. We would stay with the widow of Jean Waldaires, who ran an inn. I had not seen her, but Jean said she had red hair. Catherine and Colin would stay with us. We would take the herds. Sibelle would go with us as well. When I asked about the cats Father was stern. "You may bring Good Kitten, God help us, but the barn cats must stay. We cannot have them underfoot, nor can they be carried."

Father sensed my sadness at leaving them behind. "They are smart," he added. "They will hide in the woods."

35

Neufchâteau

It was a full morning's walk to Neufchâteau. Before we left I gathered Good Kitten in my arms, then went to say good-bye to Turnip and to the other barn cats. This was not an easy thing to do. "Be safe," I told them. "I pray to see you soon."

They seemed not to understand. This troubled me. I placed them in God's care and left quickly, as the others were waiting for me in the road.

"Hurry, Joan," said Father, when he saw me approach.

"Run, Short Legs," called Jean.

Other families from the village were leaving then as well. Hauviette was in the road with her family, as Simon was with his. Catherine and Colin would join us later. Possessions were piled in the carts as we set out, the herds before us, Sibelle, The Gray, the pony, too. We were as one, as we began our journey, leaving our beloved village behind.

Simon carried Nicholas, who was wrapped in a cloth. Only the goose's neck and head could be seen, with his serious, staring eyes. Simon said he had tried to carry his pet on a long walk the night before, but it had not gone well. Nicholas had struggled and flapped and soon had broken free, squawking and running in many directions. That was when Simon had decided on the cloth. He would wrap the goose securely, though not so tight as to bind. He would give him just the knowing that he must be still. The goose looked troubled as we walked, and a bit angry as well. It was sad to see, yet better than his getting lost. This was Simon's thought on the matter, and I agreed.

We passed the Bois Chenu on the hill to the right. Across the valley is a high hill with fields going up to near the top. A small way down the side the hill is covered with woods like a hat. On we walked, without a stop. Good Kitten stayed quietly in my arms. No sound, no struggle. This I had not expected, but for it I was most grateful. Perhaps she sensed the strongness of my need to carry her.

On the valley side, we saw a small, dark, and twisted tree with many branches. It had given up its life, but still served many birds as a resting place.

"I have my mouse," called Aimée, running to keep apace. She carried a small wooden cage made of sticks. Inside was her trembling mouse.

"I see," I answered. "That is well."

"He is in this box of sticks."

"I made it," said Simon.

"Simon made it," said Aimée, as if he had not spoken. "It has no flat sides, so he can breathe and never die."

"He will die someday," said Simon, his arms about his precious goose.

"Not soon," said Aimée. She had to shout to be heard above the noise of the herds and the wagons.

"It could be soon," said Simon.

"Not from no air, in a shut-tight box," said Aimée.

"That is true," said Simon.

"That is true," echoed Aimée.

On we went, across the fields, past the Island Castle on the right. In distant places, one could see the smoke. This was from the villages being burned. It was a fearsome sight.

Aimée was tired now, complaining bitterly and trailing behind. Her mother picked her up. Resting the weight of her child's body on her hip, she carried her. A group of cows were grazing by the Meuse, winding on the right. We passed them, moving steadily on. After some long time there came on the left a high rock ledge, which soon gets small, then disappears as you go up the hill. Up we went, then down, to enter Neufchâteau.

We stayed in Neufchâteau for many days. It was a hilly place, not flat as Domrémy. There were many more people, and many more houses as well. Mostly the houses had wooden doors, with big stone squares set around. The church was very large.

Time passed slowly, as news of the Burgundians' bloody march continued to be heard. They were proceeding, it was said, moving toward Vaucouleurs, burning all the villages, killing all the peasants and the livestock as well. It was a sorry time.

The inn in which we stayed was quite a crowded place. Many sought refuge there, merchants, pilgrims, monks, and soldiers, all manner of people. There was much to do to care for them. When I was not looking after the herds, I helped as best I could. The widow who ran the inn was kind. We called her La Rousse. She had the reddest hair I had ever seen. Our family shared a tiny room. Many nights I slept with Good Kitten in my arms. This would keep her quiet and secure.

One day was as the next, waiting, always waiting. Tending the herds, helping La Rousse, attending the church, waiting. Hauviette and I were together in many chores. Maurice was on the other side of town, which pleased her not. She feared he would forget her. I tried to comfort her in this, but I could not. Some time I spent alone. I went three times to the church of the Gray Friars Monastery. There I learned much of Saint Francis, who I loved. He had a special way with all God's creatures.

Mother and I went often to the big church. It had a tall ceiling, with grand arches. One time a bird flew in during Mass, soaring high among the arches. It flew about, chirping loudly, then stopped, resting on a top ledge to listen. That same day when we left the church, we saw two fires in the distance. More villages gone.

Each day I asked my Saints when I would return to Vaucouleurs. The answer was always the same.

Wait.

And so I waited.

After several days there came a bad surprise. I was in the dining room of the inn, helping to serve the food. Father was seated near the door, Pierre and Jean as well. There was a loud noise. I knew not what it was. Something had fallen, or been dropped. An official entered the room. He was tall, with dark hair and large, noisy boots. He stopped inside the door. "I have a summons here," he said in a loud voice, to no one in particular.

"Greetings," said Father. "And who is it for?"

"Joan of Domrémy."

My heart ceased to beat.

"Joan of Domrémy?" asked Father. His voice held worry.

"The same," said the official. He pulled a paper from his coat and read. "Joan of Domrémy. Daughter of Jacques d'Arc."

And so it happened. I was handed a summons to appear before the Bishop of Toul!

When the official left, Father read the summons. Henri, it seemed, had not taken no for the answer. He had persisted, bringing the matter to the ecclesiastic tribunal in Toul. This tribunal pronounced judgments on questions of marriage, Father explained. I had given my promise, Henri had insisted. I must be forced to marry him! I was summoned to appear in two days!

Once more it seemed a dream. It could not be! I could not marry! Not then! Not Henri! I had thought the matter to be settled. It sadly was not so.

Father urged again that I should marry. Pierre and Jean agreed.

"I cannot!" I told them. "Surely, they cannot force me!"

But this was wrong. The courts were firm in these matters, Father explained. If they ruled that I had promised, I would be forced to wed.

I felt a fury then, a fire. "No!" I cried.

"Joan," said Father, "please! Let us consider well."

"I must have time!"

"Two days. There is not much."

"May I have leave to go?"

"As you would wish."

I left the room, on fire still.

I must find Henri! I thought. I must set him straight!

He was staying in a nearby house. I found him in the yard. He was idle there, no task at hand.

"How dare you?" I said as I approached.

He did not rise. "You promised," he said.

"I did not!"

"I heard it so."

"You heard it wrong!"

"I heard it so. And now you change your mind."

"I promised nothing!"

He smiled, a half and twisted smile. "I like you and you like me. Does that not sound familiar?"

"You said that, not I!"

"You said you liked me."

"That is not a promise of marriage!"

He rose and moved toward me. "Joan," he said. "Joan, Joan, Joan."

His tone I cared not for.

"You will like marriage," he went on.

"Not to you!"

"Think on it. Let go your fear."

"I have no fear!"

"You will come to agree."

"Not so!"

"I think you will. Consider this. I like the idea, my mother likes it, your mother likes it, your father likes it . . ."

"I like it not!"

"Let us be calm."

". . . And I will tell you this! I will not be your wife!"

"You gave your vow!"

"You lie!"

He smiled again, a stupid smile. "We will let the court decide."

I went apart then to seek the help of my beloved Saints. There was a quiet place behind the church. This is where I went.

Beloved Saints! I prayed, my back against the building wall. Saint Michael! Saint Catherine! Saint Margaret! Help me! What am I to do?

Fear not.

It was Saint Michael's voice. And then the blazing light, the heavenly scent, and he was there!

Must I go to Toul?

You must.

Will they force me to marry Henri?

They will not.

How is it possible?

You will speak the truth and they will listen.

Mother and Father did not want me to go. They felt it was not safe. This I understood, yet Saint Michael had told me to go.

It must be well, I thought.

Father was firm. It was a full day's walk to Toul. A day on the road with men-at-arms at every turn, villages being burned, peasants being murdered. It was not safe.

"All this I know," I said, "but take no account of it."

"I must," he said, "and so must you."

"Let me go," I said. "I beg you! There is no other way!"

We talked for some long time. We were out behind the inn, Mother, Father, and I, near the wall, sitting in the grass.

Mother does not often sit on the grass, I remember thinking, only at picnics.

I wished it were a picnic then.

"If you were to go, you could not go alone," Father said at last. "Jean must go with you."

"That would be well."

"This troubles me," said Mother. Her face was filled with worry. I wished to climb upon her lap, to tell her all, but I could not. It would not have been a comfort.

"I must go," I said.

"I like it not," said Mother.

"Nor I," I said, "yet still I must. This marriage is not in my heart. I never promised! All my life would be untrue! I must be let to go!"

"You have no one to speak for you," said Father.

"I can speak for myself."

"It is too much."

"No one knows the truth of it better than I," I told him. "I should be the one to speak."

We sat in silence for some time. Mother looked at the grass. Then Father breathed in deep. "You may go," he said.

And so it was agreed.

The next day Jean and I set out for Toul. Mother packed the bread for us, but I could not eat. I could think only of the trial. I had no mind for food.

Hour after hour we walked, with barely a rest. The sun was hot. My mouth was parched, my lips were dry. To the east we saw the fires, but met no men-at-arms. I said a silent prayer of thanks to God for this.

Jean was quiet as we walked. He teased me not, which was a pleasant change. His presence was a comfort. He was so steady and so brave. I felt such love for him that day. My heart was filled with gratitude.

"Thank you," I said as we passed along a stretch of road on a hill. The road went through the woods, which offered welcome shade. "Thank you for coming with me."

"I want you safe," he said.

We traveled on, down the wooded hill and past the fields. There were many deer here. It was nearly evening then. The sun's rays were slanting down as we moved through the small valley with the sloping wooded hills, and out to open country. There are no towns for some long time here. At last we moved down the big hill, into Blénod Les Toul, and through. After that the road is straight, the land more flat. Then one sees the gentle hills just before Toul. Here we spent the night.

36
Toul

When we entered the court I was at first questioned by a clerk. He was short, not many years older than I, and sat on a stool. He sat before a small table, upon which rested several papers. He held a pen. Jean was some way apart from me then and could not hear. I gave the clerk my summons.

"What is your name?" he asked.

"It tells you on the paper," I replied.

He looked at me not. "What is your name?" he repeated.

"You have it written there."

"What is your name?"

I thought to tell him, lest we remain at this all day. "Joan of Domrémy," I answered.

He made a note on the paper. "What is your village?" he asked.

"I told you already."

"What is your village?"

"Domrémy."

More writing on the paper. "Father's name?"

"It tells you on the paper."

"Father's name?"

"Jacques d'Arc."

"Mother's name?"

"Isabelle Romée."

"Who will speak for you?"

"I will speak for myself."

The clerk looked at me for the first time. There was a dullness in his eyes. "That is not a good idea," he said.

"Yet I am doing it still."

"It is not a good idea."

"I know the truth of it better than anyone."

"It is not a good idea."

"I was there! I know what happened!"

"You should not speak for yourself."

"Who better to speak than one who knows?"

He stared at me with much the solemn face. "You should not speak for yourself," he said once more.

"Whether I should or should not, I am doing it," I said, "so let us move on."

He made a marking on the paper then, and led me to the court.

It was a large room, though not as large as the room of Robert de Baudricourt. The bishop sat on a raised up place. To his left sat Henri, and before him an older man with gray-white hair and many papers. Three or four other men sat behind the bishop, and in some seats, a bit to the side, were those I took to be townspeople. Jean was among those seated. There was an empty stool before the bishop. Here I sat.

The clerk called the trial to begin. He asked Henri if he

swore to tell the truth. Henri answered yes. Then the clerk asked if I swore to tell the truth. I answered yes as well. After this the man with the gray-white hair and all the papers stood. He then began to speak. He told a story of how I had promised, as a small girl, to marry one he called "this man." He pointed to Henri, who smiled a vain and stupid smile.

The man with the gray-white hair continued. He had the story written on his papers, but kept looking up to show, it seemed, how much he knew. This did not work well, as each time he looked up, he knew not what to say. He would mumble then, looking back to the papers to search for his place. This took quite some time, as he mumbled and searched. Quite soon I lost full patience. "You would do well to read," I told him.

When I spoke thus he looked not pleased. He did, however, read from that time on, moving things along.

His story was filled with lies. Many times over he would twist some point, or change the meaning. After doing this he would look to Henri and ask, "Is that correct?" Henri would say it was, and so it went. It was no easy thing to bear.

At last it was my turn to speak.

"Do you swear to tell the truth?" asked the clerk.

"I have answered that already," I explained.

"Do you swear to tell the truth?"

"Once should be enough."

"Answer the question," said the clerk.

"I have answered quite plainly already," I told him. "It must be in your notes."

"You must answer the question," said the bishop, and so I rose and gave the oath once more.

"You will tell us what happened," said the bishop.

I looked squarely at the bishop. His eyes were narrowed, nearly shut, and swollen all about. It seemed he had not slept.

Speak boldly.

It was Saint Margaret then who spoke.

"I must deny here any vow of marriage," I began. I pointed to the man with the gray-white hair, who had spoken for Henri. "I have heard this man read from his book, yet I must tell you, my Lord has a book in which there is more than in all of yours."

The bishop seemed unsure of my meaning. He shifted in his chair.

"I have never promised to marry this young man, and therefore cannot let it be believed that I have."

"That is untrue," said Henri.

Speak boldly.

"You had your turn, now it is mine!"

"You gave a vow!"

"Let her speak," said the bishop.

Henri was quiet then. I went on.

"This young man swears I gave a vow of marriage as a child. I swear before my Lord I never gave that vow. By God, and all the precious Saints, I never did! You say perhaps I did and have forgotten. I say this is not so. But what if it were true? What if I had promised as a child, a child too young to remember. How young a child was I? Had I reached the age of understanding? Could I know what marriage was? This young man does not say." I turned to Henri. "How old was I?" I asked.

"It matters not."

"How old when all this make-believe began?"

"It was not make-believe!"

"How old was I?"

"I do not remember," he answered, as if no one would care.

"Five years? Four years? Three years? Two?"

"I remember not."

"Your thinking is not sound!" I said. "And there is more!"

"What more?"

"You say I gave my pledge."

"You did."

"By what words?"

"What?"

"What words did I use?"

"I remember not." Again, his tone would say my question held no sense.

"What words?"

"I do not remember!"

"You do not remember much!"

"I do!"

"Only that I swore to marry you. *That* you remember well! The thing that never happened!"

The gray-and-white-haired man rose. "I wish to make a point," he said.

Speak boldly.

"It never happened!" I looked him squarely in the face. "I was there! In every meeting under God's great sky that ever took place between Henri and me, I was there! Where were you?"

The gray-and-white-haired man thought on that. It seemed he wished to speak, yet knew not what to say.

"You were not there! I was there! Henri was there! You were not!"

The man looked at his papers. I looked at Henri. "Henri, my friend, your thinking is not sound. You say, and wrongly so, that I, when but a child, agreed to marry you. You swear this to be true, yet you remember not the facts. How old was this child? What words did she speak? What words did you speak? You remember not! My dear friend, I remember! There was no vow! I know this, and God knows it! By all the Saints in heaven, you cannot change the truth!"

As Saint Michael had said, the bishop listened well. Without further delay, he dismissed the charge.

37

Question

When we returned to Domrémy, we found the worst had come. The town had been burnt to the ground. The fields were black, the shrubs and trees as well. The Grandfather Tree, the Troll Tree, the Piney Bush Trees, my tender friends, all burned! The vision tore my heart.

This was not all. Our church had been destroyed. Our precious church, in ruins all about!

Our house still stood, as others did, yet inside great damage had been done. Our table, bench, and stools were burned, the beds as well. The bowls and jars were smashed. The walls were black. Ashes and cinders greeted us where all had been so sweet. The air was old with smoke.

We all were silent when we came upon the sight. Not one of us could speak. We stood by the door, not moving, not able to think. After some time Father moved inside. Slowly, he set about to clean the mess. We followed after.

With all the sadness, there was good news too. The barn cats were safe! Each and every one! There was no longer a barn, but the cats had survived! They must have gone to the woods, just as Father had said, for in moments they were at the door, Turnip and all the rest, tails high, crying and asking for food. Good Kitten ran to greet them. I was not far behind.

The whole of the village worked to set things right. There was occasion for all to help each other, and this we did. There was little food, as the gardens had been destroyed. What had been put up and stored was shared, though much of this was gone as well.

As we worked to rebuild our precious church we went to Mass in Greux. The church was larger than our church, though not as large as the church in Neufchâteau. Always when I entered, the square blocks of the stone floor felt cool to my feet. At the ringing of the bells the sound was heavy when heard inside the church. It came from one could not tell where.

One Mass brought a special joy to my heart. It started sweetly, as a bird flew out as I walked in. Later I sat, Mother to one side, Catherine to the other, and listened as was spoken this. "Hold fast. Saint Michael leads the faithful angels to victory over the dragon! Saint Michael brings victory in fighting against the darkness! Saint Michael brings help!" My heart was filled with joy, as this I knew full well!

Time passed, the village gripped in fear. There was danger still of further raids. We were not allowed to go into the country beyond the refuge of fortified places. These rules lasted many months.

Vaucouleurs had conditionally surrendered. When I asked Father what that meant, he told me this. There was a custom in which the leader of the garrison would say he had enough supplies to hold out to a certain date. He would agree that if he were not relieved by that time he would surrender the town. The besiegers then would leave, sending off their men-at-arms for other work. They would return at the appointed time to take the town. Father said such agreements were never broken. He said that Vaucouleurs was holding out, he knew not how long. We could only wait and see. Time dragged on.

In early fall, there came the news. Father told us this one night at supper. He spoke with great concern. When I heard these words I felt my heart would leave my chest.

"Orléans is under siege," he said.

I dropped my bread.

"The English have taken the Tourelles."

"What are the Tourelles?" asked Mother.

"The towers at the edge of the city," said Pierre.

"On the bank of the Loire," added Jean. "With the Tourelles gone, we do not have a chance. The English will take the city."

"Is there no chance?" asked Mother.

"None," said Jean.

And Father spoke. "It all looks bleak."

"Cannot the seige be raised?" asked Pierre.

"No," said Jean.

Yes! I thought. Yes! It will be!

My heart was racing now.

Father went on to tell how with Orléans lost it would be the beginning of the end. He said we must be brave.

Orléans will not be lost! I thought. The siege will be

raised! The Dauphin will be crowned! The English will be driven out of France!

But this I could not tell.

Be still, I told myself. Stand firm.

I gripped my bowl and stared fast at my soup.

Time passed slowly. Our lives went on. Henri spoke but seldom then. He looked sad, which was not as I would have it, yet there was little I could do. I sent him a blessing from my heart.

Hauviette spoke daily of my triumph at the court. To marry Henri was a fate worse than death was her thought. Now I was saved! Saved for Michel!

I had much to say on the matter, but could of course not speak. Hauviette would carry right along. "If I were forced to marry Henri I would stab myself in the heart," she said one time.

I told her that was more than should be done.

Mengette would soon receive her husband. They would have a small house, not far from her old one. The boy was sweet, with large ears. That is how Hauviette would speak of him. "He is a sweet boy," she would say, "but his ears are large."

"It matters not," I would explain.

Time passed slowly. Orléans was under siege, and still no sign from my beloved Saints. When would they have me go? They told me not. They spoke to me, but just the simple things.

Wait. Have faith. God is with you.

These were all. I wanted so for them to tell me more.

When would I raise the siege? Why must I wait? What of the poor people suffering? These questions burned my mind, yet still they were not answered. My Saints knew best. And so I waited.

Some short time after, the answer came. It happened thus.

I was spinning with Mother at the window, Good Kitten by my chair. Outside, the autumn wind was strong. Uncle sat by the hearth. He had come to visit and bring news. It was good to see him. He spoke of winter coming, of the harvest, of the fighting in Maxey. He asked for Father, for Catherine, for Pierre and Jean. We spoke of each. He was quiet after that. He sat sipping wine, holding a piece of bread, which he dipped into the cup. At last he spoke. His joy was full. He used a quiet tone. "My wife is with child," he said.

I knew in an instant. That would be the time. I would go to care for Jeanne in her confinement. This was often done. Women needed help at that time. They felt not strong, yet had the daily chores and now the child as well. I would go. I would help. I would go to Vaucouleurs. I would not return.

Before Uncle left that day, we spoke in the yard. Mother was inside, packing up some food.

"You must help me, Uncle," I said. "You must help me once more."

"And how is that?" he asked. There was a worry to his face, but even so, a look that said he would do all.

"I must go back to Vaucouleurs! I must speak to Robert de Baudricourt! The siege is on! I must receive the men-at-arms!"

Uncle spoke not. He looked to the ground.

"Ask Father! Please! Ask him if I may go and care for Jeanne in her confinement! From there we will go to Vaucouleurs! You must take me! I must be with the Dauphin, even though to get there I have to wear my legs down to the knees!"

Uncle was quiet for a time. We stood near the burned and blackened birch, my heart pleading, and Uncle looking at the ground. The silence seemed forever. At last he spoke. "You will go no matter what," he said. "It would be best for me to take you."

Winter brought its chill. The woods grew brown. On the last mild day before the frost I sat with Hauviette to watch the flocks. Pierre and Jean were tending to the chimney, so I was needed in the fields. I started out alone, but soon Hauviette had joined me. We carried our distaffs.

It was a precious time. This was, I think, as I knew there would not be many more. I had told my Saints of my thoughts, that I would go to Burey to help with the baby, that I would go from there to Vaucouleurs, that I would have the men-at-arms. They told me yes. I asked if it was true that I would not return.

Have no fear, they answered. God is with you.

With this I understood. There were few times left to watch the gentle Meuse, to feel the breeze, to tend the sheep, to see the cows, to hear the latest on Maurice. All this was soon to end.

The sheep were near to us that day. Always they are somewhat near, but that day they kept uncommon close. I know not why.

I listened to their eating sounds. They ate quickly. I could hear the tearing of the grass and the deep rumbling, swallowing sounds. The cows ate more slowly. They were at the long grass. When on a short sward they eat more quickly, to keep their feeding size the same.

"Maurice hurt his foot," said Hauviette, working her distaff as she spoke. "It was a twist or sprain."

"What caused it?" I asked.

"I know not," said Hauviette. "Simon told me of it. I hope he told me true."

"Why wish him to be hurt?" I asked. I did not understand.

"Because he disappeared," she said. "I know not what the cause."

"He rests his foot, I would suppose."

"I would suppose," she said, her worry strong.

"What then," I asked, "if not his foot?"

"I hope he does not hate me."

"Why would he hate you?"

"He may find me young, and short, and stupid."

"I think not."

"He may. He may find me ugly, too."

"You are not ugly."

"You are my friend."

"And so is he! You are not ugly, and you are not stupid."

"I am short."

"And so is he! You are both the proper size."

Hauviette set down her distaff. She took the friendship stone from out of her skirt and held it tightly in her hand. "I hope he thinks the same," she said.

"If not, he thinks not well."

Others joined us in the afternoon, Simon, Aimée, and Little Gérard. We sat together, speaking as we had in times past. More than ever, as the day wore on, I felt a long way off. I seemed to be a distance from my truest friends, a distance from their ways, from all they held so dear. Simon was reading now. Aimée wanted to read, but Simon felt she was too young and but a girl. Little Gérard cared not to read. He wanted a cart that he could pull. If he had a cart, he could put things in it and carry them to Greux. Aimée asked if he would carry her to Greux. Little Gérard felt that she should walk. The cart would be too full of other things.

"What things?" asked Aimée.

"Important things," said Little Gérard.

I wondered what they were.

Nicholas floated on the water. His head was turned back, resting on his feathers. He seemed to sleep.

Soon I will be gone, I thought.

I watched the goose. All at once he woke. He rubbed his beak and the side of his head along his feathers, as if to scratch an itch, then burrowed his beak within his feathers, pushing many times down deep. After that he moved to the shallow part and stood, still as a statue, staring at the hills.

Soon I will be gone.

That night Saint Michael came. He woke me, the whisper in my ear.

Joan.

I woke to see him, ablaze with the light of countless suns.

Beloved Saint!

Joan.

I sat up, my feet on the earthen floor. My hands clasped, I bowed in prayer.

Sweet light.

I felt then his hand upon my head, gentle as air, warm as fire, lifting the truest part of me from deep within my heart. His light poured forth, filling me with strength. Then miracle of miracles, he took my hand. It was as grasping a gentle web of light.

Come with me.

I rose then.

We left the room and walked together in the garden.

Beloved Saint!

Tell me of yourself.

I feel this life is leaving me. I am not here, yet I am nowhere else.

You are.

I feel my friends not near. Their worries are not mine. Their joys escape my thoughts.

What worries are yours?

The question struck a deep place. Words came then I knew not I would speak.

Why did Saint Margaret suffer in the fire?

The worry had been locked within my mind. His touch had pulled it out. We were walking still, his hand was still in mine.

Daughter of God.

Yes.

In a journey through a doorway, to a place of great illumination, great splendor, of true, infinite brilliance, in such a journey, the passageway is often fire. Yet certain souls do not experience what others would expect.

And what is that?

Fire into fire does not burn.

She spoke the same to me.

Yes.

What did she mean?

She already was the fire.

There was no pain?

One speaks of the suffering of Saints.

Yes.

The suffering of mortals is far greater. The loneliness, the wars, the fear of death, which does not exist, the sickness, the confusion, all the hurt of daily life, this is the true fire. This blessed one of whom you speak, this blessed Saint, was selfless in her work. She lifted souls to heights of inspiration.

This I know.

One must see how bends the sword of the enemy, to smile when the thundering of the enemy's steed is heard, to go forth when the arrow flies so near. No one must be allowed to steal away our peace. Stand firm, and shine the light of God's love on all. This is your joy, and theirs as well. Do this and you cannot be put down. Help always comes when you are at the abyss. Sometimes before, but always then. If you have faith in this, you will be well.

He said no more that night. His words stayed in my heart.

38
Wooly Lamb

On the coldest night of winter Wooly Lamb was born. He was the smallest lamb that Father had ever helped bring forth. The mother was not well. Father spoke to me of this the morning after the lamb was born. We were having our morning meal by the fire. Pierre and Jean were not fully awake. Their night had been long. Father was full of life, as was most usual to see. He needed little sleep.

"Joan," he said, "you must visit the lamb. The smallest we have seen was born last night. We spoke of you then, of how you would love it."

"Where is it?" I asked.

"And there is the end of her porridge!" said Jean. "The lamb must now be seen."

Once more he knew my thoughts. A bowl of porridge was fine, but nothing when next to a newborn lamb.

"The lamb is in the pen," said Father, "but finish your porridge first."

After our meal Pierre went with me to find the lamb. At first I did not see him. Three ewes were there, two with two lambs each, and one, it seemed, with none. A closer look proved this wrong. Between the ewe and the fence was hidden the sweetest and tiniest lamb I had ever seen. Pulling itself from where it seemed nearly to be caught, it rose to meet me. Its face so black, its legs like sticks, it made its way. I picked it up and held it close.

"The mother may not live," said Pierre. "She has been ill. She almost did not bring forth."

This was terrible to hear. I felt a sadness for the suffering of the ewe and also much worry for the lamb. Without its mother a lamb will rarely live.

Pierre watched as I cradled the lamb in my arms. It felt warm despite the coldness of the air.

"You cannot bring it inside," said Pierre. "We went through that before."

I told him I remembered.

The next day the ewe died. I felt such a sadness, such a worry at the news. I was spinning when I heard. Jean had come to tell me.

"May I go?" I asked Mother.

"Yes," she said.

I left my work and hurried to the pens. The ewe was gone. In the corner of the pen, where the fence met the wall, was the lamb, shivering and frightened. I climbed into the pen and picked it up.

"Do not worry," I told the lamb. "I will care for you."

"How will you do that?" said Pierre. "He needs to nurse. No other ewe will take him."

I stroked the lamb's gentle head. He looked at me with eyes so true. His ears were flopping down. "I will find a way."

Father was busy with Jean. They were moving the dung from the side of the pens, spreading it in the fields. Holding fast to the lamb, I went to find them. Pierre followed.

"I must save this lamb," I said to Father, when we met them in the road with the cart.

"The mother is gone," said Father.

"There must be a way!"

"I knew this would happen," said Jean. "I knew it the night he was born."

"Without the mother the lamb will not live," said Father.

"He must!" I said.

"I know not how."

"Have you never kept a lamb alive?"

"Not without the mother."

"Never?"

Father thought a moment. "No," he said. His breath was steam from the cold.

"Not ever?" I asked.

"I have not found a way."

The lamb shifted in my arms, his look so trusting, so grateful.

"Someone must have done it," I said. "Someone, somewhere!"

Father set his spade in the cart.

"The lamb needs to drink," said Pierre. "No ewe will take it."

"Can it drink something else?" I asked.

"Like what?" asked Jean.

"Cow's milk? Goat's milk? Some other thing?"

"It needs its mother's milk," said Pierre.

"Let it be," said Jean.

Father was thinking, his hand upon his belt, his foot upon the cart. "Wait," he said. "Perhaps there is a way."

"I knew it!"

"It is only a chance."

"What is it?" asked Jean.

"It will work!" I said. "It must!"

Father pushed his hands deeper into his belt. "It had the mother's milk to start," he said.

"Yes," said Pierre.

"Then perhaps a mixture could be tried."

"Like what?" I asked.

"It must be thick," said Father. "It must be rich."

"Like what?"

"Egg yolk!" said Pierre.

"A start," said Father. "What else?"

"Oat flour?" I asked. "A paste?"

"Perhaps."

"And goat's milk," said Jean. "That would be closer to the sheep's than cow's."

"Goat's milk!" said Father. "Egg yolk, oat flour, and goat's milk!"

"Thank you!" I said. "Thank you all!"

Father warned me then. He had his stern and serious look. "The lamb must be fed as he would nurse," he said.

"I know."

"Many times throughout the morning, noon, and night."

"I will."

"You must not miss a time."

"Not Joan," said Pierre.

"A few drops only," said Father. "You must not overfeed."

"I will be careful."

"Good-bye to sleep," said Jean.

"I need not sleep!" I said. I carried the lamb off to find his food.

I named him Wooly Lamb. He liked his name and lifted his head when I called. After that, he would get up on his stick legs and hurry to meet me. Good Kitten was unsure of him at first. She would move to sniff him slowly, then touch him with her nose, and back away. At times she would watch him from behind the stool, her coat most full from fear. Sometimes she would run at him and land, then race away. Wooly Lamb would look at her with his black face, his ears coming down, waiting to be friends. In time this came about. Evenings they would lie together by the fire.

I made the food mixture and kept it in a jar outside the door. A short time only would pass between the times Wooly Lamb would be fed. I used a stick to dip in the mixture. With one hand I opened his gentle mouth. With the other I dipped the stick into the mixture, then let the few drops fall onto his waiting tongue. At first he did not understand. I feared he would never take the drink, but soon he learned. Often I would have to take the goat's milk and make a new mixture, as it should never spoil. Each night I stayed awake or slept for brief times only, ready to feed the mixture once more. If I slept too long, Good Kitten would wake me.

I found the perfect sleeping place for Wooly Lamb. I

kept him in a basket on the window ledge in my room. At first I thought to keep him in the bread basket, but Mother cared not for this idea. I changed my thought then to a different basket, one used for outdoor work. The basket fit nicely in the window, which opens wider at the inside than out. There was one trouble only, which was the height from the basket to the ground on the outside. I feared Wooly Lamb might break a leg, or worse, if he chose to climb down, and so I made a shield. Jean said this was stupid, yet I made it still. It was of crossed sticks, forced firmly in place, with space between for much fresh air, but not enough space for a lamb. This worked well. Wooly Lamb had the breeze from out of doors, so as not to be too warm or suffer dampness. I could sleep with my arm in the basket, my hand on his sweet, warm coat. As the days passed Wooly Lamb grew stronger. I kept him with me always. Father said he was not yet out of danger. This troubled my mind.

One day not long after Wooly Lamb was born, Mother and I were spinning. Wooly Lamb was in his basket. I had moved it to the hearth. There was a fire going. Good Kitten was by my feet. All was peaceful, save the strong wind without.

There came a knock at the door. My heart stopped. I rose and moved to the door. I opened it. There stood Uncle.

Oh, God.

"Joan," he said. "Isabelle! The child is here!"

I felt as I would freeze.

Now? I thought. Oh, now? Is it time? Oh, God! My mother. My father. My home. Hauviette. Good Kitten. Wooly Lamb! Now? Is it now?

"Joan," said Mother. "Find Father in the fields. Tell him good-bye."

Good-bye? Now? Pierre! Jean! Mengette! Michel!

Uncle came in. I stayed at the door. I could not move. Uncle and Mother were speaking, making plans. We would leave that afternoon. Uncle must return quickly. Jeanne could not be left alone. Mother would pack some food. We would take it back to Jeanne. How was her strength? Was the child well? A boy or a girl? A girl! How fine!

I felt as I would faint.

I fed Wooly Lamb his drops of milk and left the house.

Father! Where is Father? I thought, as I hurried through the yard. In the fields? What fields? I must look. I must say good-bye. Good-bye? Not good-bye! I cannot bear it!

I walked in such a troubled state across the road, then out into the fields. At the river was Mengette.

I must hold her. I must tell her of my love. And what of Hauviette? No! I cannot bear it!

"Joan," she called. She was gathering water then. She set down her bucket.

"Hello," I said.

"Where are you going?"

"To find Father in the fields. I am leaving for Burey."

"For Burey? Is it time?"

"It is."

"Your uncle has his child?"

"A girl."

"A girl! And when will you return?"

An arrow in my heart. "I know not for sure."

She reached out her arms. "Do well with the baby," she said.

"I pray."

We hugged.

"I will miss you," she said.

"I will miss you too."

We parted.

"Hurry back!"

I watched as she picked up the bucket and carried it to the house. Tears were coming then so it was hard to see.

I could not find Father in the fields. I walked and walked, searching as I went. Tears were coming still.

Father!

I stopped beneath a willow tree to think.

Oh, God. Father!

Daughter of God.

My precious Saints!

It was Saint Margaret and Saint Catherine both who spoke.

Must I leave now?

It is time.

Where is my Father?

You will find him. You will say good-bye.

And what of Wooly Lamb?

Mother will care for him.

And Good Kitten?

She will manage well.

I am not ready.

As you will.

As *you* will!

Daughter of God. Sweet light.

Stay with me!

We are here.

A calmness settled then. I moved from the tree and started off for home. I would wait for Father there.

When I reached the road, a man was coming toward me. It was Gérardin d'Epinal, the only Burgundian I knew. He was carrying a dung fork and a shovel.

Let him not speak, I thought.

I cared to see him not.

"Hello, Joan," he said.

"Coming from the fields?"

"I am."

He stopped in my path. "More battles," he said. "For days now. More villages burned."

"I know," I said. "I must be on my way."

"Orléans is soon to fall."

"So I have heard."

"The end is soon to come."

"Good-bye," I said, and started off.

"Why do we not surrender?"

I stopped and turned to face him. "My good friend," I said, "if you were not a Burgundian, there is some thing I should tell you!"

"What is that?"

"You must only wait and see."

When I returned home Father was there. He had left the fields early for a meeting in Greux. He sat with Uncle by the hearth as Mother prepared the food. Pierre and Jean were there as well.

"Mother fed your lamb," said Jean.

"Thank you, Mother," I said.

"He was hungry," said Mother. "I will feed him when you go."

"But that means little sleep."

"He is yours, Joan. I must care for him."

I felt so grateful in my heart. I hugged her then. "Thank you," I said.

"I love you, my baby."

"I love you."

All moved steady then. I went to my room and put on the red dress. It was the same patched one I had worn to Vaucouleurs before. Now it had more patches.

After putting on the dress, I came out near the hearth. Wooly Lamb was in the basket. I knelt to say good bye. "Mother will feed you," I told him. "Eat well, and grow strong."

He looked at me, his eyes so sweet, so thankful.

"Good-bye," I said.

He rubbed his head against my arm.

I rose then. Good Kitten was under the table. I bent to pick her up. "Be good," I said, holding her fast. She made her happy, rumbling sound, then gave a single cry. I buried my face in her fur. "You are always in my heart."

She cried once more. I set her down. She stretched then, and wandered off. She stopped by the fire to wash.

Mother put on my cloak. "Keep warm," she said. Then she gave me the food. "Give this to Jeanne."

"I will," I answered.

"Good-bye, my sweet."

We hugged once more.

"Good-bye."

"Good-bye," said Jean. "Care well for the baby."

"I will."

"Good-bye," said Pierre.

"Good-bye."

Father walked us to the door. "Take care of her," he said to Uncle.

Uncle said he would.

I held on tight to Father. "I love you," I said.

"My own," he said. "Be well."

And we were gone.

Down the road we walked, Uncle and I, just quietly, not speaking, past the half-built church, past Simon's house, past Hauviette's house beyond. Hauviette was not in the yard.

Epilogue

All came to pass as my precious Saints had foretold. Twice Robert de Baudricourt refused me, but the third time he gave the permission. I stayed in Vaucouleurs some many weeks until this came about. I then received the men-at-arms. They took me to the Dauphin. The siege of Orléans was raised and the Dauphin was crowned at Reims. I did not live to see the English driven out of France, but I am sure they were, as Saint Michael told me they would be.

My precious Saints stayed with me always, guiding and protecting me as they had promised. As was foretold, Pierre and Jean, my loving brothers, fought at my side. And there were others, too. Brother Pasquerel, Jean d'Aulon, my dear Dunois, the Duke of Alençon, Jean de Metz, and many more. All were true and good. Bertrand de Poulengy was near as well, helping always, just as my Saints had said. I thank these loyal ones from deep within my heart.

I wrote my dear mother and father before leaving Vaucouleurs. As I could not form the letters, I had it written out. I told them where I was, and what I had to do. This they came to understand, as was foretold. When the Dauphin was crowned at Reims, with me at his side, my blessed parents were there.

In all I followed my beloved Saints. They told me I had little more than a year to carry out my mission, and this was so. They told me where to find my sword, and it was found, buried at the church. They told me to wear boy clothes. They told me to carry my standard. Do not strike out, they said. Raise your sword above your head. Never point it at anyone. Never threaten with it. This I carried out.

After the siege was raised, many seemed to think I had a special way. When I would go about they pushed upon me. They asked me to bless their children. I had no special way. All is God. He is in all. This I told them.

Many battles were fought and most were won. When a bold voice was needed, so I spoke. I warned the English to withdraw, but never did they listen. It was hard to watch the killing in so close a way, yet always, since I had been born, I had known war. It now must end!

At Melun the town was taken from the Burgundians. After the battle I was upon the moat. It was Easter week.

Daughter of God.

Saint Margaret and Saint Catherine spoke the words. Be not afraid. Before Saint John's Day you will be captured. It must be. Take all in good part. God will help you.

The news brought fear to my heart. Saint John's Day was but two months hence. I was not afraid to die, as God would take me when He willed, yet I feared a long captivity.

Let it be brief, I asked.

This they could not promise.

From the day it was revealed to me that I would be captured, I left the military matters, as much as possible, to the captains of war. Their ways were fearful and were out of time, yet this would have to be. All was somehow needed. I did not tell them, however, that I had revelation that I should be taken. In this I was instructed.

In May it happened. We were fighting at Compiègne. The English who were there cut the road behind me and my men. I was caught in the fields on the Picardy side, near the boulevard. I was pulled from my horse. It was a Burgundian who did it. He demanded I submit.

"I have already made my submission, and plighted my faith," I told him, "and to Him I will keep my word."

The Burgundians took me prisoner. They put me in the tower. That was when I jumped to go and help all the poor people still suffering in France, but I hurt my ankle and could not walk.

After this they sold me to the English. They would put me on trial. They wanted to prove that I was of the devil. My Voices told me this was why. They needed to prove that our king had been ruled by sorcery, that his crowning was not true, that his claim to the French throne was not of the law. This would give the English back the power. They needed to prove my Saints were demons, but this they could not do.

They tormented me with questions, the same questions over and over, stupid questions, that seemed to have no end. The one in charge was called Cauchon. He was a bishop yet, it seemed, had lost the sense of God. His mind would push things only to his way, forgetting it was God's way that mattered. Many times I warned him, as I was told he was in danger.

"Consider well what you do," I told him, "for in truth I am sent by God, and you put yourself in great peril." He did not heed my words.

More questions then, and more, for months. I answered boldly, as my blessed Saints instructed. Always they were with me, their voices clear. Sometimes I would see them in the court. When first I entered they were there, all love, all power, pure knowing, filling the room with light. They stood behind Cauchon, who bid me speak the truth. This seemed the thing to do. I always spoke the truth. Yet I was stopped. Saint Michael raised his hand to halt my speech.

Swear not.

I needed not to think.

"I do not know on what you will question me," came my words. "It may be that you will ask me a thing that I shall not tell you."

The bishop liked this not, yet more he would not get from me!

The questions came. They would not let me rest, and kept pestering me about the clothes. My boy clothes were needed, as my blessed Saints had warned. I was a girl, living among men, with all their rough and soldier ways. I must dress as a boy as protection from their roughness. I must not lead them to behave in ways they later would regret. When I was in prison I needed the clothes most especially. They should have kept me in a church prison, where I would have been guarded by women, but this they did not do. They kept me in a lay prison, with men guards who sometimes bothered me. I must wear the boy clothes as these offered some protection. My Saints were firm on the matter.

My great tiredness would sometimes cause me to feel a sadness at my capture. This I understand, yet it was not fitting. So many in France were suffering things far worse than I. I was tired. I must stay in a cell. I was annoyed by guards. I had to answer questions. Yet others suffered tortures, death from plague, their homes destroyed, their loved ones killed before their eyes, and all these things without the Saints to comfort them. Oh, this they had, but many did not know. They suffered all alone, or so they thought. I had not cause to grieve. In my cell would be the blessed time to pray. Here all questions ceased. My Saints were with me as the moments passed. I was deep within their knowing. In this I had my rest.

At the end they took me to a burying place. It was outside the castle walls, behind the church of Saint Ouen. There were two raised-up places here of wood. They made me stand on one. The sun was hot. I had not slept and felt not well. They said my Voices were not true. They said I was a witch. They said I despised God. They told me what I feared the most. If I were not to say these things were so, they would put me in the fire! I felt such fear. It was the worst I ever knew.

Not the fire!

The bishop said I must put my mark to a paper or I would burn. My fear was great and so I put my mark.

After that they took me to my cell. They took away my

boy clothes. I was to be in prison all my life. This they told me. Then they threw me on the floor. I cared not to live. It was my lowest time. I wished only to sleep, yet this I could not do. My heart was pounding. In the pounding came this sense. I was wrong to sign the paper. I had betrayed my Saints.

No!

A wildness filled me then, a force so great. It was of fire.

No!

Tears came full as never they would end.

I have betrayed my Saints!

Daughter of God.

The purple light.

Beloved.

The smell of roses.

Joan.

And they were there! Saint Margaret! Saint Catherine! Their arms outstretched, pouring out their love.

My Saints!

Crawling to the place where they did stand, I clung to them about the knees. They spoke as one.

Sweet light.

I have betrayed you!

You could never betray us.

I put my mark upon the page!

You did not understand.

The paper was not true!

You are pure goodness.

I have betrayed you!

Never, Joan. You could not.

It was Saint Catherine now who spoke.

You did injury to yourself. You said you had not done well in what you did. This is false. You have never done anything against God, whatever you may have been made to revoke. You are goodness, Joan, sweet light. You damned yourself to save your life.

I cannot face the fire!

It is not required of you.

But I must tell the truth!

You are the truth. More is not required.

I am afraid!

Fear not. You have done well.

Don't leave me!

We are with you always. Whatever you must choose, we will not leave you.

They would keep me in prison.

Yes.

I would not see the sky!

Daughter of God.

Tell me what to do!

We cannot.

I wish only to serve you!

In this you needs must choose.

There was a stillness then. A knowing filled my every part. This brought a peace.

I choose to speak the truth, to honor you, none else is just.

They will put you to the fire.

Saint Margaret spoke the words. I gazed upon her face.

You went through the fire.

Yes.

You said there was no pain.

Only in the fear before.

Would it be as such for me?

It would.

So be it then.

It will not be easy.

Let them burn me if they must! I will not deny you!

And so I told the questioners. All that I had revoked I did only for fear of the fire. My Saints were true and good. I had been sent by God. This pleased them not. They sentenced me to burn.

The night before I was to go to the fire I had a great fear. Once more I feared the pain of burning, of losing my body in such a terrible way. But I had forgotten the most important thing. I had forgotten about how all I had to do was to give my pain to God and it would be gone, as after I jumped from the tower. I had been asked by the court to deny the truth, and this was wrong. No one must have to do this. The truth is all we have. The truth is God. God resides in all. He cannot be taken away. God is all we have, and all we truly need. He is enough. It was a lack of faith to be afraid, but I was human, and a girl of nineteen. I had forgotten, too, that my body was only something to use for a while, like my red dress, not the very most part of me. That very most part of me was being called home. My work was done, and I was being called into the arms of my Lord.

Joan.

My cell was ablaze with light, white, purple, blinding, burning all the fear. Light everywhere, in me, around me, in all.

Daughter of God.

Saint Michael!

And he was there, in all his armor, aflame with the light of pure fire. And in that same light, Saint Margaret and Saint Catherine, radiant, all love, all caring. Saint Michael spoke.

Have no fear for thy martyrdom. Give your pain to God.

Don't leave me!

My blessed Saint approached. He placed his hand upon my heart. I felt a fiery heat.

We will stay with you always. Keep your heart with purity that I may enter there and surround you with armor.

I am yours!

Ask for a cross. Fix your eyes upon it. Fix your mind upon the Lord. Only His image will be as a shield.

Yes.

You will see yourself in the flames.

I will?

Do not be afraid. It will be as it were happening somewhere else. Let all earthly cares go. You will pass through the fire into peace.

His hand was still upon my heart. His look, pure love. And more he spoke.

That which is felt by the earthly senses is not all. One must not desert the Fires of Light for the crumbs of the feast. All will be reversed. The English will be driven out of France. Your enemies will suffer. Pray for them.

I will.

Your courage will inspire many. It will heal. Be joyous for what is already set down in the pages of the future.

That night, when I went off to sleep, my Saints stayed at my side. They did not leave me. Nor would they leave the next day, nor forever. This I knew. I had no fear. I would face the fire. I would give my pain to God, and it would end. I would pray for my enemies. I would look at the cross. I would fix my mind upon the Lord. I would pass through the fire into peace. My blessed Saints had told me this. I knew it would be so.